# SECOND BREATH

## DAZZLED BY MY BLIND DATE

## DANIKA BLOOM

FIRE LILY PRESS

Published by Fire Lily Press

Library and Archives Canada Cataloguing in Publication

Bloom, Danika, 1966- , author
Second Breath / Danika Bloom

Issued in print and electronic formats.
ISBN 978-1-7774865-1-8 (paperback)
ISBN 978-0-9730619-7-0 (ebook)

1. Title

This is a work of fiction. Names, characters, businesses, and events are from the author's imagination. Any resemblance to actual people, living or dead, is coincidental. Funny … but coincidental.

Editor: Amanda Bidnall

Sensitivity reader: Reshma Gidwani-de Vries

Cover design: L.J. Anderson, Mayhem Cover Creations (ebook); 100Covers.com (paperback)

Poem / song lyrics in chapter 46: Heather Huffman

*To my HEA gals. Your feedback is brutal and I love you all for it.*

# ABOUT SECOND BREATH: DAZZLED BY MY BLIND DATE

**What could possibly go wrong when a lawyer falls in love with a young woman whose reputation he was hired to destroy?**

"Wow, what a breathtaking story! I'm simply blown away by the depth of emotions the author brought out in this book." ★★★★★
~Viper Spaulding, Goodreads

**Kama**

I never expected to meet "the one" during my research dates for my thesis. And never, in a thousand free dinners, would I have guessed I'd fall for a smooth-talking, ridiculously hot lawyer with fingers that massage my common sense right out of me. The problem is, his career goals aren't just at odds with mine—if he succeeds, he'll destroy my reputation.

**Dylan**

I've got a one-track mind and it's set on becoming my law firm's youngest partner ever. All I have to do is win a case the firm's president hand delivered to me. Problem is, once I start researching the claim, I quickly realize that to get this promotion, I'll have to crush the most intriguing, infuriating and attractive woman I've ever met.

Now I have to decide which I want more: the goal I've been focused on my entire adult life or the woman my heart tells me I can't live without.

～

"I absolutely loved *Second Breath*. Danika's writing comes alive on the page, and the world she's created in this series is so amazingly immersive her books are impossible to put down! Danika's writing reminds me of Helen Hoang, and I highly recommend it to *Kiss Quotient* fans looking for the same level of detail, feels and steam." ~Mia Harlan, Goodreads

"What a fantastic book! This was filled with humor, fun, attraction that's off the charts, action, romance and all the tension under the sun." ~Teshia Elborne, Goodreads

"Danika Bloom understands people and relationships in a way that brings her characters to life and leaves you wanting to dive right into the next book." ~Jenny G, Amazon

# 1

## DYLAN

Barb grabbed my arm as I stepped off the elevator to my office. Told me I had an unscheduled meeting with a senior partner in the firm.

"Right now, Mr. Rhodes," she said.

My stomach tensed and I smoothed my tie. A nervous tic. I thought about all the cases I had on the go, wondered which one was responsible for this emergency meeting. And whether I'd be patted on the back or tossed into the shitter. I'd not yet had my ass handed to me on a plate by a partner, and according to the other lawyers working on my floor, I was due.

In only two years as a junior litigator, I'd brought more new clients to the firm than any other lawyer except the partners. My strength was in attracting and arguing cases that garnered media attention, which was a double-edged sword. A win attracted positive attention to the firm and lots of phone calls for me. A loss was a public strike against my personal reputation. But my track record was forty-six wins and four losses. I felt confident about my goal of making partner before I turned thirty. If I succeeded, I'd be the first twenty-something partner with Premier Law Boutique. And I thrived on being first.

I dropped my briefcase on the floor behind my desk and headed for the emergency stairwell, taking the stairs two at a time. In front of the heavy metal door, I closed my eyes and struck a Superman pose for four deep breaths. It was the way I focused and solidified my confidence before entering a courtroom. I had a feeling I'd need that poise for this meeting.

Swinging open the fire door, I smiled and walked toward Shane James's office. Barb, his personal assistant, was back at her desk, and she told me to knock and go in. The door was ajar, and I noticed someone was already meeting with him.

"Mr. James. Good morning," I said to my boss. Then I reached out to the man sitting in the client chair across his desk. "Good morning. I'm Dylan Rhodes."

The guy did a head tilt to acknowledge me but didn't take my hand. I smiled. He looked me up and down, as if he were checking me out.

"Sit," James said.

I sat in the chair beside the strange man.

"Rhodes, this is Bob Booker. Bob's the son of a longtime friend of mine, and he has a case I believe your skills are perfectly suited to tackle."

Inside, I breathed a sigh of relief and did a happy dance. Being given a case by a managing partner in the firm was typically the last step before being offered a junior partnership. "Fantastic."

"Bob, tell Rhodes what you were telling me."

This guy was still giving me the side-eye. It was disconcerting. A little bit creepy.

"I'm not sure he'll work," Bob finally said. "I'd say he's out of her league. Have you got someone, you know, a little more … average looking?"

My head swung to James. I must have looked like a confused puppy with my head tilted and my eyes blinking. I think I even shrugged.

"He's in a custom-fit suit, Bob. Every man looks thirty percent better in a custom suit. Put him in jeans and a T-shirt. Add an end-of-day, five o'clock shadow. He can make it work."

"Sir?" I said.

"It's an interesting case, Rhodes. And right up your alley. This one's going to get *a lot* of media. We'll make sure of that."

"And this case is?"

Booker turned to me. "Puffery. Misleading advertising. Not fulfilling an implied contract. Take your pick. Oh, and a minor thing called breach of ethical conduct."

He had my attention. I assumed, based on my brief read of the man whose shoes looked three sizes too big, that he was being accused of one or more of these things. "What is it alleged that you've done, Mr. Booker?"

He quickly sat back in his chair. "Me? Jesus Christ! I'm the complainant. The *alleged*," he said with air quotes, "is a woman named Kama Ray. She's the one who's broken the law. And that's not alleged. I'm the victim. So are many other men. She's a class-A, lying bitch who's getting away with hundreds, if not thousands, of dollars of criminal activity every week."

I looked back to my boss, hoping he'd give me something a little more specific.

"Kama Ray is a psychology master's student at BCU. She's working on a thesis about dating." He looked down at his notes. "It's called *How to be a Jedi in the World of Online Dating.*"

I smiled. Interesting thesis title.

Booker interjected when Mr. James took a breath. "Yeah, and this chick is using mind tricks to mess with the men she dates. She gets them to say things they wouldn't normally say and *not* do things they normally would, if you know what I mean."

I turned my gaze from Booker to my boss.

"The legal issue, Rhodes, is her failure to disclose her motivations to her dates, who are effectively her research subjects. It's against every ethical and legal code for thesis research."

"She's going down," Booker said, lifting an elbow and swinging his whole arm to point at the ground, like a gangster in a rap video.

This guy was ridiculous. Even though I'd never met Ms. Ray, Mr. Booker was not a very likable man on first impression. If I were the betting type, I'd put my money, sight unseen, on Ray walking away with this one. I smiled and tried to hide a niggling sense that I was being set up to fail. "This sounds like a 'he-said-she-said' case."

"No," James said. "I want this to be bigger than that. This speaks to a systemic problem with the psychology department's research methods. This case is bigger than just the conflict between Ms. Ray and Bob. Their relationship is the springboard to a case that I believe could—and should— embarrass the entire department. And, if you do your job well, it will force the dean to step down."

I nodded. That sounded more interesting.

"Rhodes, you can go. I just wanted you to meet Bob. I'll brief you on the details. Ask Barb to book a ten-minute meeting with me as soon as I have a space in my calendar."

I stood and tried to shake hands with Bob Booker, but he repeated the same aloof head tilt he'd used to greet me. Still no smile. I reminded myself that I didn't have to like my clients. "I look forward to working on your case, Mr. Booker."

〜

I was staying late. Again. The first ten-minute opening with Mr. James wasn't until six thirty. I wasn't alone in the office, though. Not by a long shot. On my floor, twelve of my colleagues were still working away, keyboards clacking quickly.

I took the elevator this time. No need to power pose. I knew what I was walking into. Barb had gone home, and James's door was open. His office had a full wall of glass overlooking the Vancouver waterfront and North Shore mountains. It wasn't the largest office in the firm, but it had the best view. James looked up but instead of waving me in, he motioned for me to wait. I stood at his door while he typed something and closed his laptop.

"Rhodes," he said, standing, "I want to show you something."

We walked across the floor to a small office. One with a view of downtown Vancouver.

"If you win this case, this office will be yours."

I did a silent cheer. Several images rushed through my mind. My dad looking proud. Me being the first of my brothers to win Vancouver's Top Thirty Under Thirty award. A Tesla Model S with $80,000 of upgrades in my employee parking spot.

"That's amazing, Mr. James. Excellent motivation! Thank you, sir."

"Well, I can guarantee you will earn it. What was your impression of Bob ... Mr. Booker?"

How to answer that? "He strikes me as a person who grows on you."

"He's an entitled prick," James said with disdain. "The firm is taking this case for two reasons. Number one, his father is a longtime friend and was the first and largest investor in this firm. Second, I have some history with the dean of the psychology department. Her name is Starla

Spode-Sugar. She and I were colleagues during our PhD years."

James turned away from me and faced the view. "She attended my thesis defense, and because of her private feedback to my supervisor, my revisions were so onerous my dissertation was a virtual rewrite."

I inhaled a whistle without thinking.

He turned to me. "So this is also personal. Not a great reason to take on a case, but I want you to be aware why it's imperative that you win. And, since I know it won't be easy, this"—he spread his arms like a game-show presenter—"is what you'll earn as compensation."

My original feeling of being set up was confirmed. These were two terrible reasons to accept a case. "From what you know, does Mr. Booker have grounds for his allegations?"

"Couldn't tell you. Like you said, at this stage it's a 'he-said-she-said' situation, and I wouldn't bet an old sandwich on his word being more convincing than hers. So …"

I was trying to think fast but not seeing the path forward.

"So you'll have to do something a little unorthodox. You need to become the 'he-said' in the scenario."

"I don't understand."

James sat at the desk he was dangling like a carrot. There were no other chairs in the room and it felt awkward, towering above him, so I widened my stance, reducing my height to under six feet.

"Booker claims this woman follows a script with all of her dates. If that's true, then you'll have the same experience he did. As the complainant to this alleged unethical activity, you'll have more credibility than Booker and, I'm certain, more credibility than a feminist psychology student."

"Wait. I'm not sure I understand. Are you telling me that my job is to go on a date with this student and take legally defensible notes?"

"Not just one date. She carries out her research over three

dates. The first date is always in the same restaurant, and she always sits at the same table. Same with the second and third dates. She is meticulous in managing her research environment, despite being in an uncontrolled setting."

"How do you know this? How does Booker know this?"

"Let's just say he's already spent several months and god knows how much money having her followed. He gave me a file two inches thick with details and photographs. The man is..." James sighed. "He has an unhealthy obsession with this woman that has verged on, if not wandered right into, illegal territory itself."

"Stalking?"

James nodded. "So really, there's nothing in the file that you can use in your actual arguments. But it may help guide you on how best to trip her up. If these other guys she used in her research were of the same intellectual and egotistical caliber as Bob, I suspect it was easy to use her so-called Jedi mind tricks on them." He laughed.

"And you have faith in my ability to out-Jedi her?"

"You're one of the strongest young litigators I've ever seen in this firm. And I have faith in your motivation to get this office—and the status and the paycheck that come with it."

He wasn't wrong about my motivation. And in a job where compliments were rare, especially from a senior partner, he triggered me to snap my legs together like a cadet at attention.

"Thank you, sir. So I just want to be one-hundred-percent clear: my job is to bill $300 an hour to go out on three dates with Ms. Ray."

He nodded. "Plus expenses, of course. But the real job is to build a case that will take down Starla Spode-Sugar *and* give the young Booker some closure, so he can get this woman out of his system." James stood and reached his hand toward mine. "Sound good?"

My brain was processing as quickly as it could. Did it sound good? *Good* is not the word I'd have chosen. It sounded like I was being asked to stroke two men's egos with a grad student's hand. I looked around the office that could be mine. At the view that could be mine. At James, who was nodding.

"You look good in this office, Rhodes."

"Feels good, sir." I shook my boss's hand and accepted the case because, really, what choice did I have?

# 2

## KAMA

**B**urgersio was crowded, but my booth was empty, held for me with a small 'reserved' sign. I was thirty minutes early, as always, and sitting at the high table by the window, as always.

I was nervous. I was always nervous, whether it was the first, second, or third date. But each one triggered a unique kind of nerves. Date one was anticipation. Would we connect enough for him to want a second date? If not, I'd be wasting my precious time since the valuable data came from the second and third times we met.

Date two nerves were excitement. I was one date closer to graduating.

And date three? Fear. I always had a stomachache the entire time because by the third date, I'd actually started to like some of these guys. A few of them also liked me. So it was painful to end date three with a handshake and a "thanks for your time, it was nice to meet you." But that's how it had to be.

Tonight, I was especially on edge, not only because the guy I was meeting could be my very last first date, but also because he was a lawyer. He used the profile name

LegalTender and joined the service the same day he contacted me. He'd only posted two photos. In one, there were six men in bathing suits, standing with their arms around each other at a beach. They were so fit they looked like they were all part of a team. I guessed rugby or maybe skiing, since they were too pretty to be boxers, too tall to be wrestlers, and too cool to be golfers.

He'd indicated himself with a red arrow. Of the six, he had the darkest complexion, and he was also the shortest, though his profile said he was six feet one. My first reaction was that this guy had a lot of self-confidence. Who else would use a dating photo that virtually forced women to compare him to a bunch of other very attractive men?

The second photo only showed half his face. A Dalmatian puppy hid the other half. He said the picture had been taken for a fundraising event he'd organized with his brother, a fireman.

I'd seen those photos of hot men posing, bare-chested and open-hearted. Who in the world hadn't?

So LegalTender, aka Dylan Rhodes, was a lawyer and a mini celebrity with six-pack abs and the self-confidence of a lion.

All this made me more nervous than was normal for a first date.

Something else made me anxious. Dylan Rhodes was the most perfect research subject of the two dozen men I'd met in my official research because all the men in my *unofficial* control group were, like him, high achievers. But I couldn't include those first five men in my master's thesis data since I hadn't actually started my research yet. The only reason I'd even bothered to go out with them was because my advisor wouldn't approve my proposal until I'd gone out with five actual men—and not for academic purposes. She had this silly idea that my experience was too limited for me to understand the dating game.

And sure, maybe I'd not made time for men since starting university, but I had a solid understanding of app-based dating from an academic article I'd read about college dating from an economic perspective. It found that the more money a man invests in a date, the more he expects in return. (No surprise to any of my friends.) Of course, said man doesn't want to be repaid by e-transfer; he wants the transfer to be of the goods-for-services variety, payment-in-kind. And sadly, this economist's research found that most women also believed this to be a fair exchange. Dinner for sex. Sex for dinner, as it were.

It made me so angry I based my thesis research on finding a way to beat this bias in one-on-one situations, since changing the whole cultural norm would take a few more years and probably a PhD to accomplish. Hey, a girl can dream.

My thesis goal was to prove that women could game the dating system by using subtle psychological cues to convince their dates that there was no so-called debt, no matter how large his investment of time or money.

Remember that scene in *Attack of the Clones* when Obi-Wan Kenobi is offered death sticks by Elan Sleazebaggano? Obi-Wan waves his hand, mind tricks him, and Mr. Sleaze agrees to go home and rethink his life? Yeah, that's my goal. To research what it takes for a woman to wave her hand, say, "You don't want to have sex with me," and for Mr. Pushy to happily agree to go home and get off on his own.

So here I was, waiting for my first date with one of Vancouver's hottest young lawyers. He was so much more *everything* than the guys who normally replied to my dating profile, which was exciting but terrifying, since I really needed three dates with him to collect the useful data. And I wasn't convinced I'd be able to hold this guy's attention that long.

Lizzy, my best friend and a hostess at Burgersio, brought me a cup of chai with cream.

"So is this really the last time I get to spy on the early dating days of our generation's Dr. Ruth?" Lizzy hung her head and made a sad face.

"If I'm lucky, he'll be magic number twenty-four, which is all my advisor says I need. And I'm not going on one more date than I have to. But I have zero confidence he'll be my last. I mean, why would a guy like Dylan 'Have you seen his freaking abs?' Rhodes be interested in going out with me?"

"Um... because you're smart and beautiful," Lizzy said. She was the best friend and worst liar ever.

"*Riiight*. Maybe, but more likely he lost a bet."

"Shut up, idiot. So, which playlist do you think you'll be using for this tender, legal guy?"

"It's LegalTender, a totally different thing. And I'm guessing the sexy one."

At a specific moment in the date, Lizzy always put on one of two special Spotify playlists I'd created, based on whether or not I was the type of woman the guy usually dated. If, within the first five minutes, he said I was his type, Lizzy would put on my neutral playlist, one that wouldn't amp up his innate interest in me. If I wasn't his normal type, she'd put on a playlist of songs with sexually suggestive lyrics—nothing overt, since this was a family restaurant—and a beat that echoed a heartbeat. Music was one of the many tools I used to control my dates' reactions to me.

But one thing that stayed consistent from date to date was my appearance—my makeup, the way I did my hair, and what I wore. Exactly the same every time. Every date had its special uniform. But the overall look was always 'Girl Next Door': natural, unpretentious, maybe a little naive looking. The girl next door inspired a man to feel comfortable about sharing, for example, his secret interest in her best friend. She was trustworthy and—let's face it—just too plain to be the romantic lead in a love story.

I even made sure I smelled the same by using scent-free soap and shampoo—nothing that could trigger a nostalgic childhood memory for the guy.

Honestly, I had more fun making sure these dates were scientifically defensible than actually going on them. The academic element was the big turn-on for me.

The door chimed, and a man walked in.

"Gotta go." Lizzy walked to the podium where Dylan now stood.

I looked at my watch. He was twenty minutes early. My heart sped up, and I panicked a little. *Don't tell him I'm already here*, I willed Lizzy. I watched as he let her know he was meeting someone with a reservation. She walked him to my reserved table without giving me away. He smiled and thanked her as he sat down.

Then she came right back over to me, eyes wide. "He said your name right," she whispered.

"Really? You sure it didn't sound like 'gamma ray'?" I stared over at him. He was looking at the drink menu and moving his head to the beat of the song playing through the speaker above my table.

"One hundred percent, clear as day, he said Kama with a hard 'a'. He's the first one to get it right. It's a sign, Kama."

"Probably just a sign that he read my LinkedIn profile bio where I pointed out the proper pronunciation."

"Did you see him? Jeez Louise, why is he online dating? How is it even possible that he's single? After you're done with him, I want his number. Promise you'll introduce me."

"Sure, sure," I said, hoping to temper Lizzy's excitement. I didn't need her sparky energy swirling around me. "Did he ask for anything?"

"No. I offered to bring him water, but he said he wasn't sure if his date would like ice or not, so he said he'd wait.

Kama, did you *see* him? He doesn't look like a lawyer—at least not the kind you see in movies. He looks more like an action hero. He's—"

"Shush! Yes, I saw him. I know. He's way out of my league. But for some reason he asked me out, so..." I took a deep breath and exhaled slowly, trying to settle the anxiety tingling in my limbs. "Okay, go back to work. I need to get into the zone."

I waved Lizzy away with wide arms and open palms, hoping to disrupt the messy energy she'd sloshed all over me.

# 3

## DYLAN

When I asked the hostess for the table that was reserved for Kama, her eyes popped open as if I'd just asked her for a table with Scarlett Johansson. It was a strange reaction—and I was familiar with unusual reactions when people met me for the first time. And by people, I mean women. My notoriety outside of law circles seemed to be strongest with a specific demographic, thanks to my firefighter brother.

It usually went the same way:

Me: "Hi. Nice to meet you. I'm Dylan Rhodes."

Her: "Hi ... I feel like I've met you before."

Me: "I don't think so. I wouldn't forget meeting a beautiful woman like you." (Don't judge. I can be a charmer and not a player—much.)

Her: "But you look *so* familiar."

Me, striking my media-photo smile: "I've been in the news a few times."

Her, nodding: "Wait ... Didn't you do that charity photo shoot with the firefighters?"

Me: "Guilty as charged." (We lawyers love our legal jokes. Even the lame ones.)

Now, usually my mini-celebrity status in this small city worked to my benefit, but I was concerned it would work against me today. It would have been be so much easier if I was just another random guy connecting with a woman, looking for short-term love on the SmartSingles dating app. Because Kama's profile pictures were hot.

She looked nothing like the women I normally date. Okay, hook up with. I've never used a dating app in my life. I get women using my wit and charm and, quite frankly, by buying them drinks.

Anyway, based on her profile photos, Kama appeared to be quite tall. I'd say, five-eight, five-nine. And full-figured. I'd venture to guess she wasn't ashamed to eat steak and potatoes for dinner and then have dessert. And in all the photos she shared, she made me think she dressed for herself and not to impress anyone. Aside from her strikingly high cheekbones and a contagious smile, what made her so attractive was how natural and comfortable she looked. Her photos and bio made me wonder why I'd never hooked up with a woman who put more effort into looking confident than come-hither. Probably because that kind of woman doesn't hit on men in bars.

And, as arrogant as it might make me sound, I don't hit on women; I let them come to me. At least I did until my #sexyfireman brother tore up his 'Single for Life' membership card. With him as my wingman, I'd never suffered for attention. Now that I had to rely on my #awkwardprogrammer brother to help me find action … well, my close rate had dropped substantially.

Aside from looking nothing like my normal hook-ups, Kama was forcing me into all kinds of new situations, like accepting a job from my boss that felt way outside my comfort zone. I'm happiest representing the little guy who's been screwed by the big corporation. This case seemed to be the polar opposite: taking down an unsuspecting grad student who just happened to go on a date with the wrong man. Even if there wasn't a grudge to settle between the dean of her department and my boss, I could tell from three minutes in a room with Bob Booker that any date with that guy would be a date with the wrong man.

What I'd learned from the file that Booker gave James was that Kama's MO was to date upwardly mobile men. Booker had been the recipient of the Top Thirty Under Thirty award two years ago. That made me rethink my desire to win what I'd always believed to be a prestigious award.

The thing was, Booker found out that four of the men she dated around the same time were also recipients. He'd spoken to them all, and they'd said the same thing: that she'd contacted them, that they went out on a couple of dates, and that she didn't sleep with any of them. As far as Booker was concerned, this was an open-and-closed case of ethical misconduct because she hadn't disclosed her research to a single one of them.

And as much as I didn't want to believe Booker, it was beyond me why a woman with Kama Ray's bio would have ever gone on three dates with Booker unless it was for research.

The result was that Booker was a man—I used the term loosely—smitten and scorned. In his statement, he reported that he'd reminded her they had an implied contract and that he'd been quite generous to wait until the third date to collect his payment.

According to him, that's when she lost her shit and let it slip that he was the reason she had to do the research she was doing. She had to give women everywhere a fighting chance against men like him. According to his claim, she said, "You're the reason feminazis like me don't feel safe to go out on dates with generous men like you."

I suspected that his memory might not have been one-hundred-percent accurate about the exact words she'd used.

But I'd find out soon enough since I'd seen her having a cup of tea at the front of the restaurant when I came in. She was wearing the same thing as in one of her profile pictures: black jeans, a light-blue V-neck, and oxblood Doc Martens boots. Her jet-black hair was pulled into a ponytail that reached the middle of her back. I could see several thin, gold bracelets on her right arm and a watch on her left.

If her intention was to look like she could kick my ass, she was succeeding. I couldn't see if she was wearing makeup, but my guess would be that if she was, it was subtle.

Pulling my phone from my pocket, I checked the time. Five minutes to. Since she was already here, I put my phone on airplane mode, turned on the voice recording app, and placed it facedown on the table. He-said-she-said cases were always easier to win with concrete evidence of exactly what each person said.

I figured I'd have everything I needed by the end of this date, and although James had already okayed the expense of three nights out with Kama, I'd be happy to wrap this up quickly. I wasn't comfortable keeping secrets, and I wasn't very at good it. Not only that, this wasn't lawyer work. It was a job for a PI. The promotion I'd been working so hard for felt like a cheater's win since I wasn't earning it with my legal skills but with my good looks, youth and charm. I admit these had served me well in court, but as an add-on to my legal prowess, not an alternative to it.

From the corner of my eye, I saw Kama stand. I spoke toward the table, into my phone's mic. "Thursday, March fifth, Burgersio restaurant. Date one with Kama Ray." Then I looked up and watched as she walked toward me. She was a woman with a purpose. We made eye contact, and I stood to greet her.

# 4

## KAMA

Dylan's eyes met mine, and he smiled. My breath hitched. Get a grip, girl. He's just a man, not a superhero.

"You must be Dylan. Hi, I'm Kama."

He extended his hand. "Nice to meet you." Dylan waited until I sat down before he did.

"You got here early," I said, leaning my laptop bag against the wall behind my chair.

"In my line of work, being on time means being early. I noticed that you were early, too."

"I'm right on time," I said, looking at my watch.

"I saw you sitting at the tall table near the window with a cup of tea, which suggests you were here at least five minutes before I arrived." He smiled like he approved and not like he'd caught me in a lie. Still, I was embarrassed. And surprised that he'd noticed me.

"I guess, like you, I believe being on time means being early."

I mentally checked off one of my Jedi research tricks: repeating a phrase my date says verbatim. I took a visibly deep breath and made eye contact with him. "So, I'm about to catapult the most awkward five minutes of any date off the charts before we even order food, if that's okay with you." I paused and waited for his agreement.

He placed his elbows on the table and clasped his hands together, resting his chin on his thumbs. "Why not?"

I moved the wooden box that was home to the salt, pepper, hot sauce, napkins, and menus to the edge of the table. I reached behind me, pulled a purple, acrylic clipboard from my laptop bag, and placed it between us.

"Do you remember that my dating profile said that I'm a psychology student working on my master's degree?"

"I do."

"Well, my thesis is, generally speaking, about relationships. More specifically, it's about the dating stage of relationships."

"Interesting." He pressed his index fingers together and tapped his chin with them, making his hands look like he was holding a gun pointed at his nose. He also kept eye contact.

Well, I think he did. I was staring at his mouth, at the slight smile he'd had since the minute he'd caught me in my little white lie. It was a very sexy mouth, framed by significant five o'clock shadow, evidence that this man had impressive testosterone production, assuming he'd shaved this morning. I quickly listed all the other things that high testosterone levels impacted, and my breath hitched again.

I looked away from Dylan's face and spoke to the very unsexy clipboard between us. "It is. Interesting, that is. Now, because I may use some of what I learn about"—here I hedged, and feigned ignorance of what I might learn —"myself and interactions between me and my dates, I have an informed consent document I'd like you to read and, if you agree, to sign." I tapped the page and looked up at him again.

"What does the informed consent document say?" he asked.

"Well, you actually have to read it."

"I realize that. I am a lawyer, you know. I'd just like to hear you tell me what I'm signing. In a nutshell."

"Well, in a nutshell," I picked up the clipboard and read to him, word for word, what it said.

*You are invited to participate in a research study conducted by master's student Kama Ray from British Columbia University. You must be 19 years old or older to participate in this study. Your participation is voluntary. Please take as much time as you need to read this information sheet. You may also decide to discuss it with your family and friends. You will be given an electronic copy of this form.*

### PURPOSE OF THE STUDY

*I am asking you to take part in a research study because I am trying to learn more about women's personal experiences of dating as well as patterns of men's expectations on first dates.*

I read the full two pages of the document out loud to Dylan. Each time I looked up at him, he was looking right at me, attention fully focused. This was a first for me. But, given he was a lawyer, I felt fine, if not a bit self-conscious, since there was no way he could argue that I'd misled him if he got pissy at the end of the third date. Ha! Third date. That made me laugh to myself. I'd be lucky to get a second date with this guy.

*If you have any questions or concerns about the research, please feel free to contact the Faculty Advisor, Dr. Alice Balcerowski.*

"And here," I said, turning the sheet around so he could see it, "are her contact details." I placed the clipboard on the table, text up and facing Dylan, so he could read the first page himself. I waited. And waited. Finally, he spoke.

"And what if I don't want to sign this?"

My heightened anticipation collapsed like a soufflé, half-baked and hit by cold air.

"If you don't want to sign, don't sign. It's one-hundred-percent your choice to take part or not. As the form says, your participation is voluntary."

"Obviously. What I'm asking is, what happens if I don't sign? Will this date end now, or will we still have dinner together?"

"Again, I'll leave that up to you. If you'd like to leave now, I totally understand. If you're not interested in contributing to my thesis research, but would still like to have dinner with me, that would be fine." I could hear the disappointment in my voice, which Dylan clearly picked up on since he raised his eyebrows. "It would be great, I mean. Since we're both already here…" *Shut up, Kama.* "Of course, I'll pay for my own meal. Separate tabs. Well, I would pay either way, whether you sign or not, so I guess that's a moot point." *Oh my gosh, shut up.*

Dylan picked up the clipboard and pen and held them in front of his face so I couldn't see his expression. He flipped the sheet over and, I assume, read the second page.

Of the twenty-seven dates I'd started, three men had opted not to sign. Two had also opted not to dine.

Dylan placed the clipboard back on the table between us, unsigned.

"So, let's just say, for the sake of argument, I decide not to sign this informed consent document but want to stay and have dinner with you anyway. What happens if I want to go out with you again? Could there still be a second date? Are you dating men outside of your"—he made air quotes —"*experiment*?"

Was he kidding? He was making me flustered. I hated

feeling out of control. We were in my territory. This was my very carefully controlled lab. And he was messing with everything.

"First of all, this isn't an experiment. It's *research*." I emphasized the word.

"Apologies. *Research*," he said.

"And no. I'm not dating. I mean, not for real. I mean, yes, this is a date, but only for the purpose of gathering data for my thesis."

"Interesting. Why aren't you dating? For real, I mean?"

This sneaky bugger was using Jedi mind tricks on me, repeating my answer as a question. I needed water and waved to Jenny, our server. She gave me the 'just a minute' finger.

"Well, because … seriously? Would you want to date, *for real*, a woman who was actively dating other men for research?"

Dylan stared at me, and his smile grew large, showing perfectly straight, perfectly white teeth. I ran my tongue over my own bottom row of not-perfectly-straight teeth and felt self-conscious. My palms were sweating and my heart rate was double timing. I felt like I was being cross-examined and hadn't prepped my testimony. He looked totally calm.

"Well, yes, because that's how dating works," he said. "Tonight, I'm out for dinner with you. Research or not, this is a date, as far as I'm concerned. Last Saturday, I was out with a very nice woman named Tanya. I expect, at least I hope, I'll be seeing her again this Saturday. I can't say for a fact, but I wouldn't be surprised if she's been out with another man this past week. That's dating, right? Meeting lots of people until you find one you gel with. All dating is research, isn't it? Or has your dating research found something else?"

I found it hard to keep up. His logic sounded right but felt wrong. "I haven't started summarizing my data yet. I'm still collecting. So it's not showed me anything. But … Nobody's ever asked me this before. They've either been in or out. I don't know what to say. Except that you're free to not sign. I'd be happy to still have dinner with you and then never see you again."

"Ouch." He placed his hand on his heart and gave me a genuine smile.

"You know what I mean." I wanted an excuse to run to the bathroom and wished Jenny had already brought us water so I could accidentally spill it on myself. This was going to be the worst date ever. I revised my expectations from 'unlikely to get the full data set' to 'certain write-off.' I slumped in my chair.

For some dumb reason like excessive optimism, when I gave my advisor my research schedule, I'd planned on having three dates a week: one a first, one a second, one a third. At that rate, I'd have had my data collection done four weeks ago. But men hadn't been knocking down my door to meet me. And, to ensure I wasn't biasing the types of men I went out with, I had to let them approach me so I had no way to speed up the process. I needed Dylan to go the distance with me. With my research, I mean.

Jenny arrived with two glasses of water and asked if she could take our orders.

"Sorry," I said. "We haven't had time to look at the menu. And I'm not sure we'll be staying." Jenny made a sad face, which, unless Dylan had superhuman peripheral vision, he didn't see because he'd picked up the menu.

"Little Miss Jump to Conclusions," he said. "I was just asking questions, not suggesting I would walk out on you." He made eye contact with Jenny, then her name badge. "Jenny, if you were having dinner here tonight, what would you eat?"

Jenny looked from Dylan to me with a very clear 'what do I say?' face. She knew what I was doing, and that I followed a specific script. At least normally. Normally, she asked what my date wanted, and he told her. No other date had asked *her* to decide what we'd be having.

I nodded, as subtly as I could, at Jenny.

She pointed to the menu. "I was thinking about having the bison burger with a salad instead of fries. Oh, with the pickle on the side. I hate ketchup on my pickles."

When Dylan laughed, his voice dropped an octave, like it was coming straight from his ridiculously flat abdomen. "That sounds perfect. I'll have that." Then he looked at me. "Kama, I assume you bring all your first dates here and that you already know what you're having. Am I right?"

I know I was wide-eyed because Jenny mirrored my expression.

"I'll have the same," I said, sounding less than confident in my decision since I felt like every one of my actions was transparent to Dylan. But I always ate whatever the man ordered. It served a double purpose: it maintained consistency from date to date, and it was also a mind trick to build trust. We tend to like people who like the same things we do.

"And to drink? What can I bring you?" Jenny asked Dylan.

"Whatever pale ale you have on tap for me. Kama? Are you drinking, or do you like to do your research without the influence of alcohol?"

My mind was racing. I was discombobulated.

"I guess it depends. Yes, I like to be sober when I'm researching, but you still haven't signed the informed consent document, so I don't know if I'm researching or not."

Dylan looked up at Jenny. "What does she normally drink?"

"Ginger beer, no ice," Jenny and I answered at the same time.

"Then that for Kama. Please and thank you, Jenny."

"Okay ..." I exhaled. "You have definitely taken the awkward first five minutes to a new level."

"Really? I don't find this awkward at all. I'm having fun. But I have another question for you. If I don't sign now but decide I want a second date with you partway through dinner, can I provide my informed consent at the *end* of our date? Will you still be able to use the data you collect tonight if I do it that way?"

I took a deep breath, but instead of filling my lungs, it felt like all that air went straight into my frontal lobe and replaced my brain matter. The part of my brain responsible for problem-solving, language, and social behavior... vanished.

"I, um, I have no idea, actually. That's a, mmm, that's a question ... Wow, I'm not sure. Something I never considered."

I forced myself to hold eye contact and focus on things still within my control. I mimicked his hand position from earlier, placing my elbows on the table, resting my chin in my hands. "What ... what do you think? What would your law background suggest?"

Dylan burst out laughing. "You're fun to spar with."

"Are we sparring?" I spoke into the glass of water I'd picked up and realized I might actually spill it, but not on purpose. My hands were shaking.

Even if he signed, it was achingly clear that I wouldn't make it through my standard script with any kind of consistency tonight. This guy was forcing me into unfamiliar and uncomfortable territory.

He picked up the clipboard and pen, printed his name, and signed and dated the form. I held my breath until he put the pen and paper down.

"Photo of the form? Both sides. So you have a copy.

Please." I realized I wasn't speaking in full sentences. I suddenly understood the expression *airhead*.

*I am not an airhead*, I told myself.

Dylan picked up his phone and fiddled with it. I inhaled and held my breath, willing the oxygen into my lungs and out of my brain. He snapped the photo. I picked up the clipboard, casually, I hoped, and stuffed it into my laptop bag with a hard exhale.

"Don't you need to see my ID. You know, prove I am who I say I am?"

Thank the goddess, this was a question with an answer I knew.

"Nope. All I need to do, to meet the ethics committee's guidelines, is make sure the man sitting across from me understands that I might use some of what is said or done on this date—and any future dates, if we have them—as part of my thesis research. You could have signed as the *Cat in the Hat*, and it wouldn't matter. As long as you read, understood, and signed the document."

"Is that your favorite Dr. Seuss book?"

"What? My favorite ... No. I mean, I don't know. I don't think I have a favorite."

From the corner of my eye, I saw Lizzy waving at me. I looked too quickly, which drew Dylan's attention to her.

"Looks like your friend needs you."

I shook my head, first at Lizzy then at Dylan. "No. It's all good. But I have a question."

"You've got my full attention."

"I need your gut reaction. Based on my appearance and what you've learned about me in the last ten minutes, would you say I'm your normal type?"

# 5

# DYLAN

Wow, that was straight to the point. Was she my normal type? Not even close. *Should* she be my normal type? Hell, yeah.

"Define *normal*," I countered.

Kama dropped her face into her hands and groaned. It made me laugh. She wasn't looking like she could kick my ass right now.

"Normal," she said with a sigh. "I mean, are the women you usually date tall and full-figured like me? Or do you normally date smaller or petite women? Do they wear lots of makeup or not? Would she be a student or already have a career? Would she dress like I do, or would she be wearing a push-up bra and a low-cut dress? Have you ever dated a woman who doesn't have a single ancestor with blond hair? You know, do I seem like the kind of woman you normally date?"

"Are we dating?" I asked with a giant smile. I enjoyed bugging her, maybe a bit too much.

Kama reached behind her and pulled out the clipboard with my informed consent document.

"You know what? Never mind. This isn't going to work.

I'm not going to be able to use anything from this date in my data since I can't control the environment. You're too much of a wild card. I need to be able to ..." She paused.

"Control me?" I offered.

"Well, not so much *you* but the direction of our conversation. Or at least, the starting place of several conversations. This won't work, so here." She pulled off the form and placed it on the table.

"Why are you giving this back to me?"

"Without it, I can't collect information about our date. So let's just have a date. Enjoy our bison burgers. You enjoy your beer. And I'll be able to relax. Or try to since you've really thrown me off my game."

"I'm glad to hear this is a game to you, too. But I'm having fun with this game. Aren't you?"

"I shouldn't have said *game*. See. That's what I mean. Normally I know exactly what to say no matter what you reply. There's a plan. This is research. It's meant to be carried out within certain parameters." Kama sighed and hung her head. "Which include *not* drawing attention to the fact that this is research ... See what I mean? You have me all flustered."

"Am I messing with your parameters?" I said in a suggestive tone.

"You've annihilated them." She pantomimed an explosion with her hands, looked toward the ceiling, and said, "Poof."

I laughed, but when she looked back at me, there was deep disappointment in her eyes. She was taking her research seriously, and it was clear that I would not be collecting information to back up Bob Booker's claim. Not that I could prove she *hadn't* led him on—she might have— but I was inclined to think she hadn't. Everything about her felt honest, authentic.

I reminded myself that I was here for a job. And to do my

job, I needed to make it to the end of at least this date. And I was also actually interested in getting to know this woman. Either way, I couldn't let her tear up my consent and kick me out of her study.

"What if we start over, and I stop lawyering every question you ask by asking one in return? Do you think we could do that?"

"Are you asking if I think you can drop the smart-aleck attitude? Or are you asking if I can salvage this date for my research?"

I nodded. "Nicely volleyed!"

She smiled. For the first time since we'd met, her whole face lit up. Her cheekbones were even sexier in real life. Her dark-brown eyes were captivating.

"Thank you." She leaned back in her chair, looking a little more relaxed. Back in control. Then she stood, picked up her laptop bag, and walked toward the door.

"Hey!" I called after her. "Come back."

Kama stopped at the podium where the hostess was standing. They had a few words, and then Kama turned and walked back toward our table.

"Hi," she said, "I'm Kama. You must be Dylan."

I liked this woman's spunk. I stood and took her hand in mine. It gave me a bit of a tingle, a tingle that travelled from my hand to other areas. "I am. Very nice to meet you."

"Nice to meet you, too."

I tried to drop her hand so we could sit but she held firm. "So, Dylan. Gut reaction. Based on my appearance, my dating profile, and what you learned about me in the last ten minutes, would you say I'm your normal type?"

"Not. At. All."

She smiled, let go of my hand, and looked directly at the hostess, who was staring at us.

"Good. Thank you for your honesty. I appreciate it."

We sat, and before I could think of anything to say, she

asked, "So, if I'm not your normal type, what drew you to ask me out?"

*Shit, shit, shit.* I did not anticipate that question. I couldn't lie, not only because it's just not in my makeup, but also because I'd lose all credibility if it became known in court that I lied to her. Jenny arrived right at that moment with our drinks, which gave me an extra twelve seconds to think.

"Um, well ..." I took a long haul of my beer "Another man I know went out with you, and he said that it was ... umm ... an experience ... worth having."

"Wait!" Kama put her glass down with so much force some sloshed over the side and onto the table. "You knew that this date would be part of my thesis research before you even showed up?"

"I did."

"And that's why you wanted to meet me?"

"Yes."

She looked lost in thought for a few seconds as she wiped the rum and ginger beer off the table with a napkin. "Will you tell me the name of the man who suggested you should go out with me?"

"No. I will not."

"I guess that's fair." She took a deep breath and her chest expanded.

Correction: her breasts lifted and moved fractionally closer to me. Enough that I thought it best to look up, up, and away. My eyes landed on the speaker above her head. I focused on it and realized it was playing an old Buzzcocks song, 'Ever Fallen In Love.' I hadn't heard that one in years; it reminded me of summer camp. I hummed along for a few notes. She pulled my attention back to her. Thankfully, her arms were now crossed over her breasts. Not so thankfully, she looked furious.

"Are you on this date to mess with my research?"

"No! Not at all. I'm fascinated by what little I know.

Which isn't very much," I quickly added. "But I think it's interesting, and if having dinner with me will help you with your study, I'm down for that."

"Okay." She leaned back in her chair and turned off the eye daggers. "So what did he tell you? How much do you know? Did he tell you what questions I'll be asking, for instance?"

"That's three questions. Do you want me to answer them all or just the last one?" I was trying not to be a smart-ass, and I hoped she didn't read my response that way.

She turned her eye daggers back on and sighed.

"He didn't share specific questions. None. What he told me was that he felt ... used by you."

"Used?" She sat up straight, pressing her hands into her chair and those damned breasts right toward me again.

Where to look? Now she had me getting flustered. "Well, you went on a few dates with him, and he expected, you know, that there would be—"

"Sex. He expected I'd have sex with him. Am I right?"

"Yes."

Kama's eyes darted back and forth, but it was obvious she wasn't looking at anything specific. More like she was thinking and seeing images in her mind's eye.

"Okay ... that's actually valuable information. Thank you for sharing that. I appreciate your honesty."

*Whoa!* I wasn't sure how I'd pulled that out of my ass, but I was happy that she was happy.

"So how does this normally work?" I asked. "I assume you want me to be myself, but it would appear that myself is kind of jerk who likes to push buttons, which wasn't working for your research. I'm not sure what to do here."

"Well, how would you act on a normal first date with someone you'd just met online? Would you be your normal, jerkish self, or would you dial it back a little? You know, try to be charming instead of ... difficult?"

"Difficult? I never! I *am* charming."

"You're about as charming as a venereal disease."

She tried to look serious, but one side of her mouth twitched.

"Is that so? Well, your ego may think I'm disgusting, but I can tell by the way you were pressing your breasts toward me and staring at my mouth earlier, that your id is dying to kiss me right now."

Kama inhaled so quickly she choked on her spit.

Once she could breathe and speak again, we both had tears in our eyes.

"I can't believe I've never heard that one before. I thought I'd heard every psychology pickup line. Phew." She fanned herself.

"I notice you're not denying it."

She shook her head, 'No,' and blushed.

"So back to your question," I said, "You're actually my first online date, so I have no point of reference."

"I am not!"

"Honestly."

"But then how do you meet ..." she looked from my face to my chest to my left arm. I flexed my bicep for her. She looked away. "Duh. Never mind."

Okay. That was seriously cute. My ego was feeling nicely stroked. "I meet women in real life. Have you never gone to a bar and met someone who you clicked with?"

"Clicked, as in went home with? No. Never."

"Interesting. So, how effective do you find dating apps for meeting men? What's the best one you've used?"

"I haven't used any other than this one, and this is the first time I've set up a profile. And, as I already made clear, I'm only using it for research. Not actual dating to, you know, meet my *soul mate*." She made air quotes, "Or whatever."

"Whatever? You mean get laid?"

She sighed. "See, that's precisely the problem with the whole dating culture: this expectation of sex in exchange for someone's company."

"Wait, wait. There are two problems with your logic. First, what's wrong with having sex with a person you click with? And second, when it is a quid-pro-quo situation, it's not *just* in exchange for company, it's also a form of non-monetary payment for my time and the dinner I paid for."

"Payment with a woman's genitals." She rolled her eyes and hung her head.

"Well, your genitals *and* your breasts. And, depending on what the guy who bought you dinner is into, maybe that spot right below your tailbone, where your buttocks just start to take shape." I couldn't help smile. Kama looked straight at me with huge eyes.

"Off script." That's all she said.

I found her confident self-consciousness amusing. And a bit of a turn-on.

"Understood. No sexy talk on the first date. Does your research move toward sexy talk on the second or third date?"

That got a slight smile from her. "Third date. But only if you're lucky."

"Good to know. I can be patient. But be warned, I'll be researching sexy psychology pickup lines until then."

She smiled and fanned herself. I wasn't sure if she was serious or making fun of me. Either way, I liked how Kama Ray, psychology major, made me feel.

# 6

## KAMA

Jenny arrived with our burgers and offered Dylan another beer. He downed what was left in his glass and handed her his empty. I nodded that I'd have another ginger beer, too, but finished mine over the next couple of minutes.

"When I was at BCU, I took part in a few research projects, but they were all taped. I didn't see a release to be recording my voice or video, so how does this work? How can you actually analyze what you can't go back and review?" Dylan asked.

Nobody had asked that before. I was starting to realize that none of the other men in my study were as smart as Dylan Rhodes. And from the minute I saw his photo—which he lived up to, and then some, in person—none of the others were as attractive. He had a good career, he was polite and funny. This guy was a catch, and I couldn't figure out why he was single.

"How is it that a guy like you isn't already married?"

"What makes you think I'm not married?" he asked with a mischievous smile.

"Well, I'd guess you're pushing thirty—"

"I'm twenty-eight."

"—and by that age, a married man with a desk job would already be getting a little squidgy around the middle. You know, letting yourself go since you've already bagged the girl of your dreams. So I have to assume you're keeping yourself fit because you're still on the hunt."

He coughed as if he'd just swallowed his beer down the wrong pipe.

"And what do you think you know about my squidginess—or lack thereof?" he asked with a crooked smile.

"You sent me photos which made it quite clear that you're proud of your six-pack. By the way, do you surf or play beach volleyball? What kind of team are you on?"

"Team?" He looked confused. "I'm not on any teams."

"Then who were all those guys in bathing suits you're with in that picture you put with your dating profile?"

"Oh!" He smiled with his whole face. "Those are my brothers! And half-brothers. And step brothers."

"Wow," I said, trying to remember what they all looked like. "You sure won the gene pool lottery," I said, hoping the comparison landed as a compliment.

He gave me a quizzical look, shook his head and took a bite of his burger. I guess there was no snappy come-back to that.

My research required that by the third date, the man in question would want to sleep with me. And it wasn't old news that complimenting a man—or a woman—on their physicality was an easy way to increase attraction. If I made a man feel good about himself, he'd feel a little more inclined to feel good about me. So one of my standard practices during the first date was to compliment something about his body. This was too easy with Dylan. Not always as easy with other men. But I always found something that the man could puff his peacock chest about, whether it be his height, his beautiful hands, or his shamefully thick, long eyelashes. Dylan Rhodes had all this and more.

By the end of the first date, I wanted the man sitting across from me to be imagining what it would be like to have my hands or mouth touching that part of him I'd complimented.

It was a fine balance. I didn't want to come on to the man only to be accused later of leading him on. But I needed him to want to sleep with me, so I could use the Jedi tricks I was researching to convince him *not* to want to sleep with me.

The basic setup of the research was as follows:

Date one: Establish attraction.

Date two: Amplify attraction to the point where sex is desired.

Date three: Continue to amplify the attraction until it's clear that sex is *expected*, and then reverse the attraction so that sex is no longer expected.

But I had to do so not by being unlikeable. The reverse, actually. I had to make the man respect me enough to challenge the dating expectations shared by almost every person under eighty years old.

"What led you to pick dating for your thesis? I assume some bad personal experiences?"

It occurred to me that again, Dylan was asking me questions no other man had asked. Almost every other guy let me take the lead and spent at least eighty percent of the first date taking about himself. It was another Jedi mind trick I used to make the man enjoy his time with me. Again, it was old research that proved that the more a person spoke about themselves on a date, the more they enjoyed their time and the more they liked the person they were out with.

But Dylan was keeping the balance closer to fifty-fifty. And now he was asking a question I wasn't sure how to answer truthfully without telling him exactly what the research was about. It was a difficult line to walk.

"Not so much. I read a book about how economics influences sex and love. I listened to what my friends said about their own behavior on dinner dates." I shrugged. "Figuring out how a woman could game the system seemed like a fun and valuable idea."

*Rats.* That may have been too on-the-nose for a guy as smart as Dylan. I added, "That, and the movie *Moulin Rouge.*"

He laughed out loud. "You're basing your thesis research on a musical love story?"

"You know the film?" I felt an unexpected excitement that he knew my favorite movie. "It contributed to the inspiration for my subject," I admitted.

"How so?"

Dylan was halfway through his burger, and I'd barely eaten five bites of my meal. I had to figure out how to turn the focus back on him.

"Short answer? It speaks to taking control of your life. But I want to know more about you. Did you always want to be a lawyer?" I hoped he'd tell me all about his career journey, from being a precocious child, to (no doubt) an annoying teenager, to now.

"Nope. Happened by accident. You? Have you always wanted to study psychology?"

*Curse him!* "No. When I was ten—that's how old I was when I first saw *Moulin Rouge*—I wanted to be a Broadway actress."

"Quite a jump from Broadway to a BCU psychology lab. What happened?"

"This little thing called talent."

"Can't sing your way out of paper bag?"

"Oh, I can sing quite well, actually. It's the acting part that isn't so easy for me. How about you? With your photogenic good looks and all your other talents, I suppose you can also sing and dance. Own a stage."

*Come on, talk about yourself.* I willed Dylan to read my mind.

"I'm no Ewan McGregor, but I'm a shade better than Pierce Brosnan's donkey braying when he sang 'SOS' in *Mamma Mia*."

"Oh my gosh, 'SOS' was right! Stop Over Singing. He was terrible! Why in the world was he cast when the director knew it was a singing role? It must have been so humiliating for him since all the other actors have such glorious voices."

"You'd think, but I read an interview with him when the second *Mamma Mia* came out, and he said he thought people were looking forward to hearing him sing again—but just a little! He had a good sense of humor about it."

"That's some killer confidence," I mused. "With all the media attention you get, have you ever been publicly humiliated?"

"Not yet. But I'm still young. My father seems to expect it will come."

"Why's that?"

"He doesn't think much of my … well, my personal life outside of work. He's proud of my career but has this idea that one day, a woman I've dated, let's say, will do or say something to wreck my good name."

"Aren't you worried about that?"

He leaned back in his chair and made a face. "A little. I guess. I mean, reputation is everything in this line of work. People have very short memories for the good work we do, for the cases we win. But people never forget the ones we lose or the times we screw up.

"There was a senior partner at the firm where I work whose personal life was made public last year. He was in a consensual, polyamorous relationship, but when the administration at the private elementary school his two kids attended found out, they raised holy hell. It was a smear campaign that the school ultimately paid a lot of money to resolve. Unfortunately, in the end, this guy's reputation was shot—first for having a so-called depraved lifestyle and then, when he challenged the school and won, for being a bastard who stole financial resources from all those poor kids. It was a no-win situation for him."

"So he was fired?" I asked.

"No. That wouldn't be cause for dismissal, but it was understood that he was no longer considered an asset at the firm. And since that meant he wouldn't get the kinds of cases he was used to arguing, he resigned."

"That's harsh. And it doesn't scare you that a hook-up might turn bad? How do you protect yourself from being smeared by a woman you date?"

"You mean in a legal sense? Because I have no problem being smeared by a woman who's into mutual smear-ation."

The thought of Dylan smearing me with anything triggered some major Kegel contraction action. His smile was so welcoming, I could just look at his face all night. He winked, and I realized that I was staring. "Topic to hold for the third date," I managed to say. *Why did I say that?*

"Is it? Good to know. Let's circle around to it when the time is right, then. And, as to your actual question, the only way I know to avoid being smeared in the legal sense is to ask her what's on the table, what's off, and then let her lead. How about you? How do you protect your reputation?"

"By not having sex with random strangers. Kind of obvious, isn't it?"

"Why would that be obvious? You're incredibly attractive. I'm sure you could walk out of a club with your pick of any man."

I scoffed. "You're just being polite."

"I am not. Did we not establish in our first five minutes that I'm not someone who's polite for the sake of being polite? I'm a lawyer, for god's sake. I'm direct. Blunt. And honest. And," Dylan said, putting his elbow on the table and pointing a finger right at me, "you're hot."

Now I was flustered. Again.

I had a foreboding that Dylan Rhodes was going to cock up my data.

# 7

## DYLAN

Kama was squirming. She'd pulled her long ponytail over her shoulder and was twirling it. When I embarrassed her with talk about sex, she rubbed her nose—a classic sign that she was feeling stressed. But she continued to smile and laugh, and since I was enjoying putting her on the spot, I didn't stop.

Verbal sparring with her was like hanging out with my brothers or an old friend. I didn't have to put on airs around Kama. On normal dates, the end goal was a night of passionate sex, and I had to maintain a certain tone and energy that was always pointing toward the bedroom door.

And it wasn't just me. On those dates, I could tell when the woman was holding back, moderating her reactions just the way I was. If a date said something I thought was ridiculous—if she believed that dinosaurs helped build the pyramids or that *The Matrix* was a docudrama and we were all living in a computer simulation—I'd just smile and nod, smile and nod. The end goal was not to find a life partner but a bed buddy for one night. And, if the night went well and she wasn't too crazy, maybe another.

I probably should have felt more on edge with Kama

since I had more riding on my time with her. Instead, I was more myself than I could remember being with a woman. Maybe because she was transparent about her research and had no interest in sleeping with me, I could leave my virile-man schtick at the door. And that, I realized, was a relief.

I was having fun and hoped I'd pass her test to the second and third dates, not just so I could gather more intel —find a hole in her research that broke the informed consent contract—but also because I was thoroughly enjoying her company.

Yup, things were going to get complicated with Kama Ray. But it relieved me to know there would be no tears at the end of our brief, nonsexual relationship, and that there was no expectation that I was anything more than a rat in her research maze. That would make the whole 'taking her to court' situation a lot easier. She really did seem like a nice woman who was doing some interesting, maybe even important, research.

We ate our meals quietly for a few bites, exchanging smiles. She rubbed the side of her lip then pointed at mine, letting me know I had mayo on my face. I feigned deep embarrassment. She laughed and finally broke the pantomime time.

"I'm a little confused. You said that I'm not your type, but also that you think I'm attractive. Do you normally date women you find unattractive? Do you compensate for some insecurity about your own hotness by going out with women who you know will... umm..."

"Women who would be flattered that I was imagining them naked while we ate our buffalo burgers?"

Her face! It was priceless. I wished I could flip my phone over and snap a shot of that look. It was a perfect combination of shock and delight. The shape of her mouth seemed to say, "I am so offended," but her eyes darted and sparkled as if to say, "Yes, please. That."

She waved her hand between us with a motion like a windshield wiper. "You are not imagining me naked."

She said it with so much conviction she almost had me convinced. Almost.

"Aren't I?" I drawled.

Her expression immediately changed. Her chest heaved and she took a deep, quick inhale. Her eyes opened wide and she stared at me with pure terror.

"Panic. Attack. Get. Lizzy."

Then she turned sideways in her chair and laid her forearms on her thighs. Her back rocked slightly, and she mumbled something I couldn't understand. I stood up. I wanted to touch her, reassure her, but I figured that might make things worse since I'd obviously triggered this reaction. I scoped the restaurant for our server or her friend at the hostess podium. I caught the hostess's eye and pointed to Kama, who was still bent over and rocking harder now.

"Lizzy?" I called across the room.

She nodded and her face told me that she was familiar with this situation. Lizzy called out as she walked to our table. "Jenny! Ice water and a towel for Kama. Right now, please." Several people looked at Lizzy, then in the direction she was walking. At me. At Kama. Unabashedly staring. Whispering.

Another woman stood and walked purposefully toward us. She directed her question at me. "I'm a first responder. What happened?"

Lizzy was kneeling beside Kama, rubbing her back, whispering to her.

Before I could answer, the first responder knelt in front of Kama. She lifted Lizzy's hand from Kama's back, then looked up at me. "What's your friend's name?"

Lizzy and I both replied. I sat back down since there was nothing for me to do.

"Kama. My name is Sue. I'm a first responder. Can you hear me?"

Kama started to repeat the word "yup" over and over, without taking a breath. "Yup, yup, yup, yup, yup ..." Her head was down, and she was still rocking.

"Kama, can you look at me?"

"No, no, no, no, no ..."

"I need you to look up at me, Kama. I'm going to touch your shoulder. I want you to push into my hand when you feel it, okay? Can you do that?"

"Yup, yup, yup, yup ..."

Sue pressed one hand against Kama's collarbone and the other against her back and guided Kama until she was sitting upright. Her eyes were closed so tight she looked like she was in a desert windstorm, or trying to protect herself from icy snow in a blizzard. Her grimace suggested she was in pain.

"Good job, Kama. Can you open your eyes for me now?"

"No, no, no, no, no, no ..."

Lizzy had been riffling through Kama's laptop bag, dumping the contents of different pockets on the table. She held up a small prescription bottle and showed Sue. "She has an anti-anxiety med. Can I give it to her?"

"Not until she opens her eyes. You can't just put it in her mouth. I don't want her to choke."

"Kama," Lizzy said, "everyone in the restaurant is looking at you. Great performance, girlfriend. Broadway caliber."

A slight smile touched the corner of Kama's mouth.

"But their food is getting cold, and your date is clearly worried about you, so I need you to take your pill, okay?"

"Mmm-hmm, mmm-hmm, mmm-hmm ..."

Lizzy tapped Sue's leg and motioned for her to move out of the way, then squatted directly in front of Kama. "This nice lady won't let you take it unless you open your eyes, though. I'm right here. You're safe. I promise. Look into my eyes. You can do it."

Kama opened her eyes then quickly closed them again.

"See? Just me. In a restaurant with fifty concerned diners. Open again. I have your pill in my fingers. Ready to pop it under your tongue, but you have to open your eyes again."

Kama took a long, deep inhale and then opened her eyes and held contact with Lizzy until the pill was under her tongue. Then she closed them again and leaned against the back of her chair, still rocking. Lizzy wet the cloth with water, wringing out the extra on the floor behind Kama's chair. She dabbed Kama's forehead and cheeks with it.

"Feel good?"

Kama nodded and exhaled one long, "Mmmm."

"Can you open your eyes again for me?"

She shook her head. "No, no, no, no."

Sue looked at me. "Do you have a car? Can you drive her home?"

Before I could answer, both Lizzy and Kama replied with an emphatic, "No!"

"Well, she's not in a state to ride the bus," Sue offered.

"I'm aware," Lizzy said. "This isn't my first panic-attack rodeo. I'll make sure she gets home safely. Thank you so much for your help."

Sue touched Kama's shoulder. "You take care," she said before heading back to her table. Kama nodded but remained silent and kept her eyes closed.

"Memorable first date, Kama. I don't expect this poor guy will ever forget you now."

"Dylan," she whispered. "Gone?"

I silently asked Lizzy if I could talk to Kama. I was worried I might make things worse. But she gave me the thumbs-up.

"Nope. Still here."

Kama's lip twitched. "Sorry," she said.

"Sorry for nothing. I was feeling a bit uncomfortable being myself, but you just showed me I have nothing to worry about."

Lizzy gave me a thumbs-up and Kama nodded, but her eyes stayed closed.

"Does this happen often?" I asked her.

Kama shrugged her shoulders.

Lizzy answered. "It's been almost two years since the last one, wouldn't you say? She's had them ever since I met her when we were in Grade Four. So, seventeen or eighteen years."

"Five," Kama said.

"Way longer than five years—"

"Me. Five." She took a deep breath and sighed. "I was five."

"Five when they started?" I asked.

She nodded.

"Do you know why?"

She shrugged again, but Lizzy nodded and put her finger to her lips.

"Hey, Kama, what if I call you an Uber—" Lizzy said, but Kama's eyes snapped open.

"No." She looked at Lizzy then at me, and they were closed again.

"Let me finish! Sheesh. I'll call you an Uber with a woman driver, and maybe Dylan would go with you?"

I nodded at Lizzy.

"He'll make sure you get home safe. There'll be two people, a chauffeur and a lawyer. Sounds like the start of a good joke."

"You?" she pleaded.

"I can't, sweetie. I'm working. You need to get home to sleep, and I've got hours more 'til my shift ends."

Her face changed. She clenched her jaw, squeezed her eyes tighter, and her forehead wrinkled. This was not an idea that would be easily accepted. Lizzy shrugged her shoulders.

"Hey, Kama?" I leaned across the table so I could speak quietly. Her eyes met mine for a blink then closed again. "Would you be comfortable if two first responders drove you home? A woman and a man?"

"No ambulance," she said.

"No. Just in their car. My brother and his girlfriend are firefighters and first responders. In fact, Sophie's basically a nurse. I think you'll feel safe with her. And I was planning to meet them for a drink after our dinner date. I can just ask them to come here instead."

Kama didn't answer but her face relaxed and she nodded.

Lizzy touched my arm. "Good idea."

I leaned in close to Lizzy, pointed in the direction of Sue, the first responder, and whispered in her ear, "Can you please add that woman's tab to my bill?"

# 8

## KAMA

The spike and subsequent adrenaline crash from the panic attack would have been enough to make me need a nap, but with the added effect of the anti-anxiety pill, I couldn't stay awake on the ride home.

I remember getting in the back seat of a car with a woman, and Lizzy promising me she'd get me home. That I'd be safe. I trusted Lizzy, so I trusted these strangers. And Dylan? He wasn't in the back seat with me, so I had no idea if he came along or not.

I know that the woman walked me to my dorm apartment, and that she seemed worried about leaving me on my own. That made me laugh. And then it upset me, especially coming from a woman who was half my size. Did she worry about being on her own? Why do people always worry about girls being on their own? Why don't they ever worry about us being left alone *with* someone? That seemed the riskier proposition 99.99 percent of the time.

Anyway, I was fine. A little embarrassed about Dylan living through that show. But not humiliated. Panic Attacks R Us. Nothing to be ashamed about. And at this stage in my life, it was easy to find the humor in the situation most of the time. The only thing that wasn't funny was that I'd probably have to exclude our date from my research data. Not only had the odds of seeing Dylan again just dropped to zero, but now there were also far too many anomalies to make the data relevant. I'd have to ask my thesis advisor if any of it could be salvaged.

I rolled out of bed and realized I was still fully dressed. All that had been taken off were my boots and jacket. That made me feel a little more at ease. I looked around the room and didn't see my laptop bag. I experienced a moment of anxiety—had it been left at the restaurant? I'd have to wake up Lizzy and ask if she had it. But for that I needed my phone, which wasn't on my bedside table.

More heart palpitations.

I took the four steps from my bedside to the bedroom door and looked down the short hall. My laptop bag was hanging on a coat hook at the front door. Thank goodness. I started toward it and registered that my bathroom door was closed. I never closed the bathroom door.

Someone must be in it.

Quiet as I could, I pulled on my Doc Martens without tying them, took my jacket from the hook, and slipped out of my apartment. I looked in the pocket where I always kept my keys. They weren't there.

*Where are they? Where are they?*

I left my dorm apartment unlocked and speed walked down the hall to the elevator. I tied one boot while I waited for it to arrive and hit the second-floor button, having decided to find my keys in the safety of the multi-purpose room.

A handful of grad students were there, chatting and having coffee. I smiled and tried to look normal with one boot undone, my hair no doubt a wreck, and my bag and jacket all bunched up in my arms.

"Hey, Kama!" Rebecca called. "Want to sit with me?"

I couldn't very well say no, so I headed over to her couch and dropped my coat and bag beside me.

"What's up? You look kind of flustered. Wait! Did you break a research rule last night? Is this a walk of shame?" Her eyes went wide as if she'd just caught me in a dirty secret.

I was anxious. And irritated that I'd lost what may have been valuable data. And upset that I'd have to go on yet another first date and hope it turned into three dates. And confused about where my keys were. And scared that someone might be hiding in my bathroom... and I lost it on poor Rebecca.

"Of course I didn't break a rule! Don't even joke about that. What if someone overheard you and reported it to the ethics committee? That could jeopardize my research. And you know I can't afford to lose this placement."

"I'm sorry. I was just kidding around. I know you would never—"

"And what kind of patriarchal BS are you supporting by suggesting that if I had just been getting home from a date, I should feel shameful about it? Honestly, I can't even..."

"I'm—"

"No. Forget it. I need to make a call." I stood to find a new seat and upended my laptop bag. Everything in the main compartment hit the floor. Well, that did it. I lost whatever paltry amount of control I had in me, slumped back down on the couch, and started to cry.

"I'm sorry," I said to Rebecca. "I had a panic attack on my date last night. I don't really know how I got home. My keys are gone, and I think there's someone hiding in my bathroom. I shouldn't have yelled at you."

"It was just a joke. Sorry it upset you. But why do you think someone's hiding in your bathroom?"

"The door is closed. I never close the door. Why would it be closed unless someone was in it?"

"You think your date is hiding in there?"

I shrugged. "I don't know. I doubt it. It was a woman who brought me in. And the guy's a lawyer. He wouldn't mess with his reputation by being some creep. I don't think. I don't know."

"Let me text Matt and see if he's awake. I'll ask him to go check for you. Yeah?"

I nodded.

Matt was another psychology grad student who lived in our building. We sometimes went cycling together. He was a good guy. Heck, all the men who lived in the building were good guys. Men I'd trust with an unlocked door.

I realized I was still in a high-anxiety headspace. That was new. My attacks never lasted more than a couple of hours. One pill had always been enough to knock my nervous system back into alignment. But then, that was when I was taking them every day. It had been a couple of months since I'd last felt the need to take one.

"Matt's awake. He said he'll have a look."

I nodded and tried to smile.

"What happened last night? I haven't seen you like this since … well, never."

"I have no idea. This guy, Dylan, first date. He was challenging me big-time. I don't think I'll be able to use the data in my research."

"That sucks."

"Yeah. And it's too bad since from a date point of view, I was actually having fun for the first time. I mean, I am so not his type, but he's the kind of guy who'd be fun just to hang out with. Smart and funny. And …" I paused.

"What?"

"Easy on the eyes," I admitted. "I'm a hypocrite, aren't I? Getting all up in your face about the walk of shame comment but then objectifying this man by focusing on his looks. I'm a horrible human."

"Nah, just a human human."

Rebecca's phone pinged. She held it up for me to read.

> **MATT**
>
> All clear. Bathroom empty. Don't worry, nothing stolen. 😬 Keys on kitchen counter. Want me to lock up and bring them down to the MPR?

"Oh, no," I moaned.

She looked at the text. "What? This is good, isn't it?"

"Except the part where Matt saw my bathtub book." I debated taking an anxiety pill.

"Because ...?"

"*Erotic Stories for the Bath*. Waterproof edition."

Rebecca laughed so loud that everyone in the MPR turned to stare at us. I searched through the pile of my belongings to find my phone, so I could distract myself from everything going on around me. I had three text messages. The first was from Lizzy

> **LIZZY**
>
> Call me when you wake up. Don't care how early. Love you!

The second was from an unknown number:

> **UNKNOWN**
>
> Hi Kama. This is Sophie, Dylan's friend. Your keys are on the kitchen counter. Sorry I couldn't lock up. Call if you want to fill in memory holes from the drive home. Hope you're feeling better.

The last was from Dylan:

DYLAN

Text when you get up. Want to make sure you're ok.

I knew from over a decade of being Lizzy's best friend that she'd be much happier to wake up to a text from me than to her phone ringing. I replied with a purple heart emoji. It was the secret code I used to let her know I was fine. Any other reply was a red flag and warranted an immediate phone call. And if the call wasn't answered, arriving uninvited at my parents' house. I'd used it a couple dozen times, once or twice a year, until I got my residence scholarship. I hadn't used it since I moved away from home.

I replied with a simple "thanks" to Sophie and added her number to my contacts in case she decided to call or text me.

How to reply to Dylan felt trickier. I could just let him know I was fine, which was all he'd asked. But that didn't feel like enough, given what he'd had to deal with. And … Oh no, he'd paid for dinner.

Dylan—so sorry I left you with the bill. I promise that was not a sneaky way to get out of paying my share.

I read my message as I hit send and realized it was a terrible apology.

I mean, it was sneaky, but it wasn't part of the first-date plan. I'll e-transfer the amount to you.

I logged into my online banking, created a payee profile for Dylan, then sent him twenty-five dollars. More than enough to cover my burger and soda, tax, and a twenty-percent tip. I hoped he was a generous tipper.

Matt came into the MPR and dropped down on the arm

of the couch beside Rebecca, planting a kiss on top of her head.

"Thanks, babe," she said.

He threw me my keys and winked. "Your secret's safe with me."

"Thanks." I gave him a half smile and started to pack everything back into my bag. "Thanks for getting up for me."

"Hey, that's what friends do."

"Well, I'm lucky to have you guys as friends. I'll see you later. I'm exhausted. I'm going back to bed 'til class."

I was just crawling back under my covers when my phone rang. It was Dylan. I let it ring three times before deciding to answer.

"Hey," I said.

"Hey back. What's with this e-transfer? You know I'm not going to deposit it, right?"

"What? No, of course I don't know that."

"Well, I'm not. Not even sure why you sent it."

"Um, because I always pay for my own meal on a first date."

"Why? Is that part of your standardized research?" he asked.

I hesitated. Even though all my other dates had signed the same form Dylan had, they all seemed to forget the fact that they were just data points to me. Dylan was challenging everything. "In fact, it is."

"So, if I don't accept this money, what happens to your data?"

"If I can even use it now, you'd mess it up."

"And what happens if I mess it up?"

I paused, as much for effect as to think about what to say

next. I really wanted to go out with him again. I had this uncomfortable feeling that it wasn't just to collect data. "Well, then I guess there'll be no need for second or third dates."

"Rock, meet hard place," he laughed. "So, basically, if I accept your money—which, for the record, I am not happy about—I can go out with you again. But if I don't take your filthy lucre, I don't get a second date? You are evil incarnate, Kama. And, like you admitted, sneaky."

"Yup, sneaky like a repressed memory. But you could look at it this way: I'm letting you off the hook for a second date. You don't have to tell me you're not interested. I'd really prefer you accept the transfer, but if you don't want to, then don't. You won't have to see me and my anxious self again."

"But I want to see you. I think I earned a second date after what you put me through."

"After what I put you through? What did I put... Oh. The embarrassment, being the center of a scene?"

"What? No. The verbal ass-kicking I got from my brother for triggering your anxiety. He already thinks I'm an asshole player who eats damsels' hearts for breakfast."

"And do you?" I rolled over and hugged myself around my extra pillow.

"Only the ones that get left unattended on my bedside table."

"I see." I looked over at my own bedside table, "Anything to avoid a commitment, right?"

Silence for a breath. "Not true. A few months ago I fell in love with a carbon 14 expert. Even proposed to her."

"Really? I'm sorry." I felt terrible for having given him such a hard time about not wanting to be in a relationship.

"Yeah. But all she wanted to do was date." Silence, and then he said, "Ba-dum-bum."

The dumb joke made me laugh harder than I normally

would have because his timing was perfect. Dylan made me feel comfortable. Even last night, when things could have felt awkward, they didn't because he didn't make it weird.

"So a second date?" he asked.

"Are you asking me out, or are you asking if you've made the cut?"

"Is there a difference?"

"Seriously? Of course there is. An enormous difference. If you're asking me out, it means you want to see me again. But if you're asking if you made the cut, it means your ego wants to know if I want to see you again."

He laughed. "You should have been a lawyer with that level of logicking."

"You should have been a comic with your perfectly timed one-liners."

"I considered it. I even did a performance about puns in high school," he said.

"Oh yeah?" I could feel this was a setup.

"Yeah, but really it was just a play on words."

"That's terrible."

"Give me a break. I was only fifteen. Kama, can I take you out again?"

"Only if—"

"Already done. Check your account. I accepted the damn money. But for the record, it was three dollars short."

"How is that possible? It should have been more than enough."

"Then you must be a cheapskate tipper. So when do I get to see you again?"

My concern about the standardized third-date, no-kiss handshake intensified.

"Next Thursday for dinner?" I suggested.

"How about tomorrow?"

"But tomorrow is Saturday. What about... what's her name? Tanya?"

"Meh. Tanya will still be around after we've had our three dates. Or she won't. Either way, I'd rather see you again."

My heart did a little jump. A very unlike-me little jump. I put it down to fatigue and withdrawal from the anti-anxiety pill I'd taken, which made no sense at all except that everything in my system felt out of whack.

"Okay, then. Tomorrow. I'll text you details. Is seven too early?"

"Seven is perfect. Can't wait to see you again," he said. He sounded sincere.

"You too."

I ended the call and lay on my bed. I assumed he was already at his office and imagined what Dylan Rhodes looked like, freshly shaved and in a suit. Suddenly, it felt like a book-in-the-bath kind of morning.

# 9

---

# DYLAN

I decided I was going to tell Mr. James that I'd gone out with Kama and that, at least in my experience, she'd followed all the rules and then some. I didn't feel good about going out with her again with the ulterior motive of taking her down. Rather than leave a message for his assistant Barb —she always let it go to voice mail—I stood at her desk and watched her check James's calendar.

"He can squeeze you in at six-thirty for ten minutes. Does that work for you?"

I looked at my watch, not to check the time but to subtly indicate that it was only eight-thirty and that meeting time would make my workday almost eleven hours long. I could tell she understood by the face she made.

"Is he with anyone now?"

"Six-thirty. Yes or no?"

I exhaled loudly but stopped myself halfway through the breath. That was exactly how my father expressed his frustration: without saying what he was actually thinking. It was a habit I'd hated since I was a kid. "Yes. Please and thank you, Barb."

"Pleasure. Have a nice day," she said with a too-happy

smile.

"Another interminable day," I muttered as I headed back to the elevator. I pushed the button but then decided to have a look at my soon-to-be new office in the daylight.

Unlike James's office, which had opaque walls and a solid wood door that gave him full privacy when it was closed, this office was a fishbowl. Not only was the door made of glass, so too were the walls to the hallway. It made sense, since the only daylight at this end of the floor had to come from the offices. I walked along the hall, peeking in on the three other junior partners. Their heads were down, looking at laptop screens. One assistant served all the juniors. I'd smiled at her before but never said more than hello, so I introduced myself.

"Good morning," I said to the top of her head.

She looked up and then back down at her monitor. "Good morning. Do you have an appointment? I'm sorry; I wasn't expecting anyone."

"No. No, I don't. I'm Dylan Rhodes. From downstairs. I just wanted to introduce myself since it looks like I'll be making my home in the office at the end soon."

She stood and extended her hand. "Nice to meet you, Mr. Rhodes. I'm Eleanor. I guess I'll be your personal assistant. When will you be moving in? I haven't received instructions."

"To be determined. I've got one case to wrap up and then…" I gave her the universal gesture for 'we'll see.'

"Oh." She nodded and sat back down. "Well, good luck with that last case, Mr. Rhodes."

"Thanks. Do you mind if I have a look in the office? Walk around, have a seat for a minute? I want to give myself a concrete image so I can visualize my future." I laughed to suggest I might be joking, but I was dead serious.

"Make yourself at home."

I sat at the desk and opened each of the three drawers in

the filing cabinet beside it. The top drawer contained basic supplies: company notepads and pens, paperclips, a stapler.

The desk was modern, with a smoked-glass top and chrome legs. The leather chair communicated 'Very Important Person' with its high back and wide arms. The view was spectacular. I could see the whole west side of downtown Vancouver, all the way to Stanley Park.

It felt good. The bookshelf had a few of your standard law books on it. Downstairs, we shared these resources. I imagined my Top Thirty Under Thirty award sitting in the middle of the top shelf, right at eye level.

Before I stood, I took a selfie. I was seated at the desk, looking out into the hall. Then I stood and took another, framing myself with the window and the view behind me. I sent both pictures to my dad and all five brothers with a message:

> One day soon all this will be mine. Even the curtains.

Of course, there were no curtains in the office. This was an inside joke my brothers and I started when we were teens after watching *Monty Python and The Holy Grail*. In the movie, the king is standing at an open window, overlooking his land and says, "One day all this will be yours." And the dim-witted prince replies, "What? The curtains?"

Dad never figured out that while he was pointing to all the kingly positions he held on powerful corporate boards and telling us that if we worked hard we'd be able to wear the prince's crown, that we were mocking that ambition.

He'd say things like, "You're a Rhodes. You shoot higher than that."

This office, and the promotion that came with it, was exactly where Dad wanted us all to be. But one by one, we'd failed him. Everyone except me. I was still on track to join him in his kingdom one day.

Dad texted back,

DAD

Proud of you, son.

I laughed out loud and pumped one fist in a victory cheer, since that message was worth at least five of whatever drink I wanted from my brothers. It was another insider game we had. Anytime one of us could prove that Dad that had said he was proud of us, the other brothers had to buy us a drink. At first the reward was Slurpees or sodas. Now it was usually a high-end scotch or a ridiculous mixed drink that we'd have delivered to a woman at whatever bar we were out at.

Today was a good day, so it was strange that I was having trouble focusing on research for my active cases. My mind kept going back to Kama. I wondered what had triggered her panic attack. It didn't *feel* like I'd said anything trigger-worthy, but then, I had no experience with this kind of episode. For all I knew, it was just a random thing that happened to her. But that seemed unlikely.

Since I couldn't get her off my mind, I gave myself fifteen minutes to replay the recorded conversation from the end of our date. My mistake was hitting 'play' from the start and listening to the first few minutes. Once I was back with her, I didn't want to fast-forward. I pictured the way she got flustered when I knocked her off her date script. It made me smile.

Knowing I couldn't bill Booker for eighty minutes of strolling down memory lane, I sped the replay up to double time for a few seconds. But when I reached the part where she was asking me to sign the informed consent document, I slowed it back down to transcribe what she read. It might prove useful in my argument to Mr. James at the end of the day.

Once I started typing—a job that my future assistant

would do for me—I fell into the zone and didn't stop until I got to the part when Kama got discombobulated.

I listened and rewound a half dozen times, trying to remember exactly her face and body language when I joked that I was imagining watching her eat her burger naked. I'd read amusement, but obviously I'd been wrong. And I felt terrible. She was apparently much more sensitive about sex than I'd assumed.

The day dragged, and by the time Mr. James was ready to see me, I was glad I'd been forced to wait. That morning, I'd planned to tell him I wasn't willing to go on any more information-gathering dates with Kama, and that there was nothing I could add to back up Booker's testimony. If Booker wanted to take Kama to court, he'd have to do so on his own, and frankly, it was a case I had no interest in supporting and losing.

But after having spent the day thinking about her, I'd decided to try a different tack. I would still go on the next two dates with her, on the company clock, to gather as much information as I could about her integrity. That would help bring James onside with dropping the case. I had no doubt that between my testimony, her integrity, and Booker's personality, a judge would drop the case in a heartbeat, even if James didn't. And Kama would walk away unscathed.

But I still had an excellent reason to darken his doorstep after hours. Tanya—my on-again, off-again Saturday-night hookup—had called with a desperate request. Something I, as the firm's media attention grabber, could help her with.

I knocked on James's door.

"Come."

"Mr. James, thank you for seeing me."

"Something important, I assume," he said, not looking up from his computer.

"An idea. I was talking to a woman I know socially, and

she mentioned an opportunity that I think would raise the profile of the firm. Sir."

James grunted, still appearing fully focused on his work.

"Have you heard of the Vancouver Social Justice Film Festival?"

"No."

"It's celebrating its tenth year. It has a solid reputation internationally. The people who come to the films are typically university-educated, white-collar professionals."

"Rhodes. Your point," he said, finally looking up at me.

"I think our firm could get some good public attention with our target client base if we were to do a sponsorship. They have a variety of themed evenings with short films about specific subjects. The sponsor gets prime billing. We'd be the only law firm sponsoring an evening. The rest of the sponsors are credit unions, banks, and accounting firms."

James sat back in his chair and tented his hands, tapping his fingertips together in a slow rhythm.

"Financial commitment?"

I smiled, hoping to suggest this was the deal of a lifetime. "Just ten thousand dollars."

He made eye contact and held it. I leaned forward slightly and tried to mirror his breathing and facial expression.

"What's in it for you?"

That caught me by surprise. But I knew exactly what was in it for me: karma points with Tanya, a woman who I enjoyed having sex with and who had no interest in getting serious. Kind of the perfect woman. And hard to find.

"Aside from feeling good about being a member of an organization that's supporting a worthy cause?"

James rolled his eyes.

"As a sponsor, the firm chooses the films that will be shown in the themed night we're supporting. I hoped I could be on that curation committee."

He nodded. "You're interested in independent film?"

"Yes, sir. Many of my electives were in film studies." Okay, that wasn't entirely true. But I wasn't going to tell him I was hoping to watch the films naked with Tanya.

"I'll need to approve the final list of films you select."

"Of course."

"Good timing on this idea, Rhodes. Tell accounting. Say it's got my go-ahead."

"Thank you, Mr. James." I stood to leave.

"Before you go, what's the progress on Bob Booker's claim? Have you been out with the girl yet?"

"First date."

"And?"

"So far she's painting entirely inside the lines. Nothing to report to the university's ethics committee."

"On her best behavior, is she? She knows you're a lawyer, I assume."

I nodded.

"Maybe she's giving you special treatment."

"I don't think so. She had the right disclosure form for me to sign and wouldn't agree to summarize for me. I tried to trip her up, but she clearly knows the rules and is following them."

"So far," James said.

"Yes, sir. So far."

"Well, you'll find something, Rhodes. I have faith in you."

"Working on it. Thank you, sir."

James dropped his gaze back to his screen and waved me out of his office.

This was my future. Intimate, one-on-one meetings with the big bosses. All I had to figure out was how to make both James and Booker feel like they'd won without throwing Kama under the bus.

# 10

## KAMA

Dylan and I met outside *Amori a Primavera*, the restaurant I went to for all my second dates. He was thirty minutes early, which threw me off my game since I'd expected—no, I'd planned—to have half an hour to get focused and in the research zone. When I asked why he was so early, he said that since I was also just arriving, he was right on time. Then he winked. I didn't know if the wink meant 'we're on the same wavelength' or something more sinister, like 'I know your game and won't be making this easy for you.'

Our reserved table hadn't been cleared yet, so Tammy, another friend, sat us at the table she always held just for me.

"Well, I for one am happy we're both early. Gives me extra time with you," he said.

I smiled without looking at him. I was trying to figure out what to do. He'd just made things awkward, not only since I wouldn't be able to have my pre-date cup of chai, but also because I'd have to convince him to move to the other table after our drinks were served. That would be weird.

It was important that I keep as many variables as

consistent as possible, date to date. And sitting at a different table would change too many of the sensory details that people don't normally pay attention to. How clear the music is, how much server activity would pass us, and most importantly, the position of the televisions. The seat Dylan was supposed to sit in didn't have an easy sight line to any of the TVs in the place. But the table we were at was like sitting front row in a theater, and too distracting even for someone trying not to watch.

"Actually, Dylan, as rude as this might sound, I need you to come back at the right time. I'm just not ready for you."

He laughed. "Intentional double entendre?"

It took me a few seconds to understand, and when it clicked, I moaned. I'd been dreading this date more than any other second date. I already had to recover from the abrupt end to the first one and, against my best judgment, I was starting to like this guy. I was on edge, and he was pushing me over before the date had even properly started.

"Not intentional, but probably accurate," I admitted. "So, can I ask you to, I don't know, maybe sit at the bar and have a drink without me? I know it's kind of rude, but—"

"Research. I get it. I'm messing with your data again, aren't I? Sorry about that. Of course. I'll be right over there, looking like a sad man who's been stood up by his date." He pointed and pouted, then laughed and walked away.

Tammy brought me a chai latte without my even asking.

"Whoa! He's to die for. I'm shocked he needs an app to get dates," she gushed.

"He doesn't. This is some kind of setup."

Tammy leaned in, her ear seeking more details. I waved as if to say, 'Not getting into it now.'

"Well, when you're done with him, be sure to send him back here."

"Get in line. Lizzy's got first dibs," I rolled my eyes. "You realize that you people, my friends, are the reason I'm doing this research?"

"What do you mean?" she said with a smirk.

"Right. Tell me you wouldn't let him pay for dinner, go home with him, and complete your economic exchange with whatever non-monetary assets you have to offer."

"Kama, sometimes the woman wants to have sex just as much as the man does, you know… and, yes, I am one of *those* women." She looked over at Dylan, who was chatting with the bartender, making her laugh. "And with that man, I'd offer to pay for his dinner if it meant bringing him back to my place."

"I'll be sure to tell him," I said. "Now go. I need to go over my questions."

Tammy went back to her job and left me staring at Dylan's profile. He was watching the screen on the bar wall, drinking a beer. He had a friendly, welcoming energy about him. I tore my eyes off him and pulled a folded piece of paper from my purse. My cheat sheet. It only had eight questions on it. I had them memorized, but looking at them was like prepping for a play: one line could trigger an entire scene. I imagined his answers and my replies. It was both preparation and a game I played with myself, guessing what he'd say before he answered.

When I looked up, a woman was sitting on the stool beside Dylan. She had a half-finished cocktail in her hand. I looked around to see if she was obviously with anyone else. Yup. Two other women at a nearby table were gazing at the perfectly matched new couple, Dylan and their beautiful friend. The woman had her hand on his arm. Subtle. Not.

Dylan was fully engaged with her, talking, smiling, lots of nodding. And why not? She was a knockout. Gorgeous, long, red hair, flashy jewelry, painted nails. And her heels. No way could I stand, let alone walk, in shoes like hers. This was someone proud to flaunt her womanhood.

I looked down at my own hands. No nail polish, no bracelets tonight. I touched my throat and confirmed: no necklace. My hair was pulled up in a loose bun, casual, planned messy. At least I was wearing cool shoes—purple and red, kitten heel mules. Still, this woman made me feel like I'd just rolled out of bed. I was angry. Not at her, but at myself for feeling less-than by comparison.

Looking up again, I saw Dylan staring at me, making 'save me' eyes and actually mouthing, 'Save me,' while the woman rubbed his arm and, it appeared, sniffed his neck.

With that one interaction, I went from thinking I'd be having dinner alone to laughing. I shook my head at Dylan, shrugged my shoulders, and formed my fingers into the shape of a heart. I held my heart-shaped hands in front of my chest and motioned like it was beating.

Dylan took the woman's hand off his arm and leaned away, turning his back to her as he swung his legs from the barstool to the ground. She grabbed for his arm as he reached for his beer. He smiled at her but shook his head and then pointed at me.

She and the other two women who'd been watching her, all looked in my direction. I was mortified. They probably thought I was a coworker ... No, I wasn't dressed well enough. Maybe his sister's best friend. Maybe his adopted sister. I sucked up my courage, smiled, and waved back.

When Dylan reached me, he made it one-hundred-percent clear that I was not a blood relation. He looked down and whispered, "Please roll with this," as he planted a kiss right on my lips. I didn't have time to react. It was a relatively innocent kiss as far as kisses go, but it was mouth to mouth. His lips were so soft, like melting soft-serve ice cream. Without thinking I pressed into them and when he pulled away I sucked my bottom lip into my mouth and bit it to stop from sighing out loud.

He licked his lips, too. "Chai. My favorite," he said,

pulling up the chair opposite me. "I'm sorry. I know it's still a bit early, but that was getting uncomfortable."

"You didn't *look* uncomfortable," I managed to say, feeling decidedly uncomfortable myself.

"I have the best poker face you'll ever meet."

He totally ignored what just happened between us. Did he not feel what I felt? I leaned back. Of course he didn't. I felt a tinge of sadness but pushed it away. He was a research subject. And I... I don't know what I was but it wasn't what he was looking for. I knew that much.

"Don't you get hit on all the time when you're out at a bar?"

"Sure. But I'm not usually already out with a beautiful woman. I'm usually with one of my brothers. If a lady I'm not interested in comes on to me, I can point her in the direction of another set of ripped six-pack abs." Dylan flexed his pecs and darn it all, didn't I mimic him in my own way, thrusting my breasts up and out.

He smirked. "You know, it's not just women who need to learn how to dissuade overly enthusiastic suitors. Some of us guys need to learn what you're figuring out with your research, too. How to be polite but forceful. That's the problem, right? If you're nice and polite, but say no, it's interpreted as a soft no, or a no that has some wiggle room. Right?"

"Yes, that's it exactly." I felt a rush of joy. "I had no idea that it went both ways. None of the research I've seen talks about that. And all of my friends are women, so, that's... wow... that's a serious blind spot."

"Stick with me, kid. We'll change the world together."

"I suppose having a lawyer in my back pocket wouldn't be a bad thing."

Dylan shook his head and smiled. "Again with the double entendres."

I blushed and was saved by Tammy, who waved from our reserved table.

"Let's go start this date," I said.

"I don't think I've ever been out with a woman who's made me have not just one but *two* start-of-date do-overs. I kind of feel like this should count as date four, not date two."

"You wish," I said without thinking.

"Do I? Why? What happens on the fourth date?"

I answered with an eyebrow waggle and started to walk straight toward the table where the three women who'd marked Dylan as a catch sat. I smiled, wiggled my fingers at the lady with the perfect manicure, and sat in my chair. Dylan sat with his back to the rest of the room.

"What happens on the fourth date?" he asked again.

"Well, since we'll never have a fourth date, I suppose there's no harm in telling you. Date four, in my old dating life, was the milestone that made having sex okay. If we made it through four dates, that meant that there was more than just horniness at play. So sex was on the table."

"On the table?" He patted the one we were seated at. "In the restaurant? Kama, are you an exhibitionist? I'm—"

"No! Why do you do this to me? You make me say things that have the wrong meaning. That's not what I meant. I meant … Oh, never mind. You know what I mean."

"Actually, I don't know anything about you. Very little. Except that you look kind of like a guppy when you're having a panic attack." He closed his eyes and did a funny thing with his lips.

I buried my face in my hands.

"Do you know what triggers it? I mean, I figure it was something I did. Can you tell me, so I don't do it again?" Dylan's whole demeanor changed from kidding around to looking truly concerned.

That was the million-dollar question right there, and I

had no idea. Well, I knew that being alone with my brother was never safe, but my anxiety rarely hit that breaking point with anyone else. Rarely, but not never.

"All I can say is that I think it's when I feel threatened. But nothing more specific than that. It's just this spontaneous feeling and then ... that embarrassing fish act."

"Don't be embarrassed. Guppies are cute. You just want to hold them and squeeze them and call them George, you know?"

"Okay, you're insane. Guppies are not cute."

"Did I say *guppies*? Silly me. I meant *puppies*. Puppies are cute. Seriously cute. You can't argue with that."

"Honestly, stop!" I shook my head and realized that Dylan had a way of making me feel unselfconscious. Maybe it was because he didn't pretend like nothing had happened. Or that he joked about it. The only other person who poked fun at me was Lizzy. There's something that normalizes the weirdness for me when people feel comfortable enough to make jokes about it.

"Sorry. My apologies." He handed me the pepper grinder and said, "As long as you're holding this, I'll shut up."

I accepted it and pointed to the menu. "Figure out what you want."

He curled his fingers toward himself a few times, enthusiastically but silently, asking for the pepper grinder back.

I shook my head but had to laugh. I handed it back to him.

"You figure out what you want, and I'll have the same. Can I do that? I mean, that's what you did on our last date, so I figure that's fair game. You're not sexist about it... are you?"

"You're impossible. Give me back that grinder."

He handed it back and looked at the menu, pointing at options while making ridiculous faces and noises, as if trying to communicate 'that looks delicious' or 'who would order that?' without using actual words.

When Tammy came back, she asked Dylan what he'd like. He smiled angelically at her and said, "I believe it's proper etiquette to allow the lady to order first."

Not one other date had suggested I order first.

Tammy looked at me and shrugged. "Kama? What are you having?"

I stared at Dylan. He was smiling like he'd just won the most annoying little brother award. He thought he'd beaten me. Not a chance.

"I think, for a change, I'll have the kale salad. No dressing. No sides. Just a big, beautiful bowl of kale."

"Seriously?" Tammy scrunched her nose. "Nothing else? Just plain kale? Do you at least want it steamed?"

"Nope. Just raw." I nodded and gave Dylan my best 'take that' face.

He nodded back with what could only be interpreted as an expression that said, 'Challenge accepted.'

"Well, it seems we're eating family style tonight, so to go with our delightful kale *salad*"—he made air quotes—"we would like the prime rib, medium. Fries, of course, since, well, kale. And one extra serving of the roasted vegetables, please."

"Do you want the ten- or fourteen-ounce steak?"

Dylan continued to look at the server but tilted his head my way. "How much does she usually eat?"

Tammy chuckled. "If you're sharing with Kama, go with fourteen ounces."

"Perfect," he said.

I picked up the pepper grinder and shook it at him.

"How did you know I was hoping to have steak?" I asked, dumbfounded.

"Just the way you were looking at the menu. You paused and tapped a couple times on it. It was a dead giveaway.

You, Ms. Ray, have a terrible poker face. Or poker finger, I guess."

"Are you always that observant?" I asked, while my heart did a disconcerting little double beat.

"Only when it matters."

"And what I wanted to eat matters?"

"Of course it does. I figured you'd do something stupid so I couldn't, or wouldn't, order the same as you. You're kind of transparent, you know."

"I am not!"

"You're not? Apologies. I guess my superpower is seeing through your opaqueness, then. Cool. I've been trying to figure out my superpower for years."

"I think your superpower is one-upping me."

"And I think your superpower, Ms. Ray, is unlocking the cage where I normally keep my inner jackass when I'm on a date."

"Something we can agree on," I said.

The goal of date two was to ensure the man knew I was interested in him. It was easy enough whether I was actually interested or not. I had a list of questions that made my dates feel good about themselves, which in theory would lead them to feel good about me.

If I played my cards right, Dylan—well, date two— would ask me back to his place. I'd decline, of course, and his reaction was where the interesting data would start to appear. But I wouldn't use my theoretical Jedi powers on this date. This was the control date that revealed his non-manipulated reaction.

If he was gracious, our third date would take one form. If he was agitated or showed any frustration, it would take a different form.

I liked to guess the outcome of date two based on our first-date interactions. I knew Dylan was comfortable having sex on the first date since he'd said as much, but he also made it clear that his reputation as a nice guy was more important to him than a one-night stand. So I was almost one-hundred-percent certain that Dylan would be gracious about any rejection from me—if he even asked me to come over. That's what I wasn't so confident about. Since he never lost sight of the fact that these dates were research, I suspected he wouldn't ask me to sleep with him.

"So, how does this second date work? Or"—he put his fingertips together and wiggled them like an evil scientist —"can we consider this our fourth date?"

"No, we cannot," I said, as much to convince myself as to inform Dylan. "And just treat this like a normal date. That's what I'm doing." I smiled in a way I knew would highlight my one dimple.

"So I can't do anything to mess it up?"

I shook my head. "Nope. Whatever you do, whatever you say, you will be—you are—perfect."

I started to track my mental checklist of compliments to him. My target was twenty, half of which I hoped to set up so he'd give them to himself. Because my definition of a normal date, even if I wasn't collecting data, would still be as Kama-the-psychology-major first—and Kama-looking-for-a-man, never.

# 11

## DYLAN

Kama seemed a lot more relaxed than she had on our first date, even though I'd clearly thrown her off by arriving so early. That hadn't been my plan, but it seemed to work in my favor. I had no idea that Jessica would be here with her posse, but when she came to the bar to say hello, I asked her to start overtly flirting with me, to make me more attractive to Kama. She was happy to be my wingman since I'd done the same for her a dozen times during university. We hadn't seen each other since graduation, so it was nice to catch up.

"So, what does a normal date two with Kama Ray look like?"

She looked thoughtful before she answered. "Well, it looks like two people doing a lot of talking, getting to know each other, hearing each other's stories—"

"And what's your story?"

She laughed. "You didn't let me finish. Date two means me being in the driver's seat."

"You like to be in control." I handed her the pepper grinder.

"I do. That's probably why I've been boyfriend-less for so long. It can be a bit of a problem."

"But you're so self-aware. Why not just ease off the control-freak gas pedal?"

"We control freaks prefer to be referred to as *skilled situation managers*. And why don't I just ease off? Easier said than done. It's like telling a sex addict to just stop masturbating. Your brain might be saying, 'Just let go,' but every other cell in your body is screaming for you to hold on tight."

"You really should be on stage. Your one-liners are killer."

She blushed. "It's all you. You seem to trigger something that gives my inner voice permission to speak out loud."

"I'm no psychology expert, but it seems to me your subconscious is trying to tell you that this should be a fourth date."

"You'd like that, would you?"

"Absolutely. No question. I don't need no stinking subconscious psychoanalysis to know that. You make every cell in my body and brain want to get to know every cell in your body—*and brain*," I added with emphasis, "better."

"Yeah, yeah, yeah." She waved both hands between us as if shooing away a swarm of wasps. "So what's your story, Dylan? Who are you really, under the voguish clothing and the buff body and the photogenic face?"

"You think I'm buff?" I puffed out my chest for effect, hoping against hope that Kama would do the same. She was a master of mimicry, mirroring my actions and facial expressions. She was subtle about it, but since I'd used the technique to build trust and connection with both my clients and my dates, I could see what she was doing. And, as if cued by my will, Kama inhaled such a deep breath I worried —hoped—she would pop a button on her blouse.

"Uh-huh," she exhaled, acting unimpressed. "Your

buffosity has nothing to do with what I think—or don't think—about your body. It's a matter of observable fact. You're hella fit. And is that your whole story? You're just a lawyer who works out a lot? Come on, there's got to be more to you than just a big brain and beautiful biceps."

She placed the pepper grinder right in front of me and leaned back in her chair, head tilted to the side with her dimpled cheek taunting me. She knew what she was doing, playing the dimple card. Evil woman. What could I say about myself in under three minutes that would be interesting and amusing enough to keep that dimple activated?

I couldn't figure out why I wanted her to like me so badly. She'd made it clear that this would not lead to sex, that I was just a data point in her research. And maybe that was it. The challenge of changing her mind. Making her want me. Because on a visceral level, I wanted her. I was not ashamed to admit it. I found her attractive in all the right ways. And she made me truly laugh.

But I had to remember that she was also a piece of research to me. At the end of our three dates, I'd be submitting a report to Shane James about my recommended strategy for Bob Booker to take Kama's very fine ass to court. So far, all I could suggest was that Booker try to settle out of court, since putting those two up against each other in front of a judge would be a slam-dunk win for Kama. Which was exactly what I wanted for her, but... that promotion. That office. A Top Thirty Under Thirty award. I needed to figure out how I could have it all.

The part of this puzzle that didn't make sense was why Kama hadn't had Booker sign an informed consent document. Either he was lying and had signed it, or she was lying and had started her research without the proper procedures in place. Even though I should have been rooting for the client, I hoped there was an explanation and that she was the one telling the truth. I wished I could just ask her, but obviously I couldn't. Not without giving away the real reason I'd contacted her.

Kama interrupted my thoughts. "Really? Is it that hard?"

"I thought you wanted me to talk about more than just my physical assets," I said with a smirk.

She rolled her eyes, but her dimple stayed put.

"Okay. Who am I? Well, I'm the third of four brothers in my immediate family, and I have two other pseudo brothers who I grew up spending a lot of time with. And since we're such a mixed pack of moms and dads, the age difference between the six of us is only four years. I learned conflict resolution skills before I was in kindergarten. I was always the brother who wanted to know both sides of the story before choosing who'd be at the bottom of the pig pile."

"Five brothers? Wow. Did you fight a lot?"

I shrugged. "It probably looked like fighting to anyone who didn't know us. I mean, we'd wrestle and pin each other down and do wet willies. But really," I said, having a bit of a choked-up moment as I realized it, "all that rough housing was just a legit way to have physical contact. Hug each other and shit."

Kama looked at me like I was the cutest puppy in the pound. She even said, "Awww."

I scowled at her.

"So you're close with your brothers. That's lovely." She gave me a sad smile.

Even though I'd probably bury a body for any of them, it didn't feel like the right thing to tell her at that moment. "How about you?"

She shook her head. "One brother. Not at all close."

"Older or younger than you?"

"Six years older. He was a bully. So I prefer to pretend I was an only child. Just block out the whole big-brother parts of growing up." She shrugged like it didn't matter. "But I just interrupted you. You were answering my question. Who else are you, Dylan Rhodes, other than an amazing brother?"

This was hard to answer. I knew she was looking for more than the standard 'so, what do you do?', and I wanted to give that to her, but I'd never really thought about it—at least not in the context of getting to know my date. What would she find interesting? What would get that dimple back?

"Okay, well, if I were a character in a Disney movie, I'd be Woody from *Toy Story*."

She laughed out loud. "Really? Of all the things you want to share with me, you go with your Disney character avatar? Okay. For the record, I'd have pegged you as more of a Hercules or Shang or maybe a Tarzan type. You know, a hero character."

"Really? That's interesting. Do I look like a hero kind of guy to you?" I bent my elbows and pressed my fists against my hips like Superman.

"More so than a goofy cowboy toy."

"Goofy cowboy toy?" I scoffed. "For a woman who fancies herself a film buff, you totally missed the mark on Woody's character. He has many heroic qualities, including the one I feel a close connection to—"

"That you both look great in a hat and tight jeans?" She laughed at her own joke and seemed to relax a bit more.

"Why thank you. But no, I was going to say that Woody is like the glue that keeps his crazy, mixed-up toy friends and family working together. And that was my role as a kid with all my brothers and our friends."

"I love that you're so close to your brothers. I'm jealous. I wish I'd had sisters."

The corners of her mouth lifted just a little, less a smile than a look of longing. I didn't like the way her energy was moving.

"What about you? If you were a heroine from any movie at all, who would you be? Who do you most relate to?"

"Any movie?" Kama tapped the edge of her plate with her fork and stared at the ceiling. "I'd be Cindy from this indie film called *Blue Valentine*."

"Never heard of it."

"And you call yourself a Ryan Gosling fan. Tsk!"

"Quite certain I never said that… but interesting to find out that you are. So you see yourself ending up with a Ryan Gosling kind of guy?"

She shook her head. "Opposite, actually. In the film, Cindy has him then loses him, and she never figures out why. It's actually the most depressing love story I've ever seen. But probably the most honest."

"Oh, Kama, Ewan McGregor would be terribly disappointed in your mistrust of love."

"Wait! When did I tell you I had fangirl crush on Ewan McGregor? I'm sure I never mentioned him." She was wide-eyed and looking at me liked I'd hacked her diary.

"You kind of implied it when you said that *Moulin Rouge* was one of the films that influenced your life. I mean, it's an okay story, but how many times have you watched it?"

"I can't tell you," she said, shaking her head and looking at the ceiling.

"Can't or won't?" I smiled.

"Won't." She laughed. "Too embarrassing."

"But wait. Back to you thinking you're like this chick from a Ryan Gosling film. How does that make any sense?"

"It makes all the sense! In fact, even in *Moulin Rouge,* Ewan McGregor—I mean his character, Christian—has to accept by the end of the film that love is dangerous and futile."

"Hmm. So you see yourself as someone who is predestined to have a love story with a sad ending? You're going to make me cry." I was only half kidding. That was one of the saddest things I'd heard from a woman, that she had no expectation of ever falling in love. It also struck a chord, since I shared that feeling.

Kama and I ate in silence for a minute or two. I listened to the music playing in the restaurant. Like the last place, there were songs I hadn't heard in years. I made a note to ask our server which satellite station this was since I liked this playlist. It was Kama who broke the silence.

"I think you and I actually have more in common than you might realize."

"How so?" I asked, putting my fork down, giving her my full attention.

"I date for research, and you date for sex. Neither of us is trying to find our soul mate or looking for that magical life with a house and babies, are we?"

She was right, but it didn't *feel* right to agree with her.

"Which begs a question," she continued.

"What's that?" I leaned forward a little, pulled toward her like she'd activated a magnet.

"Since you know that I will never sleep with you, why are you wasting time going out with me?"

That was an excellent question, and I didn't know how to answer since I couldn't answer it for myself. Was this date still about the case and my job? Or did I just want to get to know her better because I found her fun and interesting? Could I have it both ways?

Yeah, sure I could, but I feared that I'd just end up reinforcing her identity as the lead character in a failed love story. So I answered as truthfully as I could without being fully honest. "You're an interesting riddle, and I quite enjoy trying to figure you out."

# 12

## KAMA

Our second date was a complete success from a research point of view. Dylan had made it clear that he wanted to have sex with me. When we got to the end of the night, instead of making me uncomfortable by asking if I'd go back to his place, he posed the question in the negative, answering it himself.

"You're not going to come back to my place and let me keep you up all night, are you?"

And even though I said no, he still proposed we have a third date.

I suggested the restaurant, of course. He agreed with enthusiasm. The only thing we had to negotiate was the day. He thought we should meet on Tuesday, just three days away. That felt too soon for me. He needed an opportunity to think about me and hopefully—even though I'd insisted it would never happen—consider the possibility of us getting to know each other physically, after hours of conversation.

But since my first date with Dylan had been cut short, I was nervous that I hadn't had enough time to plant the seeds of desire in him. Sure, he'd mentioned sex several times, but it was so playful I wasn't convinced he actually *wanted* me, beyond what was routine for him: have dinner, have sex. Without those seeds of desire taking root, I wouldn't be able to test my hypothesis, and all these evenings spent with Dylan would be for naught. A total waste of time.

I thought that extending the days between the second and third date would allow me to flirt, just a little, via text. And so I lied to him. I told him I already had two dates booked for the week. I also told him a truth, which was that I had a paper due that needed my attention.

He agreed to wait a week.

On Monday, I sent a 'thinking about you' text. He replied immediately with, "Looking forward to our *next* date." I debated correcting him, reminding him it was technically our *last* date, but I realized his language worked better for my third-date setup.

I sent the second 'thinking about you' text at 9 p.m. on Friday night. I assumed he'd be out but he texted back a photo of his legs extended on a couch and a television in front of him:

DYLAN

Recognize the movie?

I did. Immediately. It was *Moulin Rouge*. He was at the midpoint, a scene in which Satine has to convince Christian she doesn't love him so that the man who's bought her won't have Christian killed. It was the most heart-wrenching scene in the whole film. I couldn't even think about it without tearing up.

I replied,

You're hanging with Christian and Satine! What inspired you to watch that?

DYLAN

I thought I should be ready for the third date
with my own reference to the film.

Without thinking, I texted back a heart emoji. Then I gasped in horror and sent a quick-thinking follow-up text:

Oops. Was supposed to be the thumbs-up
emoji. Hit the one beside it by accident.

DYLAN

I'd forgotten how sad it was.

I had no idea what to reply to that. I wanted to keep texting, but I didn't want to interrupt his experience with the film. I wished I were watching with him. With anyone, really. I'd made Lizzy watch it so many times that she couldn't see Ewan in any other film without thinking of this one. Even in *Star Wars*, Ewan McGregor was a lovelorn poet first and a Jedi knight second.

Opening my streaming app, I loaded the film and, forwarded to the same scene Dylan was watching, and hit play. I was crying before the first bar of music had finished. And just as the film was ending, I got a text.

DYLAN

You need a happier spirit film. Can't wait to
see you. Just two more sleeps.

No surprise, our third date was lovely. Not just the food, but the company, too. On all my other third dates, I was so immersed in the role I was playing I hadn't truly enjoyed myself. It was all work with a clear goal. But while every other guy had been obviously on his best behavior, flattering me each time I set up an opportunity, Dylan was having none of it.

He found opportunities to make fun of me, to challenge me, and generally to treat me like an equal, a good friend, not a potential conquest. It was so fun and refreshing there were several times I forgot my purpose.

"So, how is your research coming along? Are you close to finishing?" he asked.

"I am," I said, smiling large. "I'm minutes away from wrapping up the dating part. Then I get to move on to the fun stuff."

Dylan grabbed his heart and threw back his head. "Ouch. Do you know how much energy it's taken me to be charming? And you tell me that spending time with a spreadsheet is more enjoyable than time with me?"

I shrugged. "Well, I concede that you have been, without a doubt, the sexiest and funniest of all my data points." I reached across the table and touched his bare forearm. He flipped his arm over and gently took my hand in his, interlocking our fingers.

"Just because you've finished with me as a test subject doesn't mean we can't keep seeing each other, you know," he said.

I tried to look dispassionate because inside I was doing a giant happy dance. I figured I was less than two minutes from being able to test my Jedi dating powers on the most challenging man in my research pool.

Keeping my fingers locked in his, I moved my thumb into the center of his palm and stroked it. He flattened his hand and held it open for me to see. I absent-mindedly ran my thumb back and forth along one of the creases.

"Do you read palms?" he asked.

I laughed and pressed his hand, palm up on the table. I touched the line closest to his fingers and said, "I see many beautiful women in your future. You see this mark?" I pointed to a spot that had no obvious mark. He raised his eyebrows. "This mark tells me you will make one of those women very happy one day."

"Just one of them? I'll have you know that I make all my women very happy."

I felt the smallest pang of regret that I'd not be able to prove him wrong. Or right.

I patted his hand. "Of course you do, dear," I said with my best grandmother voice. "But this one special lady? You'll make her very, very happy."

"And can you tell me how I'll do that? What does my palm tell you?"

"Well this line here," I said, running a finger along the line that bordered his thumb, "this one tells me that you'll have a difficult decision to make soon. A terrible choice that will feel like it has no win." I looked into his eyes which, surprisingly, were not mocking me. "But if you take a woman's advice, you'll find the path that causes the least amount of suffering." I smiled and was about to say, "That will be five dollars please," but Dylan pulled his hand away and rubbed it against his jeans, as if trying to erase the lines.

"Aren't fortune tellers supposed to give the client good news?" he asked. "I mean, from a business point of view, it makes sense to leave them feeling happy so they come back again and again."

He didn't look like he was joking. He actually looked a bit angry.

"What are you talking about? That was good news. You're on the right path. Or you will be—if you listen to the right woman!" I gave him my dimple.

He shook his head. "You said I have a terrible choice to make, that it's a no-win situation. My best possible outcome is the least amount of suffering, not no suffering at all. How is any of that a positive reading?"

*Whoa.* What I thought would be a silly way to create

physical contact had created the polar opposite energy I wanted to create.

"Give me your hand again," I said, laying my own hand, palm up on the table.

"Why? So you can tell me that my dog's gonna die then my woman's gonna leave me?" He made a fist and pulled it close to his chest, pouting like a kid trying to keep a candy from a mean brother.

"Give me your hand." I leaned across the table and grabbed his fist in mine, then fought with him to pry his fingers open. He was so much stronger than me I knew it was a fight I'd never win, so I changed tactics. I flipped his fist over in my hand so his knuckles were facing up and ran my index finger along them, from his index knuckle into the valley beside, then up and over the next knuckle all the way to his baby finger. Then back again.

Dylan let his hand relax into my open palm as my fingers traced his knuckles. I got so lost in the electric charge that ran up my hand that I hadn't come up with anything to say, so I did a second pass, this time with my eyes closed.

"You have a bumpy road ahead ... but the prize at the end of your journey will be ... electrifying. Be happy. This is good news. And that will be five dollars, please." His hand fully relaxed and his fingers opened, weaving with mine again.

This was going to be the hardest of all the goodbyes. I inhaled in a long, deep breath and bit the inside of my bottom lip to keep from saying what my inner voice was screaming at me. *Tell him you want to sleep with him.*

# 13

## DYLAN

"So, I know this is our last date and you were hoping never to see me again—"

"I never said that!" Kama said.

"Actually, you did. You said it on our first and second dates—that this was just research for you and that once you had your three dates, we men were of no use to you anymore." I tried to sound light, but I wasn't feeling lighthearted about it. One could argue that I'd been using her as much as she'd been using me, but the difference was that I kept going on these dates because I felt a connection and wanted to pursue it. And she'd made it clear that even if she felt a connection, she had no interest in seeing where it might lead.

"Well, okay. But you make it sound so, I don't know, narcissistic or self-serving." She made a face like this was something that had never occurred to her.

"Isn't it? I mean, I know what happens now. Even if I'd like a fourth date, or just to take this date to the next level, it's a no-go. Is that not self-serving and narcissistic?"

I had to walk a fine line here. I wanted to upset her enough to feel bad, but not so much that she got angry. I hoped my years of manipulating brothers would serve me with a woman.

"Give me a break! You know that I'm not a narcissist. And even if the dates were self-serving, you also got some enjoyment from our time together. Right? Otherwise, why would you have gone out with me more than once?" Kama raised her eyebrows and nodded her head, giving me an excellent 'gotcha' face.

"Fine. You win," I said. "But I'm hoping you'll be willing to prove that you're a selfless and giving human by bending your 'never see your date again' rule. It really is a silly rule, you know."

"No, it is not! Why would I drag out getting to know a man I have no interest in being in a relationship with? I think it's not only reasonable, it's kinder than leading him on. You can't argue that."

"Okay. You win again. But hear me out. I have a proposal for you that has nothing to do with dating me or even getting to know me better. But it would require seeing me a few more times. And it's for a charity."

She looked skeptical. "What kind of charity?"

"A film festival. One that my firm is sponsoring. We donated ten thousand dollars, and they're putting our logo on promo materials and giving us one night where all the films are 'brought to you by Premier Law Boutique.'"

"And how does that involve me seeing you more? I'm not going to attend films as your date, if that's what you're thinking, because—"

"You're not dating. I know! I've been listening. No. Part of the sponsorship means the firm gets to—has to—choose the sponsored films that will be screened. And since I brought the festival and our firm together, I've been voluntold to pick the films."

Technically, I volunteered myself. And unfortunately, Tanya wasn't allowed to be on the selection committee since she was an employee of the festival. So my ulterior motive of naked film time had blown up in my face, and now I had to watch eighty indie films on my own and choose the best ones. Nothing about that sounded appealing.

Kama didn't say anything, so I spelled it out. "I thought you might enjoy helping me pick them since you have a love of film and seem to be really smart about analyzing stories and stuff."

Kama leaned forward. Ha! I could do dating research, too. It was clear I had her interest, so I continued with my pitch. "There are eighty films, all between ten and twenty minutes long. Dramas and documentaries. They're all on the same theme. And my job—our job, I hope—is to program approximately one hundred minutes of films that work well together. I'll have to moderate a Q and A with the filmmakers after the screening."

She was nodding and smiling, and I knew I had her.

"What's the theme?" she asked.

"Well, it's one of the most popular themes in film and perfectly suited to a law firm: revenge versus forgiveness in the quest for justice."

"Ooh, that sounds like fun!"

"So, are you in? Will you be my co-curator? I'm not sure I can give you an official credit since it's a corporate thing. I may not even get individual credit myself. But it might be fun. And I sure would love to get your input and perspective."

"Maybe." She leaned back in her chair. "Where would we screen the films? Is there a screening room somewhere?"

"Um, my place? Or your place, if that's more comfortable for you."

"Hmm … So we'd have to watch eighty films times an average of fifteen minutes each … four films an hour that's … about twenty hours?"

I nodded. She sighed.

"That's a big time commitment. I don't know if I can do it. I mean, I have classes and my thesis …"

"We have five weeks. We could watch every Saturday for a month. Just half a day, once a week. Come on! You know it'll be fun. And cool. Kind of the best volunteer gig ever, don't you think?"

"It's a lot to ask. Can I think about it?" She leaned forward again, which told me she wanted to say yes but just needed a little more to motivate her.

"One of the perks for helping me is a VIP pass to the festival and all the special events, including the after-hours parties. That has a value of over a thousand dollars. And I'm pretty sure the festival starts after exams end, so you'll have all the time in the world to be a full-time film buff."

She was nodding like a dashboard bobblehead on a gravel road.

"Fantastic!" we said at the same time.

The rest of our dinner was fun and relaxed. I don't think I'd ever spent so long on the dinner part of a date. It wasn't clear to me what part of the conversation was research and what was just Kama enjoying herself, which felt both disconcerting and encouraging. I really enjoyed hanging out with her.

I never expected to have sex with her, but if she ever changed her mind, I wouldn't argue. Every time she leaned across the table to touch my arm, I wanted to grab her hand and stroke her skin. But she was, true to her word, always in control. She never lay her arm anywhere close enough for me to touch without it being awkward. But once, when she was laughing, I did lean across and take her chin in my hand so I could tilt her dimple toward me. When she grabbed the side of my index finger between her teeth, my cock jumped to attention. I wanted her. Bad.

When the waitress handed us our bill, Kama looked like she'd just been handed the bones of a dead relative.

"What's wrong?" I asked.

She dropped her head into her hands and moaned. "Nothing. Everything. I can't believe … I'm an idiot."

"You forgot your wallet, and now you can't make a sneaky escape out the bathroom window?" I tried to be funny, but it fell flat.

"You're not going to care or empathize, but …" She was breathing hard and tears pooled in her eyes. "I forgot what I was supposed to be doing. It's the end of the date, and I haven't done any of the setup."

"Setup? What do you mean?"

"I can't very well tell you, or it would ruin the data, wouldn't it?" There was venom in her tone. She looked like she was fighting a nervous breakdown.

"How can we salvage it?"

She stared at me and shook her head. "We don't." She looked away. Wiped her eyes. "I can't believe I forgot what my purpose was. This wasn't supposed to go like this."

"Like what?" I was confused. "It felt like it went really well from where I'm sitting. If you used some research dating tricks on me, I'd venture to say they worked."

"But I didn't. I didn't follow any of the actions to keep the research consistent. This was a total waste of time. Three dates. For *nothing*."

It felt like she forgot I was sitting right there with her. It felt like she didn't care that I had feelings that might be hurt since we'd actually had a really nice time together. And it pissed me off.

"Seriously? Um, I'd like to point out that I'm more than just a lab rat. I actually do have feelings, and the way you're talking about spending time with me, well, it's pretty shitty, actually. Gotta say, the narcissist label stands."

"Fuck off," she said, under her breath.

It was the first time she'd sworn. I didn't think she knew how to.

"Wow. Okay. So I know you like to pick up your own tab." I pulled my wallet from my back pocket and dropped eighty dollars on the table. "This is enough for my meal, my share of the dessert, drinks, taxes, and a healthy tip."

Kama stared at the money but didn't say anything.

"So if you're done with research subject number fuck-off, I'll be going. Let me know if you're still on for the film thing. I'll understand if you're not, since ... yeah, it must really suck wasting time with me without an ulterior motive."

I was out the door and a dozen steps down the street when Kama called my name. I stopped and turned around on reflex, but I didn't walk back toward her.

"I'm sorry, Dylan." Tears ran down her cheeks, and she was blinking quickly.

"Nothing to be sorry for. You got what you needed—or didn't, I guess. I suppose I should be sorry for knocking you off your script. Wasn't my intention to fuck up your research. I'm sorry that enjoying yourself on a date was such a downer for you." I turned and started to walk away again.

"Dylan?"

I stopped walking and waited with my back to her.

"I had a really nice time tonight."

When she didn't say anything else, I lifted a hand and waved behind me. I said, "Bye, Kama," but I'm quite certain it was too quiet for her to hear.

# 14

## KAMA

Before my third-date meltdown, Dylan and I had planned to get together on Saturday to watch and analyze films for the festival. After a few uncomfortable text messages, we agreed to meet at my place. Well, in the MPR at my residence. It seemed like relatively neutral territory, it was quiet, and the couch was wide enough for us to sit beside each other without touching.

At ten minutes to three o'clock, I was watching the front door of the building from the MPR, so I could see him arrive. At one minute past three, I assumed he'd changed his mind, so I shot off a quick text to him. Just as I hit 'send,' an Audi pulled into the residence parking lot. That was a car that didn't belong to anyone who lived here. Dylan got out, looking as relaxed as a cat in the sun despite being at least ten minutes late by his own standards.

Seeing him, I felt a mix of attraction and shame about how I'd reacted at the end of our last date. That sneaky voice that held court in the back of my mind whispered, *He'll be the one who got away.*

I opened the window and yelled down as he approached

the door. "Head to the elevator. I'll meet you down there in a minute."

He looked up, his expression flat, but he acknowledged with a nod.

I rode down, hoping he'd soften when we were face to face. *Smile, Kama, smile. You broke this, you can fix this.* The elevator door opened and Dylan stepped in, head down, as if I weren't there.

"Did you have trouble finding the building?" I asked, sounding maybe a little perkier than needed.

"Found it just fine."

We rode the rest of the way in silence. He set up his laptop in silence, which meant finding an electrical outlet and plugging in an extension cord he'd brought with him.

"You have your own earbuds, I hope. I have a splitter, but I didn't think you'd want anything as personal as my earbuds near you." His tone was biting.

I had never wanted to punch anyone as much as I wanted to clobber Dylan Rhodes in that moment.

"Look. I'm sorry. How many times or ways do I need to say it? I was wrong. I was emotional. I'm a little high-strung about this thesis since everything is riding on it. And every new set of dates not only delays my defense but costs me money I just can't afford to spend. And I had it in my mind that you were the last guy I would have to go out with. Then—"

"*Have to* go out with. Charming," he mumbled, just loud enough for me to hear.

We had a stare-down. My heart was pounding. I was breathing too fast. And him? He looked entirely impassive. I refused to break eye contact first, so when I felt myself falter, I spoke.

"You realize that the leading cause of emotionally based physical illness is holding onto anger, right? So can you please just yell at me, so I don't feel responsible when I read in the news about some hotshot young lawyer who snapped in court over someone *not* complimenting his tie or something?"

"And now sarcasm. This might come as a surprise to you, Kama, but lawyers have feelings, too... allegedly." He didn't smile, but I could see his jaw relax, just a little.

"I am so bad at apologies," I said, to myself more than to him. I leaned forward, put my elbows on my thighs, and buried my face in my hands. I felt a long afternoon ahead.

And then I heard Dylan, so quiet I had to hold my breath to make sure the sound was actually what I thought it was: a slow, steady whisper of "yup, yup, yup, yup, yup, yup ..."

When I looked up, his eyes were pressed closed, but he was smiling. It made me laugh out loud. The fact that he accepted my anxiety as a just another part of who I was, like my black hair, above-average height and weight, and the way I squeaked when I sneezed, gave Dylan that old-friend feeling.

"Worst apology ever, accepted," he said.

"Dylan, I really, *really* like hanging out with you. A lot. And I want to do this film curation thing with you, but not if being around me makes you grouchy. So do you think maybe we could start again? Like we did with the two false-start dates?"

He blinked a few times, then stood and walked out of the MPR and out of sight. He was gone thirty seconds. Sixty seconds. I knew he'd come back since he'd left his laptop, but it took him a full three minutes before he appeared at the door again.

He was smiling, and his energy was entirely different. The Dylan who had thrown me off my third-date plan appeared to be back.

"Hey, folks, I'm looking for some chick named Llama or Camera or something." He intentionally said my name wrong and again made me laugh.

The three people in the kitchen area looked at him like he'd lost his mind since they'd watched him leave.

I stood and waved like a fool. "Over here! Hi! You must be Dylan. I've been waiting for you."

I had a moment of panic, not sure whether I should shake his hand, give him a friendly hug, or sit back down to avoid having to decide. But as he got to within a few steps of me, he opened his arms wide and didn't hesitate to pull me into a tight hug.

He put his face next to my ear and whispered, "I'm sorry your research got messed up. But I'm not sorry you had a good time, because I had more fun with you last Saturday than I've ever had on a date, not-date, whatever you want to call it. This grouchy lawyer would be elated if we could be friends."

In our first four-hour movie marathon, we got through less than three hours of actual films since neither of us had considered the time we'd need to discuss each one before we went on to the next.

It was fascinating to see how differently filmmakers approached the same theme. And equally fascinating, if not sometimes infuriating, to see how differently Dylan and I interpreted the films.

We'd just finished watching our tenth film, a drama about a girl whose mother was murdered by a gang. The girl grows up and avenges her mother's death, becoming a murderer herself, taking the life of a man who had a child the same age she was when her mother was killed. The story fit the theme, but we agreed it wasn't a contender for the festival. And yet, that film prompted an argument so passionate between Dylan and I that several people left the MPR, telling us to get a room.

"The system failed her, and she had no choice but to get justice herself," I argued.

"That's not how it works, Kama. I'll agree the system didn't give her what she wanted, but haven't you ever heard the expression 'an eye for an eye leaves the whole world blind?' Would you want to live in a world where individuals got to decide the punishment for crimes against them?"

"At least have a voice in the punishment. I mean seriously, that girl lost her mother, and the guy who murdered her only got three years because he cut a deal. How is that fair?"

"How is it fair that his daughter will now be fatherless? Your idea perpetrates more violence. Now that girl may grow up to kill the woman who just killed her dad, leaving another kid without a mom."

"So you'd have her turn the other cheek? Keep taking it in the ass?" I spat, surprising myself with that second metaphor.

Dylan's eyes went wide. He reached across the couch and placed his hand on my thigh, just above my knee. He didn't rub my leg or move his fingers at all. He just rested his warm palm on my leg, which was strange since, by the sudden pressure in my chest, it would have made more sense to see his hand wrapped around my heart.

I stared at the touch point for several seconds and realized my breathing was shallow. I took a few deep breaths in through my nose, out through my mouth. When I looked up at Dylan, I saw that he was doing the same. Was I mirroring his breathing, or was he mirroring mine? He lifted his hand.

"I'm sorry," I said. "I'm just tired of …" I was thinking, *tired of being the victim*, but I didn't want to say that. "I'm tired of abusers getting away with… well, murder, of course, but all kinds of behavior that hurts others."

"I know it's a cliché, but you don't honestly believe that

two wrongs make a right, do you? It seems that's what you're saying."

"Did you watch the series *Dexter*, about the serial killer who targets only people who've literally gotten away with murder?" I asked him.

"Brilliant show," he said.

"So we can agree on that. But Dexter is all about revenge. He kills someone in every episode and yet he's a sympathetic hero. We can understand why he does it. Kind of like Batman, too, right?"

"Kama, I won't argue that shows that depict revenge aren't entertaining. They are. It's not as interesting when the victim says, 'Even though you tore my internal organs from my body, chewed them up, and did a Highland dance on them, it's okay. I forgive you.' But that doesn't mean we should bring that attitude into the real world."

I let that sink in. I wondered if he meant me, hurting his feelings. "Why did you forgive me so easily? I was an absolute trout last weekend."

Dylan's expression was a combination of amusement and confusion. "A trout? Guppy on the first date, trout on the third ..."

"A trout. A bad-tempered woman. Have you never heard that expression? My parents use it. British colony influence, I guess."

He shook his head and smiled. "Nope, nope, nope."

I rolled my eyes.

Dylan put his hand on my leg again. "The mature part of me had forgiven you before I even got home that night. I have no idea what it's like to have anxiety issues, and the fact that I somehow triggered a full-on panic attack ... well, I know that I didn't help you feel calm on any of our dates. And for that I'm truly sorry."

"You don't have to be sorry. It's not your fault."

"Yeah, well, I could have been less of a dick, even though you seem to enjoy it when I push your buttons."

He gave my leg a squeeze, and a warm rush of energy traveled right to where it had no business going. I flushed and stared at his hand, avoiding eye contact at all costs.

"But when you had that meltdown and said I was a waste of your time, you pushed one of mine. It was a double slam of feeling like I was a giant ass and, yeah, you did hurt my feelings." He made a goofy face. "Weird, huh? I'm still a baby lawyer, so I guess that's why I still have more than one feeling."

I put my hand on top of his and gave it a squeeze. I couldn't believe that a week ago I'd complained that time spent with Dylan was a waste. Once I'd accepted the fact that I couldn't use anything from our three dinners in my research, I felt relief more than anything else. Now we could be friends without triggering any kind of ethical investigation. I hadn't realized how stressful my conflicting feelings had been.

Finally able to make eye contact, I said, "Nope. Nope. Nope. Not weird at all."

Dylan gave my leg one last panty-melting squeeze then took his hand away. "So we can agree that this last film was crap, right?"

I nodded.

"And so far, we've mostly agreed on which films we think should move forward to the short list, right?"

I nodded again.

"So here's what I'm thinking," Dylan said. "We've been sitting here for almost four hours and all we've eaten is far too much popcorn—"

"Never too much popcorn," I interrupted.

"A lot of popcorn. I think we need to call it a day. How about dinner?"

I checked the time. "I can't. Sorry. But yeah, it would

good if we break now. I'm meeting Lizzy downtown in just over an hour. An extra few minutes will give me time to pick up a burger on the way. Actual food would be an excellent idea, especially since I'll be drinking."

"We can grab to-go burgers together," he suggested.

I hesitated.

Dylan stood up. "Never mind. You've got plans. And you've done your time with me. Enough is enough. I get it."

"No. It's not that. It's just that whenever Lizzy gets a Saturday night off, she and I do our girl thing. Just the two of us. Any other night we could have dinner after we do the film thing. If you want to."

"Then let's plan a post-film-marathon dinner date for next Saturday."

"Not a date," I said without thinking. "Just dinner."

"It was just a figure of speech, Kama," he said, shaking his head.

I smiled and gave him the thumbs-up, but I felt a deep stab of sadness at how quickly he'd agreed it would not be a date.

# 15

## DYLAN

K ama and I texted every day between our screenings. She sent her best message on Thursday evening, during her very last research date, when the guy she met to replace my data point went to the bathroom.

**KAMA**

Wish me luck! My last half hour of research and then I can kiss this dating life bye-bye! And what a guy to end on ...

Fireworks?

**KAMA**

More like that noise that TV game shows make when the contestant loses. THIS guy is why my research is so important.

Have you voodoo-ed him yet?

**KAMA**

Excuse me? Jedi-ed him, thank you very much. Voodoo is not real, silly.

> You sure about that? I voodooed you. That's why you're thinking about me while you're out on a date with another man…

I waited and watched the dots as she typed a reply. They started and stopped several times. It amused me, anticipating what she would say.

> KAMA
>
> You did not. I'm thinking about you because oh darn gotta go. He's coming back from the loo. See you Saturday. 😬

> Cop out! Looking forward to it. 😏

The thing was, I really was looking forward to seeing her. I liked her. A lot. Not in a girlfriend kind of way—I don't do girlfriends. But yes, in an 'I'd have sex with her in a heartbeat' way, which, unfortunately, she was still painfully clear would never happen. And that was the interesting thing. I wanted to spend my Saturday afternoons and evenings with her anyway. I was actually happy to give up a chance to hook up with Tanya when the alternative was to hang out with Kama.

On my way to the office on Friday morning, I got an email from Barb: *Mr. James would like to see you as soon as you get in.*

I'd been waiting for this message ever since I'd submitted my report on the Bob Booker v. Kama Ray file. I'd made a convincing argument against pursuing the case against Kama and suggested that the firm not represent Mr. Booker if he felt compelled to take her to small-claims court. All the evidence pointed to Kama having acted in the most professional and ethical manner possible. Asking me to stand and argue otherwise would be ludicrous. There was no way I could do so without outright lying, which obviously I would not do.

My recommendation was to submit a letter of complaint to the BCU ethics committee on Booker's behalf and let them sort it out internally. I felt certain that the situation would be quickly resolved since Booker would easily expose himself as the misogynist prick that he was.

I expected some blustering and complaining from Booker about having paid for eight billable hours plus three meals. (I put my alcohol on a separate tab so he couldn't bitch about paying for the beer). In my cover note to Mr. James, I also offered to pay for the meals if it would help make Booker more readily agree.

Barb waved me right into James's office when I arrived at her desk.

"Sit," he said without looking up from his monitor. "I didn't expect you in this early."

"I'm always in by eight," I said.

"What time do you usually check out?"

"Six. Sometimes earlier, often later."

James nodded his head. "Good. So it won't take much adjustment to get used to junior partner hours."

I said a silent, *Hoo, yeah!* "No, sir. Not much adjustment at all."

"I've read your opinion on the Booker v. Ray file." He tapped a folder on his desk. "I don't like it. Booker's not happy either."

*Shit. Shit. Shit.* "I'm sorry, sir, but there was nothing offside about any of her actions. And I swear I tried to trip her up at every opportunity. Kama Ray approached her research by the book. At least with me."

James shook his head back and forth while rubbing his chin. "Well, it was worth a shot. Would have been easier than Option B. But I guess that's what we're left with."

"Option B? You mean telling Booker to complain directly to the ethics committee?"

"No. Putting Booker up against Ray—her testimony against his."

"He'll never win, sir."

"Never say never. He has one of our most promising new partners working for him. I have faith in you, Rhodes. You'll figure something out. I want you to file the complaint by Monday afternoon. Can you make that happen?"

Thank god I had a good poker face since my entire being was saying, *No! I can't and I won't make that happen.* But out loud, I said, "Absolutely, sir. Not a problem."

"Good man. Close the door behind you."

I was fucked. I couldn't see a way to argue a case against Kama that wouldn't embarrass her. I was confident that no matter how good a job I did, she'd win. I was convinced that it wouldn't hurt her reputation as a grad student. But I didn't think it was fair to drag her into a situation that would force her to explain her behavior on all those research dates.

Unfortunately, if I walked away from the case now, I was certain that the junior partner's office on the twenty-sixth floor would not get my nameplate on it. My career drive battled my conscience as I took the stairs back to my office.

My career voice argued, *For all you know, Kama did mislead Booker. She knew you were a lawyer from the minute you met, so the fact that she went by the book with you doesn't mean she was straight with Booker.*

My conscience replied, *Not buying it. Kama has ten times more integrity than Booker has arrogance. That man is a textbook case of insecurity bred with immaturity.*

The thing about being a lawyer? I could argue either side. But for now, I had other cases to research and prepare. The Booker case might be the one that landed me the chair in the glass-walled office, but there were others to argue—and win

—on the way to that promotion. So I put Kama out of my mind and got to work.

For about an hour. And then she texted. And instead of letting it sit until my lunch break, when I typically read and responded to incoming messages, I snuck a peek.

KAMA

> Question only a lawyer can answer: How believable is Reese Witherspoon's character in Legally Blonde when she follows her boyfriend to law school to get a law degree after being a fashion bunny?

That was a setup I'd not survive no matter how I answered.

I could claim to have never seen the movie, but I'd likely get caught if she ever mentioned the film again. Which was an interesting thought since we had made no plans to keep seeing each other once our curation gig ended.

I could tell her what I really thought: that it seemed ridiculous Reese Witherspoon, aka Elle in the movie, had no interest in becoming a lawyer until a man provoked her. I'd never met a person who'd studied law as a 'fuck you,' and I didn't believe that was enough motivation to succeed.

I could tell her it was plausible since beautiful women can be just as academically accomplished as … Well, not sure how I'd end that argument without having my balls squeezed.

I could erase the message and pretend I never saw it. If she raised it in person, I'd answer with my special brand of 'question as answer.' That might work.

Or I could stall, ask my brothers, Nick and Josh, what they'd say. I forwarded the message to them both and added,

> What would you answer, assuming you're trying to convince the woman she should sleep with you?

Josh was Josh, Mr. Must-Connect-Emotionally-Before-Sex,

**JOSH**

> If I had to convince her, I wouldn't be having sex with her, would I?

And Nick, stupid-in-love with Sophie, replied in all his Nickness,

**NICK**

> I'd say, I'm a bit rusty on the film. Let's watch it together and see what we think. How about tonight? I'll bring the beer and libido.

Yup. I'd have to figure this one out alone. So I wrote back an answer only a lawyer would give:

> If you're asking if the plot device works in the film, sure. It's a perfect rom-com story. If you're asking if it's realistic for a student to swap majors in such a huge way, again, sure. Tell you why when we get together tomorrow. Looking forward to it. Do you like Greek food?

**KAMA**

> Can't wait to hear. Agapao to Greek food.
> 🩶

I showed up at Kama's residence for our film screening a full hour ahead of our meeting time. I didn't expect her to be in the MPR that early, and I needed time to make the experience just a little more comfortable than it had been the week before. I brought an external monitor to plug into the laptop, so we could watch the films on a good-sized screen at a decent distance. It was actually the flat-screen TV from my bedroom. And I'd bought Kama a pair of wireless headphones so we could sit back and watch without having to keep the laptop within arm's reach.

I moved the couch and coffee table to the far end of the MPR, to make it less likely that people would get sucked in to watch with us. Then I pulled over two footstools so we could extend our legs.

Yes, I was taking liberties in a space that wasn't mine to mess with, and I knew there were risks to being so brazen, but since I was compromising my physical comfort for Kama's emotional comfort—she refused to watch at my place, which was very comfortable—I was ready to argue my case if needed.

I wasn't an asshole about it, though. I talked to the guys in the room, and they offered to help me move things around.

At first, Kama worried she'd get in trouble, but as the afternoon rolled on and more and more people came in and saw the new layout, virtually everyone asked if the room could stay set up that way. I agreed to leave my television for the next couple of weeks until Kama and I finished our screenings. Talk about easy brownie points.

Four women congratulated Kama on having such a nice boyfriend. I'm not sure which one of us was more vehement that we were only working on a project together. We were convincing enough that I got two women's phone numbers and an open invitation to come over and watch films with them anytime I wanted.

After the second one slipped me a bookmark with her name and contact info on it, Kama paused the film we were watching.

"I keep forgetting, but I promised Lizzy I'd let you know

that if you ever want to hang out with her, she's a willing... um... Well, unlike me, she *will* have sex after just one or two dates. So if she seems like your type, I can give you her number."

I'm rarely speechless, but that little nugget of info caught me off guard. I remembered how Lizzy had attended to Kama when she was having her panic attack. She seemed like a good, caring friend. And she checked all the boxes for a good hostess in a three-star restaurant—she was pretty, with a nice smile and an appealing figure. And she knew how to swing her hips to get and keep a man's attention.

"Your best friend asked you to give your date her number?"

Kama rolled her eyes. "You were never my date, Dylan. How many times do I need to say it? So—you want it?"

Was Lizzy someone I wanted to go out with? Sure, why not? Was she someone I *should* go out with, given that in several weeks I'd likely be facing her best friend in court? Hard pass on that.

"I'll let you know after I've gone out with"—I picked up the bookmark and scrap of paper—"Tasha and Melissa."

"I'm bored with this film. Do we have to finish it, or are you happy to give it a thumbs-down and move it to the 'nope' column?" Kama asked.

"Sure. It's definitely not on my 'maybe' list."

"Since we're taking a break, you said you'd answer my question about *Legally Blonde*. So what makes you think it's reasonable for a ditzy student to suddenly switch to law?"

# 16

## KAMA

Dylan deferred his answer, saying it was one he'd prefer to share over dinner. With beer. So we watched six more films—only one of which was a 'heck, yeah' from both of us—and then I left him in the MPR for a few minutes so I could change and get ready for dinner out.

We'd been clear it was not a date. It was just two people celebrating a productive day of work and having food together. It was strange since he felt like a genuine friend now. I already knew him so well, and he knew, well, a bit about me. Not as much as I knew about him, and that was the way I liked it.

I was looking forward to our dinner but anxious, too. I was glad he hadn't hinted that he wanted more than my opinion on films and the occasional meal. But what if he did want more? What if, at the end of the date, he tried to kiss me or asked if I wanted to go back to his place? Then again, what if he *didn't* kiss me or ask me back to his place?

I realized that my anxiety about having to turn him down wasn't as strong as the disappointment I'd feel if he wasn't at all interested. Even though I didn't want a boyfriend, I felt safe with Dylan. I felt like a somewhat normal twenty-six-year-old who could have sex with a man who was nice and funny and damned attractive and smelled like a bakery, all warm and delicious.

I made a last-minute decision to change my bra and underwear to something nicer than my Hanes Her Way... just in case. In case he asked in just the right way. In case he touched my leg again, just above my knee, in the spot that had a direct communication line with my girl gear. In case my mind took a break from being on high alert for One. Blessed. Night.

When I got back to the MPR, Dylan was still sitting on the couch in front of the TV, but he had women on either side of him, sitting so close an electric current would pass right through all three of them without breaking. And it wasn't the same two who'd earlier given him their numbers. I walked over to see what they were watching: *A Star Is Born*. Zero subtlety.

"Hey! You're ready. Great," Dylan said, standing. "Nice to meet you, ladies. Enjoy the movie. And maybe I'll see you next Saturday."

"For sure," one said.

"What time?" asked the other.

Dylan didn't answer. He flung his laptop bag over his shoulder, then placed a hand on my hip to guide me out with him. It felt... yeah, like I was in trouble.

We walked down the hall and out of the building like this, with his hand pressed just hard enough against my hip to stay put. And when we reached his car, parked right below the MPR window, he opened the passenger door for me, waited until I got in, then closed it, all very nineteen-sixties-gentlemanlike. I stole a glance up at the window and noticed the two women who'd been flanking Dylan watching.

"You knew we had an audience," I said once he'd started the car.

"Suspected."

"So why make it look like we're a thing when either of them, both of them, would have been delighted had you blown me off to hang out with them?"

"For a woman researching the psychology of dating, you have a few significant holes in your knowledge."

I crossed my arms over my chest and harrumphed. "Such as, Mr. Know-it-all?"

"Well, by making those two ladies think you and I are a couple, I've just increased my desirability by a factor of"—he tapped the steering wheel a few times then took his eyes off the road to look me up and down—"at least four."

My belly did a flip. The disappointment that he'd just used me to flirt with those women was overridden by the delight that he'd just used me to flirt with those women.

"Only four? No. You're looking at my nasty side. If you'd been in the passenger seat, you'd have taken in my dimple side. That dimple adds at least one more factor of desirability since… come on, it's a killer dimple."

I turned my body almost sideways in my seat to show him.

"You're one-hundred-percent right. Six. Seven. Shit. I expect that when I drop you off tonight, those two women—and probably four of their friends—will be waiting to jump my bones. That is, of course, if you don't. Which, like I said on our second-slash-fourth date, I'd be entirely down with."

I wanted nothing more than to jump his bones right there on the leather seats of his posh Audi.

"Save it, Casanova. There already aren't enough nights in the week to accommodate all the women throwing themselves at your feet."

"Well, not if I spend one of those nights with you."

He said it playfully, but I felt a tinge of guilt that he was giving up a Saturday night to have a platonic dinner with me.

"You know, you'll probably think I'm a freak, but you're my first male friend. I mean, I feel like we're becoming friends. I hope that doesn't make you feel uncomfortable," I said, twisting my hair. Saying it made me feel uncomfortable.

"What a weirdo," he said with a cartoon voice. "You know how many female friends I have?"

"I don't know. Ten? Twenty?"

"Twenty? Are you mad? How many people, total, would you call your friends, Kama?"

"Well, Lizzy, obviously," I said. "I mean, there are all the people in my master's program I'd call friends—"

"Are there no men in your master's program?" he asked.

"Well, yeah, maybe ten guys."

"You said you don't have male friends but that all the people in your program are friends... I see a problem with your math here, psych major," he said, poking my leg.

That made me stop to think about the people I'd call in an emergency. Including my parents, six. People I'd trust with my family secret? Only one. And that made me realize that I wasn't sure if I could call Dylan an actual friend since there was so much about me I hadn't shared.

"Four genuine friends," I said. "And," I paused and looked at his profile as he drove, "that doesn't include you. But I'd like it to."

"Four seems like a solid number of friends who'd help you bury a body. Five would be better," he said, giving me a wink. "What do I need to do to make the list?"

"I don't know. I don't think you need to do anything. I think I'm the one who needs to do something, actually."

"Like have sex with me?" he said, blocking my hand from whacking his leg.

"No! I was thinking more like share more about myself with you. I know you really well but," I said, giving a one shoulder shrug, "I didn't offer you that much about me on our fake dates. You really don't know me very well at all. Not a very good basis for a friendship."

"You think I don't know you very well? Really? Interesting. I'd argue that whether or not you know it, you've shared a lot about yourself, both on our fake dates and while we've been watching those films."

"Maybe. But not the important stuff," I kind of mumbled toward my chest.

"Not the important stuff, huh? Now I'm dead curious to know what you consider the important stuff."

My first thought was a question that I'd been asking myself since I was getting dressed in my nicer-than-Hanes underwear. It was something I'd normally never talk about, but I decided I'd share with Dylan when we ordered, as an act of bravery and friendship.

"Let's get to the restaurant and I'll let you in on one of my secrets. I'll even give you a vote in how I act on it tonight."

"I vote yes!"

"You don't even know what the question is, you dummy!"

"I'm using my mind-trick powers to convince you it ends with allowing my penis to befriend your vagina."

My thong pulsed in agreement.

"You could not be more off base, playboy," I said. But, what I thought? I hope whichever option you choose makes me comfortable to say yes to your silly, persistent, scary, and intensely desirable offer.

# 17

## DYLAN

Kama was like an entirely different woman on this, our fourth non-date. She was more relaxed, she joked around more, and she spoke more. I mean, she had been a textbook example of an active listener on our three research dates, and I guess I just assumed that was the way she always was. But without having to be 'Kama the thesis researcher,' a different side of her shone through. She interrupted me and told terrible jokes. I thought lawyer jokes were lame… psychology jokes were much less funny.

"Why was Pavlov's hair so soft?" she asked.

I moaned and sighed, "Hmm … something to do with a bell or dogs? I don't know, Kama. Tell, me, why was Pavlov's hair so soft?"

"Classical conditioning!" Her entire face lit up like this was hilarious.

It was her own joy that made me laugh.

"Your turn! Tell me a lawyer joke," she said.

I had to think. I knew dozens, but I wanted one that felt Kama-ish.

She leaned forward on her elbows expectantly, encouraging me with her dimple.

"All right. A woman walks into a bar and sees a handsome, well-dressed man sitting on a bar stool, obviously alone—"

"I bet you're never alone at the bar."

"Excuse me! I'm working here. She walks up to him and says, 'Hey there, how are you doing tonight?'"

"Hey there, how are you doing tonight?" Kama said, failing to hide her glee.

"Shh. He turns to her, looks her up and down then straight in the eye and says, blind drunk, 'I'll screw anybody, anywhere, anytime. It doesn't matter to me.' The woman cocks an eyebrow and says, 'You're a lawyer, too! What firm do you work for?'"

Kama groaned and rolled her eyes, but her dimple didn't falter.

"How come lawyer jokes are always so mean toward the lawyer? Is there any profession that's both so well respected and so despised? Isn't it kind of strange that parents want their kids to grow up to either be a lawyer or marry a lawyer, if your parents are like mine? And yet everyone hates lawyers?"

I frowned. "Maybe you should reconsider that career on Broadway, because you're doing an impressive job of acting like you don't hate me."

"You know what I mean." She reached across the table, wrapped her fingers around my wrist, and gave it a squeeze. It caught me off guard because it had the feeling of a highly intimate act. A touch that had the sole intention of being soothing. It made me want to touch her back, but I didn't.

"Hey," I said, leaning back in my chair and disconnecting from Kama's fingers, "Why did you ask about that movie and Reese Witherspoon's character?"

"Oh, I forgot I asked you! Glad you reminded me. Because talking to you and watching all those films has me thinking about the way we end up choosing our careers.

Where we decide to focus all our study when we could have chosen a hundred other paths."

I didn't even try to hide my relief. "I thought you were asking as a setup to an unwinnable discussion about beauty versus brains, or something else filled with land mines."

"Why would I want to do that? No, I'm curious about what you think. I often wonder if a masters' degree in psychology is really the path I'm meant to take. Or if, maybe, I just landed here because…"

Kama looked past me, appearing to focus on nothing. Then she shrugged her shoulders and said, "Because it was easy, I guess. Broadway—or any career in the arts, really—would have been fun but …" She shook her head and scrunched up her face like she was considering something unthinkable.

"But what?" I asked.

"But I'd end up like my older brother, still living at home at age thirty-two since he can't afford to rent his own place."

"Well, just because your brother couldn't make it work doesn't mean you wouldn't. Is your brother as talented and funny and attractive as you are?" He lowered his chin and looked at me with a serious stare. "Does your brother have the same dimple?"

"Nope. Mine's one of a kind." Her face lit up, and my traitorous balls tightened. "Did you always know you wanted to be a lawyer?"

"Oh, hell no." I sat upright and used the opportunity to adjust myself.

"So how'd you figure it out?"

I laughed. "Arrogance and one-upmanship. Oh, and a healthy serving of wanting to prove to my brothers that I could be Dad's favorite."

"Is that so?" Kama tapped her full lips with her index finger. "I suspect a shot of good scotch would enhance this story. But before I order—my treat—remember I promised

I'd tell you my secret dilemma and let you decide how I handle it?"

"Yeah ..." I said, giving her a side glance.

"Well, it's no secret that I have some anxiety issues."

"Nope, nope, nope," I said without thinking. She just rolled her eyes and shook her head.

"I can't take the meds and drink alcohol at the same time. So if I have a drink with you tonight, I won't be able to take my chill pill. If I need it. Which, I hope I won't but..."

"Because being with me feels risky," I sighed. Well, that was a cock block.

"Yup, yup, yup," Kama said, pressing her eyes tightly closed and making the same face she'd had during her panic attack. Then she opened them and laughed.

"Are you asking because you feel the need to take a pill now or because I make you feel like drinking?"

"Dylan, you're special. You make me feel like I need a drink *and* my pill. So I'm asking you if you'd be willing to meet drinking Kama at the risk of seeing me do another fish-face impersonation. Or would you prefer I stay dry so I can take the anti-anxiety med if I need it?"

"Have a drink with me," I said.

Kama activated her dimple. "Thank you!" She waved the server over "Favorite brand?" she asked me.

"Favorite or favorite-affordable?"

"Excellent point. Favorite-affordable ... for a grad student."

She was adorable. "Redbreast 12."

The server nodded. "For both of you?"

"Two shots each, no ice in mine," Kama said.

"Ice on the side, please."

"You can do that?" Kama said with a look of genuine surprise.

"Stick with me, kid. I'll show you how to live like a rock star. Or at least like an overpaid lawyer."

"Back to your story. You became a lawyer to prove you were your dad's favorite son? That's kind of—"

"It's messed up," I admitted, "and ridiculously random. So you know I have three brothers in my immediate family —the brothers I grew up in the same house with. And then a kind of stepbrother because he was my half-brother Nick's, half-brother. And then another brother, Chris, who isn't related by blood, but Nick's mom and Chris's mom lived together, so he's also as good as a brother. The six of us hung out all the time."

"One day you'll draw that family tree for me," Kama said.

"Better, one day you'll meet them all. Then this story will make a lot more sense. But the quick version is that we all have some pretty obvious strengths and abilities. Nick, who's a firefighter and first responder, is hands-down the calmest under pressure. And Josh, who's a video game designer—he's the most creative. And we're all super competitive since we're so close in age, so we wanted to prove which one of us was the smartest."

"And becoming a lawyer makes you the smartest?"

"I'm not so sure about that. But we decided that whoever got the highest grade on the LSAT could call himself the smartest."

Kama threw back her head and laughed out loud. "You're all crazy! And you won?"

"I did."

"But if you hadn't planned on becoming a lawyer before you did the test, why go into law?"

"That's where Dad comes in. He decided for me. And since he and I had … an up-and-down relationship through my teens, it was nice to get his full support and approval for something. So I finished my bachelor's degree in philosophy and did my master's in law. And here I am. A guy who'll screw anything, anywhere, anytime."

"Literally and figuratively," Kama said with a smile.

"No, no, no. Literally, I am exceedingly particular and have exceptionally high standards. Figuratively? I do what my boss tells me to do. Sometimes I agree with the position I'm told to argue, and I feel positive about helping the client. Sometimes … well, it's a job."

"What's a case you didn't agree with but represented anyway?"

*There's this case right now I'm supposed to be arguing. I'm representing a misogynist pig and have to discredit a woman who, as far as I can tell, is nothing but honest and kind and is one of the most interesting and sexiest women I've ever met.*

I held eye contact with Kama and pressed my glass against my lips while I allowed myself that thought. "You know I can't talk about cases."

"I know. So if you hadn't won the Smartest Brother award, what do you think you'd be doing instead of being the butt of shark jokes?"

"Probably living in an ashram in India," I said without thinking. I wasn't actually serious, but it wasn't a joke either. That had been my original plan after getting my bachelor's degree—a year traveling the world with three- to six-month stops in India, Costa Rica, and Portugal. Kama was the first person I'd told about my ashram dream. I steadied myself, expecting her to laugh at me.

Kama clapped. "You should totally still do it. I did a one-month karma yoga program at an ashram when I was sixteen. I guess it was more of an ashram-*lite* experience since it's just a few hours away, not the full India experience. Still, it was amazing. I think everyone should take a month, or two or six, to connect with what's important to them. Meditate, work in service, harvest food … it's life changing." She paused and tilted her head. "In the best way possible."

And that was the moment I realized that I didn't just want to sleep with Kama once. I wanted to fall asleep and wake up with this woman every day. My guts twisted with a familiar fear, but something else felt stronger: desire. And not in my cock. In … my heart?

Even though she still had her secrets, I knew more about Kama than any woman I'd ever met. I liked everything about her, and there was still so much more to learn. It was a strange feeling, being this interested. Strange and dangerous since, for the first time in my life, I wanted to date monogamously.

*Whoa.*

What kind of Jedi mind trick had she played on me? If her goal was to make men walk away, her skills had backfired, because she had the opposite effect on me. I wanted to stick to her the way tiny arachnids cling to a web.

I rubbed my face, which felt itchy at the thought. Then my entire body seemed to feel itchy. I squirmed in my chair.

"You okay?" Kama asked.

I pushed what was left of my scotch toward her. "Pass me one of your panic-attack pills, will you?"

# 18

___

# KAMA

The end of our Greek dinner was both lovely and disappointing. After Dylan asked for one of my anti-anxiety meds—which I did not give him—he withdrew and reined in the flirting. At the end of the evening, he drove me home and kissed my cheek. This was after we'd stood for twenty minutes, chatting in the residence parking lot.

Every day in the week between our film marathons, we texted back and forth. Nothing sexy. Nothing flirty. Just check-ins, the way friends do.

We were in the middle of screening the fiftieth of the eighty films when my phone rang. It pulled me right out of a scene where a young woman was cursing her god for allowing her to make a dreadful decision. I would have been totally immersed if Dylan hadn't kept moaning and saying things like, "Give it up. Take ownership for your actions."

"Shoot! What time is it?" I looked at my watch. "Oh, no." I answered the phone.

A venomous tone bit my ear. "Seriously. Where the hell are you?"

"I'm so sorry. I lost track of time. I'll be there in ..." I looked at Dylan. "Can you drive me downtown? I was supposed to meet Lizzy at a karaoke bar twenty minutes ago."

"Who are you talking to?" Lizzy chirped. "Are you still with Dylan?"

"Yeah. Sorry. We got sucked into the films. I didn't notice the time."

"Well, you owe me a drink. Get here as soon as you can. And I'm picking your first song, so prepare to be humiliated."

"Half an hour max. See you then."

"Is she seriously mad?" Dylan asked.

"She'll get over it. We know lots of regulars, so it's not like she'll be sitting by herself. I'm not worried. Well, except for the song she chooses for me to sing. That will be brutal."

"What would be the worst she could pick?" Dylan asked as he packed up his things.

"Anything by Led Zeppelin." I poked my finger into my mouth and made a vomit sound.

"Not a fan? Me neither. But I sure would like to see you belt out 'Immigrant Song.'"

"For you?" I sang the opening screams, but instead of nodding my head I shook it side to side and I added an 'n' in front of the sound. "Nah-*ah*-aaah, aah. Nah-*ah*-aaah, aah."

Dylan smiled so big I could see his uvula.

"That is freaking amazing. You nailed it!"

I took a bow, then curtsied. "I have to go up to my room and change. I just need five minutes. You really don't mind driving me down?"

"Happy to. I'll just wait here."

"Thank you! Be right back."

I threw on a clean T-shirt and my skinny jeans. Changed from my old Doc Marten boots to my fancy kitten heels and called it done. I didn't bother with makeup since, by the time I got on stage, nobody would notice if I was wearing lipstick and eyeliner.

Dylan dropped me off at the bar with a wave. "Good luck."

Lizzy was sitting with friends and acknowledged me with just a chin tilt when I dropped my jacket on the chair beside her. I looked at her glass—a Moscow Mule—ordered one for each of us at the bar, then sat down beside her with my peace offering.

"You mad?"

"Heartbroken. You promised that you'd set me up with Dylan once you'd finished with him. But you're keeping him to yourself. He's my soul mate. He doesn't know it yet, but he is."

I laughed at her award-winning performance.

"I didn't put dibs on him. This is purely work. Well, it's fun, but it is not dating. Not even close. And I offered to give him your number."

"You did not," she said, raising her eyebrows.

"As if I'd lie! I did. And he said he'd take it as soon as he'd gone out with the two women who were hanging all over him when I left him unattended in the MPR."

"You're the best! I'll let you pick the bridesmaids' dresses."

I nodded and lifted my copper cup. We clinked our drinks and turned to watch the person on stage. She was singing 'Hello' by Adele. She was braver than I would ever be.

"Have you been up yet?" I asked Lizzy.

"Nah. I was waiting for you. And I think you'll be up soon." She gave me a wicked smile.

"You going to tell me what you've got me lined up to sing?"

"Nope!" Lizzy popped the 'p' with great enthusiasm.

Two songs later, my name was on the board, and Lizzy bust a gut laughing as I walked to the stage. The cued-up lyrics made me laugh, too. Not Led Zeppelin, thank goodness. Actually, the polar opposite. It was the Captain and Tennille song 'Love Will Keep Us Together.'

Lizzy and I usually sang it to each other. But never on stage. It was our inside joke about never letting a man come between us—and the perfect song for me to perform as an apology.

I started singing with all my heart, pointing first at Lizzy, then myself. After the first stanza, I took my eyes off my best friend and sang to the room, looking around to make eye contact with those bar patrons who were paying attention. I knew how to hold a crowd.

When I got to the verse about how one day Tennille's lover would be old and not so beautiful anymore, I turned to sing to Lizzy again. But as my arm reached out to point to her, it landed on the person sitting beside her. In my chair.

Dylan.

I inhaled a gasp, choked on my spit, and coughed as I tried to sing the next line. I continued to cough, staring at my best friend and Dylan. I couldn't recover because Lizzy was splitting a gut, which made me laugh, too. Dylan grabbed one of the copper mugs, jogged it up to the stage, and handed it to me. I was mortified. As I tried to get myself together, he stepped up in front of the mic and carried on with the rest of the song, thoroughly humiliating himself, singing the words but to the tune of the opening scream from 'Immigrant Song.'

If his intention had been to take the attention away from me, I guess it worked. The entire bar was now watching him. When the song ended, he took my hand in his and forced me to bow with him. Lots of laughter from the room, but an equal number of rolling eyes and head shakes. Some of these people were serious about their karaoke and didn't appreciate Dylan's jazz treatment of a classic song.

I thought it was brilliant and hilarious.

Back at the table, I noticed that Lizzy was sitting with a man I'd never met. I reached to shake his hand.

"Hi," he said. "I'm Josh. Dylan's brother."

Oh. My. Gracious! Were all the brothers in this family descendants of Adonis?

"Hi. I'm Kama—"

"Duet! You and Dylan have to sing a duet," Lizzy interrupted, heading just over the line from tipsy to topsy-turvy.

I rolled my eyes at Lizzy and turned to face Dylan. "Thank you for saving me. But why are you here?"

"I was hoping to catch you singing Zeppelin. Did I miss it?"

"No. She picked the song you just saw me destroy. I am so embarrassed."

"Why? You were killing it until you saw me." His head tilted back in a full-body laugh.

"Well, thank you for saving me. Your performance was … singular."

"I can do better if I know the song."

"Duet. Duet. Duet." Lizzy chanted.

Dylan shrugged and smiled at me. "I'm game if you are. But you have to let me pick the song."

"Nothing with screaming," I said.

Dylan jogged over to the guy with the music library and came back with an enormous grin. "Got the perfect one."

"What is it?" I said, feeling giddy. Part of me wanted to be irritated that he'd budged in on my girl time with Lizzy, but that part was whomped away by the feeling in my belly when he'd sung-screamed the lyrics that he really loved me and would be thinking of me. Toni Tennille meets Robert Plant. That mash-up was one baby so ugly you had to love it.

"Not telling." He winked.

I felt something that was not appropriate to feel for a friend. "What if I don't know it?"

"Oh, you know it. Guaranteed."

We sat through five more songs and then we saw 'Dylan and Kama' on the call board.

I stepped onto the stage and saw the song name: 'Elephant Love Medley.'

"I don't know this song," I whispered to Dylan, panicking.

"You sure do. Just wait 'til the music starts."

Dylan started to sing before the music even started. He got down on one knee and belted out that he was made for loving me and I was made for loving him. The next lyrics up were the woman's part, and that's when I knew the song he'd cued up for us.

It was probably the hottest duet in the history of movie love songs. It was from *Moulin Rouge*, the song where Christian, who's never been in love before, declares his love for Satine, the star courtesan at the Moulin Rouge.

My karaoke confidence was normally high, but it was quickly slipping away. I can sing, but I'm no Nicole Kidman.

I turned my back to Dylan, who was still on his knees, and sang my line—that the only way to love me was to pay. Then, like in the movie, I turned around to face him.

He asked for just one night.

I called him a crazy fool.

Back and forth we argued in song, just the way we did in our non-date conversations. He challenged me line for line, declaring love while I pushed him away.

He sang that we could be happy.

I sang that it would never work.

He sang that we should be lovers.

I sang that we couldn't do that.

Of all the songs, all the duets he could have chosen, there

wasn't one that was more perfect for me. For us. Except that we weren't actually in love. But the sparring felt like us. And the song was an appropriate metaphor for my thesis. It had never occurred to me, but this was practically my theme song.

And when we got to the beginning of the end, when he took my hands and we sang in harmony, staring into each other's eyes? That's when it happened. A feeling that rose from my lower abdomen to my throat and then swirled around and through my whole body like first-night, stage-fright jitters.

The song ended, with our noses touching, and just before the moment when Ewan and Nicole kissed, I whispered Satine's final line in the song, with a minor change: "You're going to be bad for my thesis, I can tell."

And then he kissed me. Dylan Rhodes pulled me hard into his chest and pressed his lips against mine. His tongue tested my open mouth, touching my tongue for a second before retreating. My hands found his waist, and my fingers curled hard into his flesh while my tongue sought and found his.

Our end-of-song embrace lasted considerably longer than the on-screen kiss between Christian and Satine. Long enough that when I could hear past the adrenaline rush, my heartbeat, and the applause and whistles, Lizzy yelled, "Get a room!"

Our lips parted, but Dylan didn't release me from his hug.

"Your place?" I whispered in his ear.

He put his hand on my bum and pulled me against his groin. I interpreted his hard-on as a yes.

But he shook his head and said, "Don't you want to sing another? I lined up five more duets—including Buzz Lightyear and Woody's 'You've Got A friend in Me.'"

If he'd started with that song and eased into Christian

and Satine's song, sure. But I was feeling too light-headed to speak. I shook my head. "Home. Now. Please."

Monosyllables. That's what he had reduced my brain to.

Back at our table with Lizzy and Josh, I grabbed my purse and jacket and told Lizzy I was going home with Dylan.

"Damn straight you are! Have the time of your life."

"You, too," I said meaningfully, glancing at Josh.

She shrugged and made a disappointed face. "Not happening."

I made a sad face.

Dylan rubbed my back and asked if I was ready to go.

"I love you," I said to Lizzy, as Dylan took my hand.

"Love you, too," she called as I walked away, leaving my best friend with my not-date's brother.

"My place or yours?" he asked.

"My bed is a single."

"My place it is, then." Dylan hailed a cab.

# 19

## DYLAN

In the back seat of the cab, Kama tried to kiss me, but I placed my hand on her shoulder and gently pushed her away.

"What? You don't want to kiss me? I thought ..." She trailed off and looked embarrassed.

"Oh. I do. More than you can know. But that's not how tonight is going to go," I said, even though my body was screaming for me to shut up.

"Why?" she whispered, looking at her hands.

"Kama, look at me. Two reasons. One, I'm not sure you're sober, and I don't want our first time to be when you've been drinking."

She looked at me, her dark eyes smoldering—angry or hungry, I couldn't tell.

"Assuming we have a first time," I said. "Sorry. I feel like that's where the is headed but I shouldn't assume."

"But I want to," she said, desperation thick in her voice.

"I'm glad. And I promise that we're on the same page. But the second reason is actually about me. You've been in control of all our dates until now. Where we go, what we talk about. Everything. I don't know how much of what's happening here is real and how much of it you manipulated with your Jedi dating tricks."

"Nothing. Honestly. Nothing since the third date. Not even the third date."

"I'm glad, but I need you to let me be totally in control for one night."

She stared at me, blinking with wide eyes. I realized that might have sounded a bit scary.

"What I mean is, can you trust me to guide you on this date, or non-date? I don't care what the fuck you call it, but can you give me control the way you've been guiding our other not dates?"

Kama looked at me with apprehension and whispered, "I'm the boss of my body."

"Yes. I promise not to make you do anything you don't want to."

"I want to kiss you right now."

"I see that." I pressed my palm against her lips so she could kiss my hand, which she did. "As much as you're the boss of your body, I'm also the boss of my body, and right now I need to slow down so I can *stay* the boss of my body. Does that make sense?"

"I want to be the boss of your body."

"I know, Kama. You want to be the boss of everything. You like to be in control."

"I need to be in control." She said it more to herself than to me.

"You can control your body, but the rest? That's mine tonight. Tonight, you're handing that crown of yours to me, and you're going to let me guide. Can you do that?"

She nodded. "Yes?"

"No way! You do not get away with a question. I want to hear, "Hell, yeah, Dylan, you can be in charge tonight."

"And if I say no?'"

"If you say no, we drive past my place and get you home

where you can continue to be the boss of whatever you decide to do with the rest of your night."

She sucked in her bottom lip. I pushed a strand of hair away from her face. She shivered.

"What do I have to say?"

I breathed a sigh of relief. I hadn't realized I'd been holding my breath. "I need you to say a convincing, 'Hell, yeah!'"

"Hell, yeah," she said, matching my smile.

"I need you to say, 'Dylan, you can be in charge tonight.'"

"Dylan, you can be in charge tonight."

"Thank you. And now I'm going to kiss you. But just a nice, getting-to-know-each-other kiss."

I took her face in my hands and guided her head toward mine. I leaned forward and brushed my lips against hers. Just a touch. A breath. And then I pulled away and looked into her eyes.

There was definitely a hunger. It was a familiar look, one I often saw from the women I slept with. But the longer I stared into her eyes, the more I saw. Not just sexual hunger, but a longing.

"When was the last time ..." I wasn't sure how to ask without embarrassing her.

"Two years. Give or take," she said with a shrug.

"Why me?"

"I don't know. I trust you, I guess."

"Why?"

"You're different."

The cab pulled up in front of my place. "Hold that thought." I paid and took her hand as we walked through the lobby of my building. Kept her hand in mine as we rode the elevator to the twentieth floor. We rode up in silence, but I had a hundred questions I wanted to ask her.

I showed her around my small condo, which took all of thirty seconds. I just stood in the middle of my entrance/living room/dining room/kitchen and pointed at the bathroom and bedroom doors.

"Have a seat," I said, pointing at the couch. Even though I was in charge of the evening, I knew I needed to give Kama some control to feel comfortable.

"Hey, do you use Spotify?" I asked.

She nodded.

"Do you want to connect your phone to my Wi-Fi and put on one of your playlists? Something chill, some background music."

"Really, you're letting me set the mood? But I thought—"

"Stop thinking, woman. Tonight is about turning off that giant brain of your yours and just going with the flow."

I squatted down in front of her and took her knees in my hands. She shuddered.

"Obviously, I hadn't expected you over tonight. If we'd planned this, I'd have asked you to do a few things beforehand to make sure you were comfortable. So, I know it will sound strange, but we have to work with what we've got," I said.

"Okay…"

"Do you normally shave your legs, or are you more natural?"

"Seriously?" She tried to pull away from me, but I held tight.

"Yeah," I smiled, hoping she'd not interpret any judgment on my part.

Giving me the side-eye, she said, "I shave them."

"And are they, you know, up to your standards tonight? Will you feel comfortable if I'm touching them and looking at them in the light?"

Her eyes went huge. "That's three questions with two different answers."

"My bad," I said, realizing my mistake. "Have you shaved your legs in the last twenty-four hours?"

"Yes."

I breathed a sigh of relief. Asking her to shave here might have shut the night down. "One more question, and please read nothing into it. I promise I won't read anything into your answer. Did you wear comfortable—as in to lounge around in—underwear?"

"Oh my god. I will not be lounging around in my underwear." She slapped my hands off her knees and tried to stand up. I pressed my hands onto her thighs and held her in place.

"Well, you can't wear skinny jeans and a T-shirt for what I have planned."

"Obviously!" She said.

"Not so obvious. You have no idea what we're going to do, Kama."

"Have sex."

"Actually"—I closed my eyes and steadied myself for a long night—"we're not having sex."

She slumped, and her head fell forward like a rag doll's.

"Don't worry. I won't let you go home with tales of how unsatisfied I left you. But I need to get a few things ready in my room." I jumped up, grabbed a pair of boxers from my dresser, and tossed them to her. "I need you to put these on. When I come out of my room, I'd like you to be sitting here in nothing but your bra and my underwear."

"Dylan …"

"Kama, you promised to let me lead tonight. And I promise you'll love this. Just go with the flow. Trust me."

"Can I have a safe word?" she asked, making a face to suggest she was half joking.

"Fair enough. How about *stop*? If you say, "Stop," I will. And I'll call you a cab and you can go home. Deal?"

She nodded.

"Okay, sexy woman, put on my underwear and pick

your playlist. Wi-Fi login is Telus8484. Password is Tenderlegal84 with a capital T."

I left Kama looking skeptical. To be honest, I was feeling skeptical about pulling this off, too. It was something I'd tried and failed to do many times. But I'd never felt so committed to success as I did right now.

I pulled a shoebox from my cupboard. It contained everything I needed: tea-light candles and a lighter, a diffuser with three scents to choose from, scent-free massage oil, and an inflatable donut pillow.

I lit a dozen new candles—I'd learned the hard way that a woman will notice a previously lit candle and that no amount of assurance will convince her it hadn't been burned for another woman's pleasure. I added water to the diffuser and chose the orange/lavender/cinnamon blend, not only since it claimed to be calming but also because those scents felt the most like Kama.

I pulled my duvet off the bed and placed a fleece sheet down. It would protect my sheets from oil stains and be warmer for Kama when she first lay down. And then I changed into sweatpants and a clean T-shirt. I needed to be comfortable too, and giving my cock room to react without being all up in her face was critical to the successful completion of this experience.

Before I opened my bedroom door, I knocked. "Are you ready? Can I open the door?"

"Hell, yes?" she said with a slight laugh.

Good call, keeping my underwear on under my sweats, because Kama looked fan-fucking-amazing in my boxers and her bra. I would be rewarding myself with a bottle of Glenlivet single malt if I made it an hour without losing my focus. And my pants.

"Wait. Why are you still dressed? That's totally not fair." Kama grabbed the blanket off my couch and wrapped it around herself.

"Tonight isn't about me. It's about you." I reached out to take her hand. "Leave the blanket. There's one on the bed for you to cover up with. If you need it."

I led her the seven steps to my room. She sat on the bed then swung her legs up and pulled the blanket down over her. She was entirely covered but for her eyes and the top of her head.

"Kama, when was the last time you were touched?"

"Five minutes ago. You had your hands on my legs."

"I mean sensually."

She blinked but didn't speak. I reached my hand under the blanket and touched her leg. Her calf muscle tensed under my fingers.

"When was the last time you had a massage?"

She pulled the blanket down enough that I could see her whole face but nothing more. "Never."

"You've *never* had a massage?" I couldn't hide my shock. "How is that even possible? Massage is my go-to mental health care practice. I have at least one full-body massage a month."

She squinted and scrunched her nose. I knew what she was thinking.

"Not *full* full-body. Therapeutic with a registered massage therapist, covered by my extended medical insurance. That kind of full-body massage."

"I've never had one," she said.

"Woman, you will be a massage addict by the time I'm finished with you."

"You're going to give me a massage?"

"From the top of your head to your baby toes, I will touch every inch of your body tonight."

Kama's eyes opened wide.

"Except what's under my boxers and your bra," I added.

Her expression changed. "You're not going to touch *anything* that's covered?"

I shook my head. "Nope. These clothes create the boundary lines that I will not cross. So even though I'm in control of the massage, you have full control over where I don't touch you. Fair?"

"A massage? Seriously? That's all we're doing tonight?"

"You look disappointed. Don't worry. You won't be once I get started."

I, on the other hand, could tell that I would need to take a cold shower between her back and front sides. I wasn't sure how I'd pull that off, but my cock was already pushing hard against my boxers, and I knew it wouldn't stand down anytime soon.

"If you're ready, roll onto your stomach and get comfortable. I'm starting with your feet and legs."

As soon as she was facedown, I pulled my cock out of the fly on my boxers to give it some breathing room.

# 20

## KAMA

Once I was comfortable, with the duvet still covering my body, Dylan folded the bottom half up to expose my feet and legs from the knees down.

"What I'm giving you is called a sensual massage. It's not the kind you'd get from a massage therapist, and it's not a sexual massage, either. I'm thinking that there would be no better way to get to know the real you in just an hour or two."

He squeezed a line of oil on my leg from my knee toward my foot. It tickled and I squeaked. I couldn't speak very easily since my face was buried in a ring pillow. It was comfortable, though. Dylan suggested it had been designed specifically for me since I'd have no choice but to stop thinking and just feel. He was right. Without the ability to talk, I fell into a kind of trance.

It didn't matter where Dylan's hands were, how lightly he was brushing my skin, or how hard he was kneading my muscles—it was all ecstasy inducing. He kept laughing because I was a nonstop moaning machine.

He was also right that I would be booking a massage every week for the rest of my life. I could totally understand why this was his mental health go-to. What he was doing made my entire body feel loved. And I was happy with the playlist I'd chosen. It maintained the mood perfectly since it was the same one I'd used on our first date: the one with the heartbeat backtrack and lyrics about love. When Dylan asked if I was ready to roll over, I knew that he'd spent fully forty minutes caressing my back. It felt impossible to have zoned out and just *experienced* for that long.

I lifted my head so he could hear me clearly. "Not if that means you're already half-finished."

"You are seriously the most touch-starved woman I've ever met. No one has ever been as responsive to this as you are," he said, lifting the blanket so I could roll over more easily.

And that pulled me right out of my body and back into my brain. How many women had he done this with? Why did I think I was the first, that I was special? I rolled onto my back with my arms pressed against my sides. Dylan smiled and picked one up. Without thinking, I resisted.

"Whoa ... What just happened? My bendy girl just got all stiff."

"I just realized that this is part of your schtick," I said with a weak smile.

"My what?"

"Your foreplay. I'm an idiot. It felt like this was something special to me, but ..." I shrugged my naked shoulders.

"Oh, no you don't," he said, lightly placing his hands on my collarbone. "Get out of your head, Kama, and back to what your body is desperate for. This *is* special to you. I promise you that. Sure, I've given sensual massage to other women, but never for more than ten minutes because they just weren't into it like you are. They were here to take off all their clothes. And my clothes. I tried to get to know them better. I tried to let them get to know this side of me.

But they just wanted to fuck. So, yeah, this is special, and not just for you but for me, too. This is very fucking special."

A lump formed in the back of my throat. I held my breath to keep from crying.

"How many men have you been with?" he asked.

That was a tricky question. If I said too many, I worried he'd think I was a slut. If I said too few, he might think I was a prude. I didn't want to answer since I didn't want him to judge me either way. I hesitated long enough that he rephrased it.

"Kama, have any of your lovers ever taken the time to get to know your body to the extent that you get to know people's minds? All those questions you ask. All the listening you do. You're great at getting to know half of a person. The parts they want you to see. And letting them see the parts of you you're willing to show. But have you ever relaxed like this before? Moaned so freely and unabashedly?"

I shook my head. He took my face in his hands.

"On our third date—you probably don't remember—but the Foo Fighters came on the radio. The song 'Everlong.' There's a line in that song that's been on repeat in my brain ever since; I want to breathe you in, so I'm going to kiss you now," he said, bending over and pressing his lips gently against mine for several heartbeats.

There was no hunger. It was more like he was listening to me with his mouth. I could feel him match his breathing to mine. When he pulled away, I knew exactly the line he was thinking of.

I sang the lyrics to him.

He smiled and leaned back over me. I lifted my head toward him. We kissed again, this time with a clear intention to breathe each other in. Hold each other in. That was the moment I realized I never wanted to kiss another man. I never wanted another man's hands on my body. Every inch, inside and out.

When he pulled away, I was his, if he wanted me. His past was irrelevant. My past, so forgettable, was also irrelevant. I had the words *I love you* on my lips, but I knew better than to say them.

"Can I get back to exploring you? The top side is the best side. Getting to know your hands, feeling the beat of your heart, exploring the contours of your hips, and running my fingers through your hair as I massage your head."

I moaned again. "Sounds amazing. And then do I get to explore you?"

"Not tonight. Tonight is all about you."

I so wanted to tell him I loved him.

"Did you know that babies who are held and touched lovingly grow bigger and healthier than babies who are not? Humans need touch to survive. We need it to thrive. You've been deprived of a vital life force, Kama, and tonight I'm helping you refill your well."

"But I feel like I'm doing all the taking and not giving anything back. You're doing all the work. I'm getting all the pleasure."

"That's where you're so wrong. You'll see. When you've got me under your hands, you'll understand. I'm getting just as much from this as you are. I promise you. Your reactions to my touch are feeding my spirit too. This is a mutually beneficial experience."

"Then shut up and get back to work. I'm starving here."

Dylan took my left hand and pressed his thumb into my palm, gently tracing my life lines. My eyes were almost closed but not quite. I could see his face, as if through gauze, looking at my hand as if it were the most interesting thing he'd ever seen. When he changed the direction of his strokes up to my fingertips, I got a chill. I opened my eyes to smile at him, but his eyes were closed. His focus was singularly on me. On getting to know me.

I tried to fall back into the altered state I'd been in when he was rubbing my legs and massaging my back. But my mind was working, and I needed to think my thoughts before I could slip away again. I had an epiphany about my research. While I was trying to prove that a person's interest in another could be controlled and manipulated verbally, Dylan had just proven to me that it could be equally controlled and manipulated without a single word.

I'd had no intention of falling in love with him. He was a research subject I had actively pulled toward me but always intended to hold at arm's length. I wondered if his gift of touch was just a reaction to him feeling seen and heard by me. And if what I was experiencing right now was nothing more than a counterpoint reaction. An example of the action-reaction principle in effect.

Dylan had come into this situation with the full understanding that he would be a subject upon whom I'd be testing communication techniques. He'd figured out pretty quickly that the goal was to keep him from my bed. And here I was, in his bed, experiencing the most profound connection I'd ever had with a man. The most profound heart connection I'd ever felt with anyone. It suddenly seemed obvious that his eagerness to go the distance with my research, and then to go farther with the film project, had been a setup from the start.

It occurred to me that he'd participated in my research to make me part of his. He wasn't just sharing his stories and being heard—he'd been actively listening the entire time, and not just to my words, but to the environment I created. To my music. The music that expressed all the thoughts and feelings I held to myself. My hopes and dreams. He heard my call in those songs and responded.

I was the observer put under a microscope to be observed. I was the researcher now being researched.

"Kama." His voice was gentle. "I've lost you. Where are you?"

"What do you mean? I'm right here." I knew exactly what he meant. My skin was still under his warm hands, but the rest of me had retreated.

"Talk to me," he said, placing a hand on my heart area.

"This isn't real." I felt like those three words summed up everything.

"This? What do you mean, 'this'?"

I lifted his hand from my chest, placed it against his own leg, and let go. My body contracted. I felt like I'd shrunk without his touch. The feeling surprised me, and I made a small gasping sound.

"Kama? Are you having a panic attack? Did I touch a place I shouldn't have?"

Did he touch a place he shouldn't have? Yes. He touched a place I didn't know I even had in me. A place I didn't have a word for. He touched it, and now he was going to leave it for me to find again. I didn't even know where to look.

"I'm not having a panic attack. I'm having … an epiphany."

"That's amazing," he said, laying his hands on my collarbone. "Tell me. What have you realized?"

He was smiling. He had no idea that I'd figured him out. Did I tell him, or play him the way he was playing me? I was too tired of the game with him to play anymore.

"You're using me," I said.

He kept smiling. "See, I told you you'd understand. You're filling my well as much as I'm filling yours."

"No. I know what you're doing, Dylan. You met me and went on those dates with an ulterior motive. You said from the beginning that you wanted to go out with me because a friend had met—"

"He is not a friend," Dylan said with force.

"Okay, but at the end of that dinner, you said you wanted to go out with me again because I was a puzzle you wanted to figure out. Why? What's in it for you to care about understanding me?"

I was right; I could see it on his face, and I felt his energy contract. He watched me pull the blanket over my exposed body, and then he took off his sweatpants and T-shirt. He stood in his boxer briefs.

"Move over. I'll tell you everything, but I want to be spooning you. I need to feel your breathing, your heartbeat. I'm still not done with our skin-to-skin contact."

"No." I sat up. "No more manipulation. I'm not having sex with you so you can distract me from answering."

"No sex. I promise. We're keeping the sexy bits covered, I promise. *I promise*, Kama."

"Why should I trust your promise when I know you've not been honest with me?"

"I never lied. I just neglected to share one minor detail. Hear me out. Please, Kama. I want to tell you everything. I've been wanting to tell you since ten minutes into our first date. But ..." He lifted the blanket and touched my back, coaxing me to lie back down and roll on my side. "Just let me lie down with you. Hold you. I'll tell you what you want to know."

# 21

## DYLAN

This was it. I had to tell her the truth, the whole truth, and nothing but the truth. Come what may. If she hated me, better now than in eight weeks, right?

I'd thought about how I'd tell her a hundred—a thousand—times. But now that I had to confess, none of the rational, logical words I'd use in a court of law seemed good enough.

I pressed my chest against her back and wrapped one arm over her body to hold her close. She resisted for a few seconds but finally relaxed into me, placing her hand on top of mine, above her abdomen.

I matched her breathing for a minute or two as we lay in silence. And then I slowed my breath in the hope she'd follow, which she did. Good start. Both calm. Her fight, flight, or freeze hormones went back to sleep. I just had to keep it that way—not just for her, but for myself.

"Remember on our first date, when I told you I wanted to meet you because someone I knew had gone out with you?"

"Mm hmm," she said.

"I told you he was a guy who'd been upset that you wouldn't sleep with him."

"Yeah," she said, tensing her stomach muscles, holding her breath.

"Keep breathing, Kama."

She exhaled hard and then inhaled a full breath.

"That man's name was, or is, Bob Booker. Do you remember him?"

"Bob Booker?" She lay quietly for several heartbeats. "I didn't go out with anyone named Bob."

"Well, he says you did. And he knew enough about you to suggest you had three dates with him. He told me which restaurants you'd take me to."

Kama rolled out from under my arm and turned to face me. She looked confused. "Well, then he didn't use that name on our date or when he signed his informed consent document, since that's not a name I have in my research."

"See, that's the thing. He claims you never got him to sign that form."

"That's impossible. Every man I dated for the research filled out ... oh." A look of knowing and repulsion took over her expression. "Robert. He was an ass."

Kama sat up and crossed her arms in front of her chest. I needed her calm for the next part.

"Hey," I said, touching her shoulder, "will you lie back down with me? I want to hold you."

She shook her head. "I need to see you. I don't like where this is going."

"No. Neither do I. That's why I want to be holding you." We locked eyes. She didn't look angry. Yet. "How about this?" I sat up and pressed my back to the headboard. "Will you sit between my legs? That way we both get what we need: you get eye contact, and I get to rub your back. Please?"

"You're kind of freaking me out, Dylan."

"Come here." I spread my legs and guided her into the open space. Thank god she was wearing my boxers and I was in sweats because all it would have taken to ... I exhaled and bit the inside of my lower lip.

"Is that uncomfortable?" she asked.

"No. It's perfect." I leaned forward and breathed in the smell of her hair. Almond. I had to resist running my hands through it. Now was not the time. God, I hoped that after I told her I'd still have the chance.

"Okay," I said, "remember how I told you that sometimes I have to take cases I don't agree with?"

"Dylan."

"Booker claims you misled him. He says you used him in your research without his consent—"

"I didn't! He was never one of the subjects. He was an actual date." She tried to pull away, but I held onto her. "He is actually the perfect example of why I pursued this topic since he was such a textbook asshole, expecting—no, *demanding*—that I owed him sex for the time he spent with me. 'Wasted with me' is what he said when I made it clear that I would not give him what he wanted."

"So, you didn't use your Jedi mind tricks on him?"

"Obviously not!"

"And he's not included in your research?"

"Well, not in the data. I mean, I used that specific date in my rationale to my thesis advisor for why this line of inquiry was important and would be interesting. But no, he's not included."

"I'm confused. You told me you hadn't been on a non-research date in something like two years. So, when did these dates with Booker take place? Was it over two years ago?"

Kama shook her head and sighed. She closed her eyes. "No. This is embarrassing. My thesis advisor told me I had to go out with five different men on actual, regular dates before she'd let me submit my idea. She claimed I needed more real-world dating experience to, I don't know, be convincing as a normal dating human and not just a researcher. So they weren't research, but they also weren't real. Does that make sense?"

She looked so vulnerable. So sad. I couldn't help it. I leaned forward and kissed her. She gasped in surprise but kissed me back. I moved my hands to her cheeks, and she put her hands on my temples and held me close.

She whispered into my mouth, "Breathe out. I want to breathe you in."

With our mouths open, our lips touching lightly enough to inhale but firm enough to explore each other's tongues and teeth, we kissed like that, breathing each other in for so long I got light-headed.

"I want you," I said.

"I want you, too," she whispered. But then she pulled back and looked me in the eye. "Dylan, why are you asking me these things about that guy?"

I bit my lip. I held Kama's shoulders gently but firmly, made eye contact with her, and took three deep breaths. And then I said it. "Booker is suing you for unethical conduct and breach of an implied contract."

Kama gasped and squeezed my biceps. Hard.

I closed my eyes and prepared for the attack. "And I'm the lawyer assigned to represent him."

# 22

## KAMA

I was speechless. I couldn't process what Dylan had just said. One minute ago I was falling in love, and now … he was representing the biggest jerk I've ever met—against me. I decided I'd not heard him properly. I mean, I'd just spent the last ten minutes breathing recycled air, so my brain was oxygen deprived. That's what was happening.

I stared at his chest and could see his heart beat. It was pounding hard and too fast. He was stressed. I placed one hand on his sternum and one on my own. I studied his face. His brow was furrowed, eyes sad, jaw and mouth soft. He looked as confused as I felt.

"So you went out with me because you were expecting to find something to back up Booker's claim?"

"At first. I contacted you for that first date, expecting to find out you weren't following all the research rules—"

"But I was. And you saw that."

He nodded. "You were perfect."

"So … why did you go out with me again? Why not just tell the client he didn't have a case?"

"That's what I'd planned to do. I went to my boss—who assigned me this case—and told him you were by the book.

I'd intended to tell him it was a waste of the client's money for me to go out with you again."

"So why didn't you?" In the seconds it took for Dylan to answer, I ran through all the reasons he might say yes to a second and third date, even knowing I wouldn't give his client a win. "Were you being paid to go out with me?"

He nodded. "Technically, yes—"

I pushed out of his lap and wrapped myself in his duvet, leaving him sitting exposed.

"Kama, I wasn't personally being paid. The firm billed him, and I just got my normal salary. But, yes, those were billable hours. The best billable hours I've logged in my entire time at the firm. That's why I didn't quit that case. I legitimately wanted to see you again."

I scoffed. "You could have done both, you know. You could have walked away from representing that ass and still had two more dates with me."

"Technically, you're right. And in my defense, after our first date I did encourage my boss to tell the client to drop his case since I didn't see any way for him to win since you were one-hundred-percent by the book. But he, my boss, told me to continue dating you. He thought that since you knew I was a lawyer you were on your best behavior. He wanted me to trip you up. I just wanted to see you again."

"Then you could have told me that before we went on our second date and I'd have taken you out of my study to avoid … I don't know, being all mixed up in this mess," I said.

"Um, no, I couldn't have. You were one-hundred-percent clear that if I wasn't part of your research, I had exactly a zero chance of seeing you again."

I thought back to that sparring we did before Dylan had even signed the informed consent document and had to accept that he was right. But if we'd had that conversation on the second or third dates, I would have said something different.

Maybe.

He reached across the bed and forced his hand under the duvet, onto my thigh. I let his hand caress me. We sat in silence for minutes. Dylan was the first to speak.

"You know what? You're right," he said. "I could have walked away from the case but kept pursuing you. But in my defense, I honestly didn't think you had any interest in me other than for your thesis. And you said that, in exactly those words, at the end of our third date."

"I'm sorry. I was confused, and—"

"I'm not looking for an apology," he said, leaning forward and giving me a kiss on the cheek. "And that was only half the truth. I also have a promotion resting on this one stupid, frivolous case. So I figured, why give up a promotion for a woman who may be doing nothing wrong— and who also doesn't care about me as more than a set of data points?"

I couldn't be mad because it was true. Or had been true. That's when I had a flash of insight. Our dates were also billable hours, of a sort, for me. It was my work. I couldn't judge Dylan without doing the same to myself.

"But things have changed," I said. "At least for me they have. Obviously, I wouldn't be lying in your bed virtually naked if I still thought of you as just a set of data points." And then I had a terrible thought. "Which begs the question: are you still trying to win a case against me? Are you going to argue that I've abused my position as a researcher to lure you into my bed?" I felt like I was going to hyperventilate. "I need to get my purse." I tried to get up from the bed. Dylan wrapped himself around me and held me tight.

"Kama, you didn't hear me. Or maybe I wasn't clear. I'm not arguing a case against you."

"But this entire relationship—or whatever this is—it's

built on us both using each other. I was honest about it, but you're right, I was using you." Emotion clogged my throat, and all I could do was whisper the rest. "None of this is real. Why am I even here, Dylan?"

He took my chin in his hand. "Who says this isn't real? It feels more fucking real than anything I've ever felt. As to why you're here, I hope—I believed—it was because you felt something for me, too. After our third date, I recommended that the firm give Booker back his money, and that he drop the case. He refused, and I was forced to submit a request for a court date. I've been hoping that the court will see it as frivolous and reject it. I hoped I'd never have to tell you about it. But I'm glad I got the case. Otherwise I never would have met you."

He looked and sounded sincere. I wanted to believe every word. And why shouldn't I? I tried to think back to any moment that suggested he'd lied to me. I couldn't think of any. Maybe he hadn't told me all the facts, but then, I hadn't told him everything about what I was doing when we had those dinners, either.

"I'm glad, too. But what if the courts agree to let Booker have his day in court? I'll need to get a lawyer. I don't have money for a lawyer. And," I almost yelled, my frustration finally overtaking me, "I haven't done anything wrong."

That's when the tears started. Dylan wiped my cheek with his thumb but didn't speak. We sat in silence. Again.

"Now do you understand why I didn't date for all those years? I can't do this. It's too hard."

"Stop thinking that way. Look. If the court thinks this is worth their time, you won't need a lawyer. I can't represent Booker now. I have an obvious conflict of interest. And even though I can't technically represent you either, nobody can stop me from coaching my girlfriend…"

My laugh—more like a disbelieving *pfft!*—left me before I registered I was doing it. "Yeah, right. You don't have girlfriends. You made that painfully clear every time we went out."

Dylan's eyes, his touch, and then finally his words convinced me he'd changed his position. "And you don't date. But it looks like I finally found a woman who I'm willing to break my rule for. How about you? Are you willing to break your 'I don't date' position for me?"

"If you hadn't noticed the virtually naked woman sitting on your bed, I already have. And if I'm honest, I broke it weeks ago. So what do we do now?"

"You mean about Booker? Or about the fact that I am feeling so freaking grateful that you don't hate me, and I want to express that gratitude by giving you a reason to call me your boyfriend?"

"Yeah. That second one," I said, unwrapping myself from the duvet and pressing as much of my almost-naked body against Dylan's as I could.

# 23

## DYLAN

"Will you lay on your back again and let me finish the massage?" I asked, pulling myself away from Kama's hug.

"Would you be disappointed if I said I really, really want to have sex with you *right* now?" Kama asked.

My cock jumped.

"I'm delighted, overjoyed, that you want to have sex. But, yes, I would be disgusted with myself if I didn't give you the gift of the rest of this massage. Kama, your body is so fucking responsive to my touch it's like medicine for my nervous system."

Kama gave me a shy smile with questioning eyes.

"I can't explain it. And I've never had this sensation. But the energy from your body as I touch you ... It's like being in a trance, like deep meditation. I'm here with you, obviously, but also, I'm not. I'm in another world. I know it sounds insane, but—"

"It doesn't sound crazy at all. I feel it, too. But the spell keeps breaking when you lift your hand to jump over my bra strap; when you stop where the underwear starts. Can we compromise and finish the massage without the bra and underwear, so I can feel your hands on all of me?"

My breathing hitched. Keeping my cock in my pants was already a Herculean challenge. If I were touching her breasts, her nipples, her mound ... Jesus, not her slick folds ... Just the thought brought me to full erection. Instead of answering, I pulled my boxers down and let Kama see what her suggestion had done to me.

She flushed and her mouth opened, but the only noise she made was a whisper. "Oh."

We locked eyes as she undid her bra. I let my boxers hit the floor and stepped out of them. She pushed the duvet aside and lifted her hips to pull down her boxers. We maintained eye contact as she finished the move. I wasn't ready to look at her fully naked body, so I pulled the duvet up and covered her.

My breathing was ragged, and my voice didn't sound like my own. "Same deal as your back. I'll start at your feet and move up."

I exposed her right leg up to the hip bone, making sure to keep her pubic area fully covered. I'd let my hands slide there, but I couldn't let myself see. Not yet. I reached for the massage oil and dripped a line from her ankle up to the blanket, poured more in my palm, then rubbed my hands together to warm them. I started by rubbing the line of oil into her skin in long, slow strokes, never allowing skin contact to break. While I raised one hand to start the slow draw up her leg again, the other gently caressed the spot where it had stopped moving.

I looked up at her face. Her eyes were closed. The duvet was rising and falling over her chest, showing me that her breaths were slow and deep. This was trust. This was vulnerability. This was a connection I'd never expected. I had to close my eyes to settle my breath, which had become shallow.

It took several minutes before I could let myself relax into a space where time had no meaning, where I was no longer Dylan Rhodes, the lawyer who lived in his brain, but simply energy moving from one body to another and back. Thoughts came and went. Images appeared and disappeared. Feelings rose and fell.

When I finished massaging Kama's left leg, I had to fully come back to the room to adjust the duvet so I could massage her abdomen, ribs, shoulders. That's when I registered the music in the background, and Kama quietly humming the love song duet by Lady Gaga and Bradley Cooper. I lingered at her hip bone longer than I'd planned, listening. And when she reached the part where Bradley's character sings, I hummed the part with her. I didn't plan or expect to. In fact, before this moment, I'd have said I hated the song.

Her eyes opened slowly, and she smiled, humming a little louder. She lifted her arm from under the duvet and motioned with two fingers for me to come closer to her face. I was wholly, unconditionally under her spell. She kissed her own fingers, then placed them lightly on my throat.

"Keep humming," she whispered. "Put your fingers here." She showed me the spot on her own throat.

This was next-level sensual massage. My cock, which had settled down once I was in the zone, remained soft. The strange thing was, at that moment I wanted to be on Kama, inside her, and wrapped around her, with every inch of my body touching hers. But not in a horny way.

My free hand touched her shoulder, and I looked at the empty side of the bed. She understood. Without letting our fingers move from each other's throats, she wiggled to the side, and I slid in beside her. Two naked bodies. Such a familiar thing, and yet like nothing I'd ever experienced.

We lay covered, her on her back, me on my hip and shoulder facing her. The song ended, and we lay for several heartbeats, motionless. Then she slid her hand down my neck to my sternum and pressed a flat palm against me. I mirrored her action. Slowly, deliberately, she traced her palm down my body, stopping at the bottom of my rib cage, then again on my belly. She turned her hand so her fingers were aimed down. She touched my pubic hair. That's when my cock came to life. Fast and hard.

I moaned.

Kama pushed herself up on an arm and then sat forward on her hip before tossing the blanket off our bodies. Wordlessly, she pressed my chest down, so I was flat on my back—flat except for my erection. She straddled my thighs, holding most of her weight on her knees.

"I want to feel your heart beat against my chest. Can I lie on you?"

I pulled her down by her shoulders and wrapped my arms around her back. Her chin rested on my shoulder and I buried my face in her hair, breathing in the warm scent. She kissed my neck. My cock ached to be inside her. I squeezed her ass and tried to pull her body down low enough for her folds to press against my hard-on.

She resisted with a gentle bite to my neck and a quiet, "Uh-uh. I promised I'd let you massage every inch of me. I'm not breaking that promise. I was just giving your hands a little rest. And I needed to put my mouth on you. To taste you."

She pulled herself back onto her knees, leaned forward, and kissed my lips with an open mouth. Our tongues found each other and swirled together. She nudged my tongue back in my mouth and explored my teeth. I felt the shape of her mouth change, a smile, when I gently closed my jaw and caught her tongue between my teeth.

And then, without warning, she pulled her lips from mine and pushed herself up and off me, back to her side of the bed. My head fell against the pillow and I closed my eyes, disappointed. My body, which had felt so grounded under her weight, suddenly felt lost in space, grasping for something to hold on to. But that feeling lasted less than three seconds because before I could reach to pull her back to me, her hand wrapped around the base of my cock and then her warm mouth took me inside.

Her tongue continued the same rhythmic dance on the head of my cock that it had been doing inside my mouth. Although my eyes were still closed, I could see lights and colors and movement. It was like seeing my emotions. This was not just a blow job. It was full-body, mind and spirit arousal. Kama was performing Jedi mind tricks on my cock.

Her hand, working my shaft, wordlessly said, 'You are enough.'

I thought, *I am enough.*

Her mouth, sucking my head, whispered in moans, 'You are worthy.'

I thought, *I am worthy.*

Her tongue, swirling on my tip, silently communicated, 'You are valued.'

I thought, *I am valued.*

I never wanted her to stop.

When I felt myself ready to let go, I reached forward and grabbed her shoulders. "Kama, I'm going to come."

Instead of pulling away and finishing in her hand, she took me deeper in her mouth and moaned. The vibration shook me. And it clearly said, 'You are unconditionally loved.'

I felt it, unconditionally loved, perhaps for the first time in my life. Certainly for the first time with a woman.

I knew in that moment that I would do anything for Kama Ray.

# 24

## KAMA

If anyone had told me that my dating research would lead me to the man of my dreams, I'd have told them they were crazy. I'd have taken any bet, for any amount of money, knowing I'd win.

But here I was, less than eight weeks since my first date with Dylan Rhodes, and I couldn't imagine life without him. I could barely *remember* life before I met him, and I didn't see any possible future without him in it. I couldn't explain it, but he made me feel complete.

When I was too in my head, he helped me find my heart. When I was anxious, he calmed me with just a touch, the right word, or a wink that said, 'I've got your back.' When I wanted to hide behind research and my student persona, he coaxed me out and made me realize how much I'd been missing by not being fully present as Kama-the-woman-who-is-so-much-more-than-just-a-future-PhD.

Since that day we first made love, I'd been accidentally moving in with him, T-shirt by T-shirt. Each time I spent the night—which was several times a week—he insisted I put my previous day's clothes in his laundry basket instead of taking them back to school or work with me. And as the days and weeks passed, the dresser drawer he'd emptied for me filled until I needed a second drawer.

And when Dylan noticed, instead of squashing his own clothes into a smaller space, he bought a matching dresser and moved my clothes into it. It may have seemed quick if one was counting days on a calendar, but it didn't feel quick in real life. It felt right. Natural. Easy.

Mostly.

I still had my room at the residence, and I made a point to spend two or three nights a week there since I knew it was risky to trust these early relationship feelings. I knew better than to believe that after less than two months together, Dylan and I knew each other well enough to tackle life's serious challenges. We'd had minor arguments but hadn't faced any of the kinds of stress that a couple has to weather for a relationship to survive—a death, a job loss, a move, or even a vacation together. Statistically speaking, if a couple could get through those four challenges, they could survive anything. Dylan and I had a long way to go before putting our new status to those tests, so I let myself get comfortable living with Dylan only part-time.

That said, the nights I spent in his condo were the highlight of my week. I loved cooking, and having someone to make food for was a joy. At least twice a week Dylan would have to work until seven or later. He'd text me mid-afternoon to let me know when he'd be home, and if I wasn't working, I'd have dinner ready for him.

He insisted on picking me up after my evening shifts at the university library. I'd finish at nine, never having eaten, so we'd go back to his place, where he'd either have made dinner or picked up something delicious.

Always, even better than the food, was the company. We ate at the table. Sometimes we had music on in the background, but never a screen—no TV, no news, no streaming movies. Dinner time was 'talk about your day' time. After dinner, we'd sometimes watch a binge-worthy series, sometimes sit on the couch together, working on our laptops, and sometimes we'd go to bed early. We needed our seven hours of sleep, and making love with Dylan Rhodes was not an experience I ever wanted to rush.

With Dylan, foreplay was a misnomer since the word suggests something that comes before the main event. The hour—or two—of touching, tasting, and teasing each other's bodies made the orgasmic part even more intense.

Today had been challenging for me, and even though it wasn't a night I'd normally spend with Dylan, I needed his company. I'd submitted a draft of my thesis to my advisor the week earlier, and today she'd given me her comments and recommendations. They were significant. I was deflated. Dylan was the perfect person to vent to, since he knew my research so intimately and would understand exactly what my advisor was concerned about.

"She's questioning the objectivity of my research methods. It makes no sense. She approved the approach, so why, suddenly, is this a problem when it wasn't before?" I wasn't sure if I was more infuriated or devastated. Since I didn't feel like crying, I decided anger was my primary emotion.

"Has she suggested a way to prove the objectivity or somehow ensure it? Or is she just being a dick and saying, 'This doesn't work. Fix it.'?"

"Total dick." I stabbed my barbecued chicken breast for effect.

"How can I help?"

I loved this guy. For someone who was probably five times smarter than me, not once in all the hundreds of hours we'd talked had he ever mansplained to me. He asked questions and only offered suggestions if I asked him directly.

"Put yourself in my shoes. You're one paper away from

getting your master's degree. One lousy paper—I mean, one kick-ass research thesis—away from your degree and suddenly, your advisor does a one-eighty. She's all but said in her comments that, based on what you've submitted, she thinks you should rethink your thesis topic and start again."

"Ouch."

I stabbed at my food but before I took the bite said, "I should resubmit a research paper on how to Jedi-mind-trick a thesis advisor into going home and rethinking her life." I did the open-palm hand sweep that Qui-Gon Jinn used when he mind-tricked the death-stick peddler.

Dylan inhaled, expanding his chest so it was obvious. Then he smiled and made the same hand motion at me. It was our unspoken, non-judgmental, and highly effective way of saying, 'Breathe.'

"Okay," he said, after I'd mirrored his breaths for several seconds, "so a bit of a sidestep, but not a rhetorical question." Dylan held up his hands in prayer position, our silent way to communicate 'don't be mad when I say this.' "If you were just starting fresh in your master's program today, what would you focus your thesis on?"

"You think I should start again?" I ignored his silent plea. I was angry and didn't hide it.

He smiled and shook his head. He may have rolled his eyes, but I was too busy rolling mine to tell.

"Maybe my question wasn't clear. Let me rephrase. If you were just starting fresh in your master's program today, what would you focus your thesis on?" He was still smiling. His eyes twinkled.

"You said exactly the same thing!" I wanted to be mad at his snark, but it was hard to be angry when he was so patient. "Okay. Fine. If I was just starting out today, with all I now know and all the experiences I've had in the last six months ..." I stopped to think. What would I research? A phrase popped into my head as I stared at Dylan. Words that felt entirely unrelated to his question. But I'd learned early in my psychology program that thoughts that seem random never are. So, despite how irrelevant it sounded, I said, "Understanding begins with a shared breath."

Dylan leaned back and shook his head. "That's beautiful. And kind of inspired. And it's so perfectly … you." He stood, then leaned across the table and kissed me. "So can you see any way to weave 'understanding begins with a shared breath' with the thesis topic you've been researching?"

This is what made Dylan so darned perfect. He had this unique ability to move me from anger and frustration to hope, and even solutions. Three minutes ago—and for the full day since meeting my advisor in the morning—I'd been fretting and fuming and stressing. Now I was imagining possibilities. I wasn't sure what the answer was yet, but I knew, with this man as my sounding board, I'd find one.

"Thank you," I said. "That was exactly what I needed."

"I have every confidence that your solution to that wicked-witch advisor's challenge will kick ass and take names."

"Has anyone told you today that you're the best? Seriously. Better than a Lady Gaga duet."

"Really? Better than that? I find those words kind of abstract and hard to believe. I think I need you to show me what you mean."

I stood and stripped naked, right there at the dinner table. Then I took Dylan's hand and led him to the bedroom.

# 25

## DYLAN

As I undressed, Kama stood beside the bed and stared at me with an intensity I'd never before seen from her. It was clear she was pondering, weighing something important.

"What? Just say it," I said. I was getting concerned about where this might be headed.

"I don't know how. I don't know what words to use to not sound... like a freak."

"Just say whatever is in your head right now. Go!"

She pursed her lips and inhaled fast through her nose. Then she squeezed her eyes closed and said really quickly, "I want you to go down on me." Before I could answer, she jumped into the bed and pulled the covers over her head.

I crawled in and spooned her, pulling the covers over my head, too, so we were both in the dark.

"Is that okay?" she whispered.

Was that okay? I'd wanted to give her oral a hundred times, but she always pulled my face back to hers when I tried, saying, "Not yet."

"Of course it is. Are you kidding? I've wanted to eat you since—"

"Please don't say *eat me*."

"Okay then, I've wanted to explore the tip-of-the-tongue phenomenon with your pussy since the first night I had you in this bed."

Kama shook her head but chuckled. I held her in a non-sexual hug—non-sexual but for the fact my semi was pressed hard against her tailbone. She wrapped her arms around mine, which pulled her even tighter to my body. Her muscles were tense.

"The fact that you speak with a forked tongue, lawyer, makes me even more toe-curlingly curious about what it will feel like. I've never let anyone do that to me."

I pulled the covers down to our shoulders so I could see her. "Seriously? Why not?"

She shook her head. "It's always felt … mmm … just way too intimate, I guess."

I kissed her head and breathed into her neck. No perfume, just her natural, sweet-and-spicy scent.

"It is that. But it's no more intimate than a blow job and, thank you sweet Jesus"—my cock got hard at the thought of her mouth on it—"you sure seem to enjoy giving those."

She wiggled her bum against my engorged cock. "That's entirely different."

"How so?"

"Well… what if you don't like how I smell or taste? What if it grosses you—"

"Stop. I promise you that won't happen."

"But what if it does?"

"It won't. I love how you smell and taste. I already know how you taste from touching you. On mornings after I've had my fingers inside you, I'll be at the office and pretend to scratch my nose, hoping even a molecule of your smell is still on me. Kama, I love how you smell, and I know I'll love how you taste."

I felt her relax, so I pulled my hand out from under her

arm and gently tried to nudge it between her thighs. She pressed them tightly together.

"Let me at it, Kama Ray," I said, rolling her onto her back. She laughed but continued to fight me, so I changed tack, straddling her just over her hips. She relaxed and tilted her chin up, mouth open slightly and lips pursed. I ran my index finger lightly along her bottom lip. She twisted her head, sucked my finger into her mouth, and swirled her tongue around the tip, the same movement she used on my cock, which was now painfully engorged.

In one hungry motion, I pulled my finger from her mouth and pressed my lips to hers, giving her my tongue. Her breathing was shallow. Mine was choppy, coming in quick, short bursts like a heartbeat.

"I love how you taste," I said into her mouth.

She reached up and put her hands on either side of my face, ran her tongue along my teeth, then pulled away enough to kiss the corner of my mouth. I knew this move. She was about to push out from under me, roll me onto my back, then kiss and suck my cock. And there was only one thing that could keep me from letting her do that.

"Not this time," I growled, pressing her shoulders back against the mattress. "Now it's my turn." It took all my self-control not to dive between her thighs, but I knew for her to enjoy this she had to get over her fear. I'd have to move slowly.

I dragged my tongue along her collarbone until I reached the spot right above her armpit. I buried my face into that space and breathed in as deeply as I could. "I love how you smell," I said.

From her armpit, I nibbled and licked down her side rib, right to her hipbone, moaning my pleasure. She held my hair between her fingers. I could feel them flex and relax as I moved. When I bit just a little harder right on her hip, her hand fisted, pulling my hair.

"See how good it feels when my mouth is on your body? Feel my cock against your leg? That's how good you taste."

She moaned and arched her hips.

I placed my hands on the bed, on either side of her hips, keeping my mouth always connected to her stomach, and slid down the bed to get into a position I could comfortably hold as long as she needed. Her legs were pressed flat on the bed, straight out in front of her. I placed my hand on her pubic bone then slowly slid it down, toward her thighs. Without a word, she bent her knees and spread her legs, just a little, for me.

"I am so hungry for you, Kama." I exhaled hot breath against her inner thighs. Her ass pressed against the bed, pushing her sex away from my face. *Slow down. Don't scare her.*

Pushing up on my hands, just high enough to look up Kama's body, I smiled. She was wide-eyed, fisting the sheets. She gave me a weak smile. No dimple. I needed to make her so comfortable that she showed me that dimple, so I put my mouth on her lower abdomen and nibbled and licked my way up to her belly button. I turned my tongue into a probe, circled the indent then pushed into it. The corners of her mouth lifted.

Opening my mouth wide, I pressed my lips tight against her skin and blew a loud raspberry on her. She made a surprised squeak and then laughed. A real laugh. A dimpled laugh. We held eye contact while I wordlessly asked, "Are you ready?"

She nodded, exhaled, and pulled her knees up, so her heels were close to her ass. That was my invitation to enter.

I'm not normally a vocal licker, but I wanted Kama to know exactly how much I enjoyed having my mouth on her sex. "Mmm." I lay my tongue flat against her folds. Not intruding, not licking, just there. I breathed in deeply through my nose. "Mmm... so good." Her ass cheeks tightened, pushing her hips up and her sex a little harder against my tongue.

I exhaled hot breath half an inch from her skin. "So, so good." My fingers replaced my tongue, and I felt how engorged she'd become. I was harder than I thought possible. I licked a finger then opened her lower lips, touching her in a way I knew she was comfortable with. I circled her clit until she moaned, then slid my finger against her opening. She was wet and so ready for my cock, but I pushed one finger in. She tightened her inner muscles around it. I pushed a second finger in, and she moaned and arched a little higher, inviting me to go deeper.

I dropped my mouth back onto her, this time using my free hand to spread her labia, I ran my relaxed tongue, back and forth, up and down, from her clit to my fingers, humming against her. The way her body responded, I knew she wasn't worried about how she tasted. And I wanted more of her to taste, so I pulled my fingers out and pressed my stiffened tongue into her.

For minutes I licked and sucked while Kama made encouraging sounds, small squeaks, breathy exhalations, and groans. Twice, when I felt like I had her close to coming, I eased off. I just wasn't ready to stop eating her. The third time I had her on the edge, just as I was about to slow down, she yelled.

"For fuck's sake, finish."

I'd only ever heard her say *fuck* once, and the desperation in her voice made me laugh. But only for a beat. I didn't want us to lose the moment. The tip of my tongue flicked her clit quickly while my index and middle fingers massaged her G-spot. When I pressed the heel of my thumb against her asshole, she arched high and came hard, right against my mouth.

I couldn't let her push my face away from her sex. Having her orgasm against my flat tongue was the hottest thing I'd ever felt. I held my fingers and tongue still while she rocked against me. When the contractions had slowed from tremors to a vibration, I lifted my head and crawled back up into the bed beside her.

Kama stopped me from assuming our go-to position with me behind her. Instead she sat up and pushed me onto my back. Before straddling me, she grabbed a condom from the bedside table and threw it at me.

"I need you inside me now!" It was a command, not a request, and one of the hottest things she'd said during sex.

A far too short amount of time later, Kama lay her head over my heart and her arm across my abdomen, which was rising and falling like I'd just run a marathon. Or just had marathon sex. Her fingers ran gently up and down my side from my hip to armpit. Electricity ran through my body. The effect slowed my heart rate and breathing back to something resembling normal.

"Thank you," Kama said.

"Thank you."

"It was okay?" she asked.

"Are you crazy? If you asked me to choose between booze and eating you, I'd never drink again."

Her hand ran down the length of my body and as far down my leg as she could reach. I shivered. She looked up into my eyes.

"Tell me something you haven't told me about yourself."

I thought for several seconds. "You know everything. In fact, you know more than Nick and Josh know about me."

"Really? Like what?"

"About my lost dream of living in an ashram in India."

"Why didn't you ever tell them?"

I laughed. "Number one, I don't think either of them even know what an ashram is. And number two, if they did, they'd torture me with it."

"That's not cool."

"You know how brothers can be, sometimes jokes can go too far and get hurtful. I can only imagine how they'd take every chance they could to call me something like, I don't know, Guru-la or Swami Rhodes.

"Yeah, I know how brothers can be." She exhaled a long, sad sigh. "Well, thank you for trusting that I wouldn't mock you."

"I'm jealous that you've had the experience."

"Not quite the India immersion, but one day, I hope." Kama kissed my chest and neck and then pressed her lips to mine. "Breathe out," she whispered.

We kissed in that way that left us both light-headed. Eventually, I had to turn to take a deep breath of fully oxygenated air.

"Can you take a few days off work?" she asked.

"To spend like this? I could take off an entire week. A month. I'd quit if there was a way to get paid to just hang out with you."

"Seriously. What would it take for you to get three days off work? A Monday to Wednesday or a Wednesday to Friday."

"A bit of planning. As long as I don't have a court appearance, it shouldn't be that hard. What are you thinking?"

"My exams end in two weeks. I'd love to go away for five days. With you. On a road trip."

I felt my chest tighten. Unconsciously, all of my muscles contracted. I didn't realize I was holding my breath until Kama spoke again.

"Okay. Bad idea, I guess." She lifted her head and looked me in the eye.

I exhaled hard. That was an unexpected reaction. And altogether unwarranted, my brain said, but my body wasn't done arguing. I needed to move, stand, run, hit a punching bag.

"I need to pee." I rolled off the bed and headed to the bathroom just three steps away. I closed the door and stood, staring at myself in the mirror. Thoughts and feelings swirled in a chaotic mess through my body. I tensed and relaxed my biceps, made fists, opened my hands wide, shook my arms. Repeated the motions half a dozen times.

"You okay? Can I come in?" Kama sounded sincerely concerned.

I felt bad to be hiding from her. But what would I tell her? 'Hey, sorry I freaked out but, you know, *road trip* is a trigger word for me.' How lame would that be?

"I'll be right out. I think I got a little too deoxygenated from that kiss. Just give me a minute." I splashed water on my face and took three deep breaths, faced myself in the mirror, smiled, and opened the door.

"Road trip, huh? Where do you want to go?" I crawled back under the covers and spooned myself around Kama's warmth.

"I want to take you to the ashram I went to as a teenager. I want to have that experience with you. And I want your first experience to be with me."

I squeezed against her even harder. She lifted my hand from her rib cage and pressed my palm against her lips, kissing the center of my hand then each of my fingers, never letting her mouth lose contact with my skin. I focused on the energy moving between us, and my body relaxed.

"Please say yes,'" she whispered into my hand.

Fear squeezed my chest. "I would love to go on a road trip to an ashram with you."

# 26

## KAMA

Since meeting Dylan, I hadn't been home for dinner with my family once. My mother was expressing her displeasure in her special way, never telling me directly that I was disappointing her. She preferred to tell me cheerful stories she'd heard from her friends about how their adult children still made time to visit their mothers and fathers at least once a week.

The guilt trip finally worked, and I promised to go for dinner the day before Dylan and I left on our ashram-lite road trip. He'd hoped to come and meet my parents, but we both knew it was fifty-fifty at best. He'd be scrambling at the office until the eleventh hour in order to leave work behind for a few days.

"Where's this man who's stolen you from us, Beta?" Mom asked, looking around me to the street.

"He had to work. He sends his regrets, Ma. He really does want to meet you and Papa."

"Rohan will be disappointed. He was looking forward to meeting this man to make sure he's good enough for you, Beta." Ma shook her head and I knew she was disappointed that Dylan wasn't Indian.

"I thought Rohan would be at work tonight." I felt a sudden tension in my stomach. I'd planned tonight specifically to avoid having to see my older brother. Of course, I could never ask my mother directly if he'd be home since she and dad refused to acknowledge that there was anything unhealthy in my relationship with my brother. They had no idea he was the reason I lived on campus instead of at home.

I heard his feet on the stairs, coming up from his suite in the basement.

"Baby sister, I've missed torturing you," he said, throwing an arm around me and giving me a side hug.

Hiding in plain view, I thought, as Mom laughed at Rohan's joke. I jerked my shoulder out from under his hand and glared at him.

"Why aren't you at work?" I asked him.

"I quit two months ago. I work for myself now. From home. Want to see my office?"

I stiffened. "No, thanks. Where's Dad?" I called to my mom. She'd gone to the kitchen, presumably to let me catch up with my brother.

"In the garden. Go now to see what he's planted, so I can save you when dinner is ready. If you wait until after dinner, he'll keep you out there all night," Mom called back.

"Hey, Papa," I called as I rounded the house to the backyard.

"Beta! Come. See what's growing."

Dad and I chatted about his flowers and vegetables. He didn't ask about Dylan or my schoolwork. His garden was his happy place and here, it seemed, nothing else existed. When Mom called us in for dinner half an hour later, he said, "But you haven't seen anything in the greenhouse yet. That will be the after-dessert tour."

Mom had dinner on the table by the time Dad and I had washed our hands. Rohan was already eating.

"You took too long. It was getting cold."

I wanted to tell him off for being rude and disrespectful to Mom, but I was also relieved that he might finish quickly and leave me to have a nice dinner conversation without his know-it-all opinions and suggestions about how I should live my life.

I waited for Mom to sit and give the signal for us to take food from the platters and bowls. I missed her cooking and knew I'd be going back to Dylan's place too full to sleep well.

I filled my plate with enough basmati rice, palak paneer, lamb curry and aloo gobi to feed me for three meals. I tried to pace myself, but couldn't move from flavor to flavor fast enough.

"Ma, this is delicious. Thank you so much."

"You should come home for dinner more often. Next time I'll make garlic naan and tandoori chicken."

"Mm-mm," I said, mouth full.

"So, this Dylan boy. Is it serious?" my father asked.

I shrugged. "I think so. I hope so."

"When your mother said you were taking him to Aurobindo Ashram, I said, 'Get used to the idea that our daughter might not marry an Indian man, Saira.'"

"Papa! Stop. It's not that serious. He's always wanted to go to an ashram in India. And even though Aurobindo isn't everything a traditional ashram is, I had such a good experience there—thank you again, for the hundredth time, for sending me—that I thought it would be a nice thing to do together. It doesn't mean more than that. It's a holiday."

"Oh, Beta," Mom said, shaking her head. "If you think this is just a holiday, you learned *nothing* when you were there."

Mom was right. *Holiday* was the wrong word. But I didn't want to explain, so I nodded my agreement. Yes, I hoped that these five days with Dylan, like a holiday, would let us both relax and recharge, but I also hoped to get some clarity about my next steps with school, my work, and my life. And to see how well Dylan and I traveled together since, between surviving a death in the family, a job loss, or moving, it was the most appealing relationship stressor.

I also hoped Dylan would have an a-ha moment about his career since he didn't seem in love with his work. He seemed, to me, to be doing it from a sense of obligation, and not with his full heart. It made me sad to think he might spend the next thirty years doing a job he didn't love. So I hoped he'd be able to catch a glimpse of what might make him happy enough to leave the bed when I was in it. As it was, I was a big reason he was having to work late so many days.

"I need to meet this man to give my approval, Kama," Rohan said with his mouth full of spinach and cheese.

I looked away, and not only because it was disgusting. If he saw me tense my jaw, he'd escalate to asking questions about why introducing Dylan stressed me out. Mom and Dad said nothing. I finished my mouthful of paneer and said, "Of course, big brother. Your opinion is of the utmost importance to me. And if this relationship gets serious, you'll be the first to know."

The only joy I got speaking to Rohan was when I could use sarcasm. He was so arrogant it seemed impossible for him to detect it.

After an uneventful dinner, I helped Mom clean up. Dad sat down to watch television and Rohan, thankfully, disappeared back into his cave.

"Go visit with your brother, Beta. He misses you," Mom said, once we'd put away the dishes and food.

"I don't have time. Dad wants to show me his greenhouse." I called out to the living room, "How about that tour now, Papa?"

I heard the television switch off, so I kissed Mom on the

cheek. "Thanks for a delicious dinner. I promise I'll come home more often now that school is out." *And now that I'll have someone in my corner to take Rohan's focus off me.*

Dad and I stood in his greenhouse and he pointed at a handful of plants, telling me what they were. Then he said, "Sit. Let's talk."

We sat on gardening stools, facing each other in the small space. Like me, Dad was born and raised in Vancouver, but he'd accepted his parents' desire that he marry an Indian girl. At nineteen, he flew back to his family's home city to meet my mom. They got married and moved to Canada just a few months later. Since Mom held on to Indian traditions more than Dad, he was a lot easier to talk to about relationships and career.

"How have you been, really? Your anxiety and panic attacks—are they under control?"

"I had a panic attack a little while ago. But it was a particularly stressful night." No need to share details.

Dad frowned.

"Papa, it's okay. Only one time in two years. It's not like it used to be."

He shook his head. "No. But I hoped that once you moved away from Rohan, they would stop. I hoped you wouldn't need the pills at all anymore. I know he's hard on you."

Hard on me? I wanted to scream. He used to lock me in the little half-bathroom with the backwards hung door, when they left him to babysit, so he could go out with his friends. I'd told Dad, but he hadn't believed me. Or maybe he had. Rohan insisted that both Mom and Dad knew what he did, but since I was safe, they didn't care if I was uncomfortable or not. I didn't want to believe him, but after a while it made no difference who believed what. Mom and Dad would go out for dinner or to a party. Rohan would lock me in the bathroom for hours with nothing but a book—that he'd chosen—for me to read.

He stopped locking me up when I was twelve, the same age he'd been when he first babysat me. But he never stopped torturing me, making me anxious, and sometimes even triggering full-on panic attacks. In all the years I'd had them, I'd never figured out what the trigger was. It always seemed so random. Just like the one I'd had with Dylan. That was a question I decided to sit with at the ashram.

I smiled at my dad and took in a deep breath. Dad mimicked me.

*Understanding begins with a shared breath.*

"Rohan is hard on everyone. Ma the most. And I'm just fine, Papa. Happy and healthy. I want you to meet Dylan soon." I pointed a finger at my dad. "Don't tell Rohan, but I don't care about his stupid approval. I hope you and Ma like him, though. Don't tell Ma since you know how she gets, but I really hope he's the one. I think I'm falling in love with him."

Dad stood up and looked around his greenhouse for a few seconds, mumbling to himself. He tapped me on the shoulder to stand up so he could get by, then pulled two small pots off a shelf and handed them to me.

"These are lavender plants I grew from seeds. They offer happiness, love, and peace. One is for you and the other is my gift to Dylan. Will you give it to him?"

I accepted Dad's gifts as a sign of his approval of Dylan, even before having met him. A way of saying he trusted my judgment. Nothing could have made me happier.

# 27

## DYLAN

I worked until after midnight to get my files to a place where I wouldn't have to think about them for a weekend and three workdays. Basically, in the last week I'd done two weeks of work, just to get three days off. Somehow holiday time didn't feel quite the way it had been advertised when I'd been hired. Three weeks a year plus nine stat holidays looked pretty sweet on paper. In reality, I think I worked two extra days for every day I took off.

But my laptop was closed now, and I wouldn't open it again until Monday morning. I tried to believe I wouldn't think about work either, but I knew that was a false reality. Kama was already asleep when I crawled in to bed. I curled up against her and fell into an easy, deep sleep.

Kama woke me with a kiss on my mouth.

"Morning, handsome. Coffee is brewing. Omelet is keeping warm in the oven. You excited about getting your woo-woo on with me?"

I opened my eyes and brought her into focus. She was in her robe and smiling. She was beautiful, even first thing in the morning.

"If by woo-woo you mean making use of my morning woo-woo-wood…" I pulled back the duvet to show her.

She opened her robe and let it drop to the floor. I wiggled over, and she crawled back in with me.

"If you want to make it to Kootenay Bay in time for a burger before five days of vegetarian food, we've got"— Kama reached behind her, pulled my phone off the bedside table, then squinted and looked at the ceiling—"exactly one hour and eighteen minutes before we need to be out the door."

"And if I forgo the burger in favor of giving you multiple orgasms, how much time do we have?"

"Enough," Kama said, opening the bedside drawer and pulling out a condom.

Despite the unplanned, pre-trip cardio, we still arrived in the small town an hour too early to check in to the ashram retreat center. So I still got my burger. Then we went to a family-owned, homemade ice cream shop.

"Do you know what kind you're having?" Kama asked before we went in.

"Tiger Tail if they've got it," I said without hesitation. It was my favorite, and a flavor I could only ever find in specialty shops. Orange ice cream with black licorice stripes.

"Or," she said, "how about we start the enlightenment experience now?"

One thing Kama wanted us both to do while we were on this adventure was open our minds to things we'd never considered, or ideas we'd considered and rejected; basically, to give up what was known and comfortable and try unknown and even uncomfortable things.

"You're not going to let me have Tiger Tail ice cream?" I pouted. "No fair! I want Tiger Tail."

"But you don't even know what you're missing. Let me choose for you?"

I scowled at her. Jokingly but, I hoped, effectively.

She gave me her joyful, dimpled smile.

"Fine. And I get to choose for you, right?"

"Of course."

Kama whispered the order for my scoop to the server and asked me to turn my back so I wouldn't see. When I got toward the bottom of the candied bacon in whisky scoop—an excellent flavor I'd never have chosen—and saw a peek of orange and black in the cone, my heart melted faster than the ice cream.

"Lesson number one about finding your joy," she said, "is that life doesn't have to be about choosing between what you know you love and what you might love if you gave it a chance."

It took everything I had not to be flippant and say, 'So I can love Tiger Tail and love Kama tail?' I wanted the first time I told Kama I loved her to be a moment she'd be excited to tell her best friend about.

At the retreat center registration desk, they asked us to wait until a few other program participants arrived so the host could give all of us the rules and regs spiel at the same time. She didn't use those words, of course. She said something like, "I invite you to browse the gift shop until other transformation seekers arrive, and then I shall guide you around the property to share our wish for your stay."

Kama smiled and gave the hostess a very slight bow with prayer hands, so I did the same, even though it felt strange. I was eager to get to our room. We'd booked one of only two private rooms. Apparently most people did not attend the programs as part of a couple. That was clear when the hostess swung open the door to our space and showed us ... a double bed.

At my height, I need a queen-size mattress to sleep

without my feet hanging in the air. Kama was also tall, so the two of us in this bed would be hell. And not just for the sleeping part.

"Does the other room have a larger bed? As you can see by our sizes, this bed will be a challenge for us."

"I am so sorry, sir. This is the largest bed we have in the center. But I think we can find a solution for you." The hostess asked us to walk around the gardens or explore the lakeside for twenty minutes then meet her back at the registration desk.

The solution was a semi-private room with two double beds. Before I could say a word, the hostess said, with what I interpreted as a shit-eating grin, "This is a much better option for you. In fact, it's the room we should have given you in the first place. We don't just *invite* sexual abstinence during your retreat." She pointed an accusatory finger first at Kama and then at me. "We *insist* on it." She dropped her hand then brought both up into prayer position. "We'll see you for dinner in the main hall at seven."

The harbinger of hateful news turned and left.

Kama couldn't contain her laugh, which helped me dial back my spontaneous frustration from a nine-point-nine to about a three.

"What the hell? Four nights and no sex? Not happening! Why didn't you tell me this was part of the deal?" I wasn't angry. Not really. But suddenly, enlightenment felt a whole less appealing.

Kama was still laughing. "I had no idea. I was sixteen when I came. Sex was a non-issue back then."

I grunted. "Well, what the hell are we supposed to do between now and dinner then?" I was trying to be funny, but I sounded more like a whiny teenager.

"Walk on the beach? If my memory is right, there's a pretty cove about ten minutes away that's private enough for us to go skinny dipping. And since the program hasn't officially started yet, I think we could, perhaps, get away with a blow—"

"Grab your towel, woman!"

~

By bedtime on Friday, we'd completed one evening and two full days and nights of mindfulness activities: full group meditation and yoga classes, smaller group workshops on a variety of subjects, self-reflection time, and community meals. Kama and I chose different workshops, but we were together the rest of the time. We even did self-reflection together, sitting on the beach, each with our own notebook. Kama wrote nonstop, except to wipe her eyes from time to time. I wrote in mine a little but mostly just stared at the water, allowing thoughts to come and go. I did also spend some of my self-reflection time staring at Kama and letting thoughts of a future with her come and go, but each time I tried to gently push one of those thoughts from my mind, a voice in my head screamed, *Don't push this one away.*

As much as I'd originally rebelled against having celibacy imposed on me, I didn't feel like I was being punished once the program started. Kama and I cuddled, naked but non-sexually, in one bed before we separated to sleep. I still got the benefit of the skin-to-skin contact that fed and calmed my nervous system, and even though I woke up with a woody—and walked around to let Kama see because it made her laugh—not using it showed me that my desire for her was so much more than sexual.

At the end of our retreat time on Sunday, Kama asked the check-out hostess if we could stay on the property for a few more hours.

"You're welcome to use any of the common areas. You won't have access to your room anymore, though."

Kama beamed—the smile that highlighted her dimple—

which meant this news thrilled her. We left our packed bags at the reception desk and she took my hand.

"I've wanted to do something since the day we got here. Are you willing to take a risk with me?" Her eyes sparkled in the sun.

As a lawyer, I heard a loaded question. Was I willing to take a risk with Kama? *What kind of risk?* A voice in my head asked.

"Yes?" I hoped my answer didn't sound as tentative as it felt.

We walked to the far edge of the retreat property where the shared dorm rooms were. We'd only walked by them once, the afternoon we went on the tour. There was nothing interesting here that I could see. Kama dropped my hand when we reached the outdoor community showers.

"We're here!"

I looked around. All I saw was a small building with two walls that connected at their centers to create a cross. I walked around it and noticed that inside each of the four open rooms was a bench and a shower head. Only two of the open-air showers had curtains. I circled back to Kama and asked, "Where?"

"This may sound kinky … Actually, I know it's kinky, but when we walked by these showers, I had an overwhelming urge to soap you up and wash you down."

I didn't care that I didn't have a towel to dry off. I was pulling my T-shirt over my head before she finished her sentence.

Kama laughed. "It's not too depraved for you, I guess. The other thing I pictured was that I'd be naked with you since—"

"Since take off your clothes, you twisted, beautiful woman."

"We might be seen, you know."

"Clearly this building was designed to be open to the

world, so if anyone walks by and sees nudity, they can't be surprised or offended. The only question is, curtained space or—"

"No curtain," she said.

My cock was at full attention.

Kama took my hand and led me to the shower stall the least exposed to passers-by. The space in the quad was the perfect size for what I had in mind. Attached to the wall was a soap dispenser, the same kind we had in our room and the only cleaning product permitted in the septic system. It was hand soap, body soap, and shampoo all in one, scent-free and fully biodegradable. It was probably edible too, and that worked for me.

We placed our clothes on the ground outside the shower. Kama turned on the water, and while we gave it time to heat, we stood naked in the fresh air, holding hands, looking at the forest.

"Just to be clear," I said, after she kissed me, "did your vision include sex in this shower or just washing me?"

"Just washing," she said with a crooked smile. "I know, probably disappointing, but ..." she shrugged, "I saw a two-part process. First, washing you with soap, using my hands. Then washing you with love, using my mouth."

The blood left my face. My knees literally went weak. This woman's Jedi powers were forcing me to re-examine my life. I couldn't imagine ever wanting another woman's hands or mouth on any part of my body. But the implication of that feeling was immense. Life altering. And terrifying.

We stood under the water in silence as she pumped soap into her palm. She reached up and started by massaging my scalp. I leaned forward. Her fingers moved in small circles all over my head and temples. The sense of fear I'd felt just a moment earlier vanished, and I thought this should be my new meditation practice.

"Rinse," Kama said, stepping aside to give me the full benefit of the water.

"God, I want to kiss you," I breathed out.

She placed her hands on my shoulders and pressed her lips to mine. The water was landing on top of our heads, so breathing was a slight challenge. I tried to move her out from under the flow, but she pulled away.

"Later."

Kama soaped up again and touched every conceivable inch of my body with her hands. Including my painfully erect cock, making it even more desperate for relief. With a swirl of her tongue, she made an unspoken promise that she'd be back again once her mouth was washing me. I moaned and steadied myself by placing my arms behind me against the shower stall wall.

"Good?" she asked.

I replied with a kiss. Hungry and impatient. She pulled away, but only far enough to put her mouth on my neck. She kissed below my ear down to my shoulder, over to my Adam's apple, and up to my chin. She planted one quick kiss on my lips and went down the other side of my neck. At my shoulder she moved across my collarbone, sucking gently with each contact. She moved to my left nipple, took the pebbled nub in her mouth, and teased it with her tongue. I don't know if it took two minutes or twenty before she reached my cock. Time felt as fluid as the warm water flowing over us.

Even though there was a bench she could have sat on, she knelt on the wood-planked floor with her back to the open doorway, allowing me to look out at the dense, green forest—that is, when my eyes weren't rolling to the back of my head. The water pouring over me, the sight, sounds and smell of nature surrounding me, and Kama's tongue and mouth working my cock were as close to a religious experience as I'd ever had.

It was a good thing Kama had left me with my ass facing the bench because when I started to come, still in her mouth, my knees buckled. I collapsed backward, landing on the bench like a panting mess of noodles.

Kama laughed so hard that she, too, had to sit. Once we'd both regained muscle control, I washed her, first with my hands and then with my mouth. Each time I closed my eyes, I saw colors, like the Northern Lights, dancing around my brain.

"I want you to orgasm under my tongue, but I don't know how we can do that on this bench," I said, as I gently bit her inner thigh.

Kama placed her hands on my shoulders, encouraging me to stand. "I'm too self-conscious anyway. You can finish when we get home."

*Home.* My home, since her home was just a long-term hotel room.

"Give up your residence. Don't renew for the fall semester." I'd thought about asking Kama to officially move in about a hundred times, but I'd always let the voice of fear override it. After the last five days, I couldn't imagine anything too big for us to tackle and beat as a team. We were living a movie love story—the kind women cried over since it was so perfect, and the kind guys said was bullshit and too good to be real. Guys were idiots, I decided. Sometimes life could deliver a happily ever after.

Kama pressed in tight against my chest and stomach. Held me hard against her body so I couldn't see her face.

"But what if—"

"What if nothing. I've never been more certain of anything. I want you here with me, every day, every night."

She laughed and then sang lyrics from the 'Elephant Love Medley,' suggesting she might start to drink all the time or I'd become mean. And then she said, "Yes."

"You'll move in with me full-time?"

"One hundred percent. You had me at hello."

We stood, kissing and touching each other, until the water ran cold.

# 28

## KAMA

Living full-time with Dylan was both better and worse than having my own space.

Falling asleep in his arms and waking up to his smile—and his erection—felt divine. It also had an obvious, positive impact on my mental health. I hadn't felt the need to take an anti-anxiety pill in weeks. Dylan made me laugh every day, listened to me groan about my now-stalled thesis, and even offered helpful advice, always in the form of questions that let me know he had confidence in my problem-solving skills.

On the downside, I was never alone. Even as a kid I'd had my own bedroom. In residence, though I'd shared common areas with fifty other students, my room was mine. When I put something down, I knew where it would be when I wanted it again. I knew how many times my facecloth had been used. And if I just wanted to drink chai and eat two-bite brownies for dinner, I could do that without feeling guilty.

Dylan's condo was just a glorified bachelor apartment. Sure, it had a bedroom separate from the open living area, but it was tiny. Too small for true privacy. Sometimes I missed being able to fully relax; to pass gas if I didn't feel like holding it in.

One night, after a couple of drinks, I mentioned that to Dylan. So, in an effort to show me he didn't care if I farted, he started doing so. I don't care how much you love someone, there is nothing as unsexy as free-flow flatulence.

Thankfully, that only lasted a week before he figured out that not only was I never going to be a public piffer, but that it grossed me out when he did it.

Overall, though, the plusses far outweighed the minuses, and after almost a month, I was feeling settled. My anxiety about having given up my dorm apartment dissipated until one day, I realized I hadn't worried about what would happen if things didn't work out with Dylan.

When I'd first left home, my mother insisted that it made no sense to pay for a room when I had a perfectly good one for free with them. ("With home-cooked meals, Beta!") But I swore I'd never go back as long as Rohan was living there, and as far as I could tell, he had no intention of ever leaving. I couldn't imagine any woman who'd be interested in dating a man who still lived in his parents' basement at age thirty-two. It wasn't my problem to worry about, though it had potential as an interesting research topic for my PhD. But first I had to finish my master's thesis.

I'd been considering how to blend my 'understanding begins with a shared breath' thought into my research to see if that would solve my advisor's issues with it, but I hadn't come up with anything concrete. Her concern was that I hadn't effectively articulated how I maintained objectivity with my actions or consistency with my date's reactions on these research dinners.

Right after Dylan and I got home from the retreat center, I'd had an insight. I'd argued that objectivity and consistency were irrelevant except in the last ten minutes of the third date, since the remainder of the time was merely a vehicle to get to this critical moment in the research.

My advisor, Dr. Balcerowski, still maintained that I'd failed to provide a neutral situation against which to draw conclusions from my data. She wasn't wrong, but I didn't feel that neutrality was necessary. My aim was simply to test —and hopefully prove—that I could manipulate a situation that had a universal culturally expected outcome: sex in exchange for a meal. And I'd done that by convincing every man in the experiment to graciously accept my 'thanks, but no thanks' when he made the offer. Seventy-two dates, forty-two offers or requests, twenty-four men, and not one condom opened for my benefit.

I'd even amped up the introductory section about my personal experience. The first draft had included just one sentence about an unnamed date who'd stalked me after I'd refused to go home with him. I expanded that to almost a full page about his actions post-date, to reinforce how accustomed men had become to this unspoken agreement. Thank you, Bob Booker.

Based on these experiences, I argued, my Jedi-mind-trick approach had worked. I didn't need to prove anything more since none of the women I knew had managed even five consecutive dates with different men without being strong-armed into a 'sex for drinks and dinner' conversation that only a handful had the strength of will to walk away from.

I sent Dr. Balcerowski my compelling rationale. And today, I'd find out how effective my argument was.

"Good luck with your meeting today," Dylan said, giving me a kiss. Then he held me at arm's length and looked me straight in the eye. "Remember that you are not your thesis. If your advisor still has problems with the research, it does not mean she has a problem with you or that there is anything wrong with you."

Sadly, I really needed to hear that.

∾

Dr. Balcerowski's door was ajar when I arrived a few minutes before our scheduled meeting time. I stood to the side, where she couldn't see me, and inhaled deeply to center myself. Dylan had suggested I strike a Superwoman pose before engaging in a challenging conversation so, as silly as it felt, I gave it a try. Just another mind trick to influence an outcome, I told myself.

Once I felt adequately *super*, I knocked on my advisor's door.

"Come on in, Kama."

I exhaled and put on my most enthusiastic smile, making sure it reached my eyes.

"Hey, Dr. B. How's the summer term starting? Good set of students?"

She returned a much more reserved smile and a nod. "So we have to make a decision today, Kama, about this thesis of yours. I've read your thoughts"—she patted some sheets of paper on her desk—"and considered them. But while I hate to say this, I'm still not convinced."

My guts twisted. I fought the urge to react the way that felt most natural: like a three-year-old throwing herself on the floor and screaming, "I hate you!" Instead, I visualized my inner Superwoman, calm and composed, and asked, "What do you recommend I do to salvage my research, Dr. Balcerowski?"

Her nostrils flared and her cheeks reddened. "Kama, honestly, I'd advise you to give it up and refocus your efforts on a new topic."

The force of my inner three-year-old was strong. My heart seemed to vibrate rather than beat. Tears spontaneously blurred my vision, so I opened my eyes as wide as I could and blinked quickly to wash them away.

Without thinking, I reached for my purse to find my anti-anxiety pills and realized I hadn't packed them.

"I know it's frustrating," Dr. B. said, pulling a box of tissues from a drawer and pushing them across the desk to me. "I'm not making this recommendation lightly. I've …" She paused and covered her mouth with her hand.

"What? You've what?" Superwoman had left the room.

"I've spoken to the dean of the department about this, and she is adamant that there are too many flaws in your model to proceed."

Dr. B. stared at the papers on her desk.

I wanted her to look at me, to feel my fury. "Six or seven months ago you approved my thesis statement and research outline. You even seemed enthusiastic about it. I don't understand. What's changed?" I didn't give her a chance to answer before I raised my voice. "I followed all the parameters the ethics committee asked for. I was meticulous. This is so unfair. You … your job was to make sure my thesis approach was sound. Mine was to do the work based on the proposal. I did my part. You cannot do this to me now. This will cost me two full semesters."

"Kama, I'm sorry you feel that way."

"Feel *what* way? Like I've been gaslighted? Like you didn't do your job and I'm the one who suffers?"

"The university does not believe your research meets the standards to approve your thesis defense."

"The university? What does that even mean? I haven't even finished writing the thesis. How can anyone even draw that conclusion? The *university*," I said, making air quotes, "approved the research methodology. And now the same university has changed its mind?"

"Kama, getting angry at me won't help you. I'm your ally here."

"My ally? You're my ally? Then why aren't you defending my research—research *you* approved?"

I believe the correct psychological term for how I reacted is *apoplectic*.

We sat in silence for over a minute. I used the time to settle my heart rate and re-oxygenate my brain.

"Okay," I said. "The problem, it seems, is that I don't have a control group to compare my manipulated group against, is that right?"

Dr. B. tipped her head toward one shoulder then the other. "That was … one concern."

"Fine. What if I go out with five more men and use them as my control group? Then I'll be able to compare data from my original research group to these men. And for these five control dates, I'll act like a normal woman on a normal date, just the way I did with the first five who are not officially in the study. I'll let the man pay if he offers. I let him choose the restaurant. I'll have at least two drinks that cost more than a soda. Virgin cocktails. I'm still not going to drink alcohol."

"Kama." Dr. Balcerowski shook her head. "I'm not sure that that will make a difference. You may do all of that work only to still find the …" She hesitated and shook her head. "The panel judging your thesis may still not pass it. And then you'll have invested more weeks or months in this work. As your advisor, I strongly suggest you let this go and that we find a new topic for you to explore."

"Are you *telling* me I have to stop, or are you *recommending* that I give up all the work I've done?"

She sighed. "I'm urging you to redirect your research. But no, your thesis proposal was approved and you are within your rights to complete it." She held up a finger to stop me from interrupting her. "But if you continue," she said, "you'll need to find a new advisor because I cannot support this thesis."

We held silent eye contact for several seconds. My heart was racing. I felt like I'd been chased twice around the campus by an invisible predator. And as my mind settled, a random thought came to me.

"Does this have anything to do with the fact that I'm now dating a man who was in my research pool?"

She avoided my question. "If you want to earn your master's in psychology from this university, Kama, let go of this topic."

I took a cab home since there was no way I could ride the bus in the state I was in. I texted Dylan, but he didn't reply. That wasn't unusual when he was at work, but it made me more upset.

All afternoon, my monkey mind chattered, and by the time Dylan walked in the door at six o'clock, I'd figured out that he was the reason my research was being challenged. As angry as I'd been at Dr. Balcerowski, I was ten times angrier at Mr. Rhodes.

# 29

# DYLAN

I'd had a day from hell, and all I wanted to do was eat dinner, have a couple of beers, and watch some mindless television. I was starving; I hadn't had time to get lunch or even grab an afternoon coffee.

Mr. James had dropped a surprise case on my desk at lunchtime. The lawyer who'd been assigned was found to have a conflict of interest while the case was in court. The judge adjourned and gave our team three days to pull in new counsel. It was an embarrassment—at least inside the industry, if not publicly—which made James's interest in it my problem.

I spent all afternoon getting up to speed, trying to find anything in the previous lawyer's argument that might smell of unlawful bias. It should have been a relatively simple settlement of assets between a former husband and wife who'd married when they were both broke but were divorcing with assets of several million dollars to split between them. I was arguing on behalf of the husband, who'd been the one to earn the millions while his wife took care of the kids and home.

It had been a nineteen-fifties-style marriage, right down

to the mid-afternoon scotch and receptionist this fine husband partook of several times a week. He argued that since he'd earned the money, he should get to keep most of it. His ex-wife—and the law—thought otherwise, and were arguing for a fifty-fifty split of all assets.

The conflict was that the lawyer from our firm was the sister of the woman our client had been sleeping with for five years. I got to figure out a way to argue this shit show of a case that frankly, I wanted nothing to do with. I thought the client was a douche and would have liked to see him lose more than half to the woman who gave up her career as a trilingual flight attendant to be at his beck and call as chief cook and bottle washer.

And, to top it all off, when I checked in with James at the end of the day to give him an update on Kramer vs Kramer, he gave me an update on Booker vs Ray. When I'd last spoken to him, he'd assured me the case was being dropped. James had no idea Kama and I were still dating, let alone living together, and I'd intended to keep it that way. But he made that impossible with one sentence.

"The Booker case has been resurrected as Booker vs BCU. Since you know the file, you're back on it."

"What? But Booker walked away. He doesn't have a winnable case. Why in the hell is he onto this again?" I was visibly angry.

James was impassive. "There may not be a case against the young lady specifically, but there's enough unusual and, well, questionable activity in her research that Booker was willing to challenge the psychology department's overall management of thesis projects."

"Why the hell would he do that? What's he got to gain?" I asked, realizing too late that I was speaking to my boss, not a colleague.

"Well, because I forgave the twenty-five hundred dollars you racked up on the goose chase in exchange for him allowing me to put forward this new argument. But I can't personally argue it since... well, it may be construed as personal given my history with the dean. And frankly, between you and me, it is personal. I want to see her burn. So I need to be arm's length with no direct influence on the case. And you're the man I trust to act in my stead."

*Dammit.* There was no way now to withhold my relationship status. And James took it about as well as I'd expected.

"Goddammit, Rhodes, this complicates things."

*You're telling me.* I'd promised Kama that everything had been settled with Mr. Asshat, Bob Booker.

James and I sat in silence, him tapping his pen, me biting my lip to keep from yelling expletives at the situation and directly at him. He spoke first. "How serious is this? Is it just a summer fling, or do you expect to be together in the fall?"

I stood, clasped my hands behind my back, closed my eyes, and inhaled a deep breath. As I exhaled, I opened my eyes and looked directly at Mr. James. I could sense that my promotion to junior partner was hanging in the balance. And in the seconds that I silently debated what to say, James spoke up.

"Your first three to five years as a junior partner leave little room for serious relationships, Rhodes. You realize that, right? One reason we chose to promote you over other lawyers who have been here longer is that two months ago you were single and appeared to be happy to stay that way. No ticking baby clock on the horizon like for some of your female colleagues." James closed his eyes and scowled. "For Christ's sake."

"Sir, are you saying that the offer of the promotion was based less on my skills as a lawyer and more on my lack of a relationship status?"

I needed a minute to process this.

James rubbed his eyes. "Rhodes, you're a talented

lawyer. You've got solid potential. You're good with the publicity bullshit. But if you think you work long hours now, in six months you'll be laughing at how naive you were to think a fifty-hour week was working overtime. So yes, your happily-single status carried some weight in our decision. I'll ask you again. Is this thing you have with Kama Ray serious?"

On the one hand, I was appalled by James's blatant gender discrimination. If the wrong colleague heard this, he'd have his ass sued off. Which led to the other hand feeling, that he trusted me implicitly with information that, if I wanted, could bring him down. He'd pulled me into his inner circle. This was huge.

And Kama. How the hell was I supposed to know how serious it was? Was the relationship going to outlast my career? Statistically speaking, probably not. Maybe she'd hang in there for a year, maybe ten. But I planned to be a lawyer for at least twenty-five years. Did I think Kama and I could pull that off? I hoped so, but everything with her was still so new.

"I just don't know, sir."

As soon as I said it, I felt like a shit. Not a liar, but certainly a shit.

And walking into my condo after that bullshit kind of day to find Kama glaring at me was just too much. She looked as if she'd been in my meeting with James, listening in on both my thoughts and our conversation.

And Jesus, I was hungry. Hard conversations should never be had on an empty stomach.

It was clear that dinner was not on Kama's priority list, and since I didn't have enough patience to do more than open a bottle of beer, I dialed our favorite takeout restaurant and ordered for us both. The first words I said to her were, "Dinner will be here in thirty to forty minutes."

She responded with nothing more than two blinks. No

"thanks, Dylan." No smile. Just two blinks like a goddamn cat.

A cat. Interesting. No truly random thoughts, Kama always says. They all have some meaning. And what I know about cats is that they blink to communicate affection. It's their way of saying 'I love you.' Maybe Kama was unconsciously telling me she was happy to see me and thanking me for taking care of dinner on a day that must have been pretty awful for her, too.

I took a chance. "I love you, too. I'm sorry you—"

She literally leapt off the couch. "Seriously? Sarcasm? After everything you've done, you think this is the time to be sarcastic?" Then she gritted her teeth, growled from deep in her throat, and closed herself in the bathroom.

She obviously didn't want to talk and frankly, I had no interest in dealing with this, so I dropped onto the couch and turned on the television. *What did I used to watch when it was just me on my own?* I flipped through the menu and stopped on *Top Gear*. I'd watch three Brits goof around and drive cars until dinner arrived. And then, if Kama joined me... fuck it, I'd just keep watching until the episode ended. I was so tired of negotiating. For one day, I just wanted to do what I wanted to do, at work and at home. One day. Why was that so hard?

Thirty minutes later, when the front door phone rang, it startled me. I was on my second beer and had virtually forgotten that I'd ordered pizza.

"Be right down," I told the delivery person. I hung up and yelled into the bedroom, loud enough to be heard through the still-closed bathroom door. "Back in three minutes with your dinner."

Kama was dressed in pajamas when I got back up to the condo. Her hair was wet, and the steam escaping from the bedroom was a good tip that she'd spent the last half hour engaged in hydro-relaxation therapy.

"Good bath?"

"I'm sorry I yelled at you. I love you, too."

"I'm guessing your day was as shitty as mine. Maybe worse."

"What happened to you?" she asked.

I scratched at my ear. I really didn't want to think or talk about work right now. I wanted to eat and hear about what was bothering Kama.

"You know, stuff lawyers have to do. Two cases that are pissing me off. Nothing out of the ordinary. But two on one day makes me want to come home and rethink my life." I hoped my reference to the *Star Wars* scene that inspired her to take on her research would make her smile. I realized too late that joking about her thesis was probably a terrible idea.

She slowly waved her hand between us and said, "You don't want to represent a-holes."

I repeated, "I don't want to represent a-holes," but in my head I thought *assholes*.

She did another sweep with her palm facing me. "You want to come home and rethink your life."

"I want to rethink my life."

Then she smiled. "You want this crazy woman to stop waving like a maniac so you can eat your pizza."

Dinner was relaxed, as if Kama's outburst of anger had never happened. On the one hand, I was glad, but on the other it freaked me out. Unexpressed feelings never stay that way forever. In my experience, they build until one day you're cleaning up a high-school chemistry experiment gone terribly wrong. Except instead of Pop Rocks and Coke, it's an explosion of emotions you're trying to push back in the bottle.

"Kama, I need you to tell me what happened when I got home. Why you got so angry with me. I have no idea what I did to trigger that."

She put her slice down, placed an elbow on the table and

her chin on her hand, covering her mouth so she couldn't talk. She hemmed and hawed for several seconds before sitting up straight again. "I got it into my head that I'm being blocked with my thesis because you and I are together."

"Why would you think that?"

"It was in Dr. Balcerowski's body language, and the fact that she didn't directly answer me when I asked her that specific question."

The muscles in my guts tensed. My inner voice told me that this new lawsuit, with James behind it, was the problem. James with his personal vendetta, out for blood. And Kama would be the sacrifice.

It was so obvious that had Booker not met her, and had she not rebuffed his demand for quid pro quo, her thesis would be in front of the reading committee by now. She'd have her degree before the autumn.

I hated the guy. Then again, had Booker not been such a douchebag, I'd have never met Kama.

It was such a shitty situation. Even though what I knew would help her understand what was going on, I couldn't tell her what was happening behind the scenes. For one, it would be a serious breach of confidentiality, and for two, there was nothing she could do about it anyway since she was not specifically named in the case.

"What does she want you to do?" I asked.

"She wants me to scrap all the work I've done and find a whole new research topic. She *literally* wants me to start from square one and submit a whole new proposal. She said she won't stay on as my advisor if I keep working on this topic."

"And what do you want to do?"

"All I want is to have my ideas heard. Heard and believed, or believed in. Either. Both. I don't know." Kama dropped her face into her hands and I could hear her breath catch in her throat. She was trying not to cry. "I'm so tired of having to fight to be heard."

"Do you feel like you have to fight for *me* to hear you?"

Her eyes were glassy. "No. Not at all. You hear me. Heck, you even hear what I don't say, and sometimes it freaks me out. It's like you actually get me." She lowered her head and wiped her eyes. Then she looked back at me and blinked twice before speaking.

I rolled my eyes and exhaled hard.

"What? What did I do?" she asked.

"Nothing. I mean … you blinked," I said, realizing how idiotic that sounded.

Her eyes opened wide. Not in surprise. It was more like 'this man has lost his damned mind.'

"You blinked twice, to be specific."

"I blinked twice." She paused. "You mean like this?" And she did it again. One blink, a heartbeat spent looking into my eyes, and then a second blink.

I nodded.

She smiled.

"It's the same thing you did right before you freaked out and left the room." I shrugged. "I thought it was your cat way of telling me you loved me, but—"

"Shut up." She stood. "Stand up, please," she said, giving me her dimpled smile.

I stood.

"I need to hold you. Or I need you to hold me. I'm not sure which." She took a step toward me. "Both. I need both."

We hugged. She held onto me like she wanted our bodies to meld into one. Or maybe that was me since I was holding her just as tightly. I buried my face into her wet hair and breathed in her scent, her warmth, her energy.

She tilted her head back and raised her lips to mine. As we kissed, she whispered, "I love you. Exactly as you are. All of you." Then she pulled her head back and blinked twice. "Except the farts. I'll never blink twice after you force a fart."

Jesus, I loved this woman. How could I even wonder if she'd still be around after the summer? In that moment, I couldn't imagine anything big enough or bad enough to tear us apart.

# 30

# KAMA

The day after my last exam, back in early May, I'd interviewed for a full-time job as a child protection worker with a government department. One of the job's prerequisites was a master's degree, so Dr. Balcerowski sent a letter on university letterhead with my application. It stated that if they offered me the job, she had no doubt I'd have the required academic qualifications before my three-month probation period ended.

I'd only been in the position two weeks before Dr. B. dropped the 'start over or I'm resigning as your advisor' bomb. I still hadn't told my boss since I still intended to meet that deadline come hell or high water. I kept working on the thesis, analyzing my research, and added 'find a new advisor' to my workload.

I'd met with four, and it was clear this would not be an easy search-and-replace exercise. The first two questioned why Dr. Balcerowski had stopped supporting me, saying that the work I'd done was strong. I couldn't answer that since I had no idea why. I worried that my non-answer made it look like I was a difficult student, but I assumed they'd ask Dr. B. directly, which eased my mind. Sort of.

They both agreed that adding the five control dates would strengthen my conclusions. That struck fear in my heart for so many reasons, but it was something I said I was willing to do if, after they read my draft, they thought it was warranted.

I left each of those meetings with the advisor's implied support only to get emails from them days later saying they were sorry but they'd have to pass. Oh, and "good luck."

The other two advisors met with me but kept the meetings short and focused on guiding me toward a new thesis topic.

"I feel like my thesis is cursed," I said to Dylan after the fourth failed advisor interview.

"I think you're right."

That was exactly *not* the thing I wanted to hear. There was no support in that response. He didn't ask questions about ways forward like he normally did. I felt abandoned in my greatest time of need.

And, because I was now working an eight-to-four job and doing my thesis work in the evenings and on weekends, I suspect Dylan was feeling abandoned in a different way. I did my best to leave work at work, so we could at least enjoy dinnertime together.

I was surprised to find him home early on a Thursday, already making dinner.

"Court situation took two hours less than I had scheduled, so instead of going back to the office, I thought I'd make your favorite takeout."

Dylan stood at the stove in sweatpants and a T-shirt, flipping meat and vegetables in a wok. He looked like a god with a wooden spatula.

"You don't know how happy this makes me. I'm starving. I could smell it from the hallway but assumed it was coming from suite 2016." I tried to grab a piece of meat from what looked like kung pao chicken with red peppers and peanuts. Dylan smacked my fingers with his spatula.

"It still needs about four minutes. Think you can wait?"

"If you distract me, I think that could work." I grabbed him in a full-body hug and coaxed him two steps away from the stove. Five steps from the bedroom door.

"Four minutes. Not forty."

I put my mouth to his ear and whispered, "You'd be surprised at what I can do in four minutes given the right motivation." Then I moved one hand from his lower back to his lower front and wrapped my fingers around his sweatpants-covered cock. To my delight, it was responding.

"You are a wicked, wicked woman. Just let me put the burner on low." Dylan went back to the kitchen and gave the food a quick stir. "Four minutes," he said.

I pulled him into the bedroom and dropped to my knees in front of him.

"Five, tops," he moaned as I pulled his sweats down and took him in my mouth.

Before meeting Dylan, I'd never enjoyed giving blow jobs. After only two nights with Dylan, I realized that my sex life with my previous, and only, serious boyfriend had left me with a core, false belief about sex that had heavily influenced my thesis research.

Prior to Dylan, sex was always transactional. My ex would do something nice for me, then expect me to thank him by opening my mouth or my legs. I wasn't sure if the worst part was that it was so boring or that there was never real intimacy with my ex. It was as though he'd read a textbook about how to insert tab A into slot B, and that's all he did.

I couldn't be too angry at him, though, since I'd done nothing to educate myself about how to make sex fun or something more than physical. Sex with Dylan was so much more. I hated even to categorize it as sex. He'd shown me that a simple touch, like slowly running his finger down my spine, could create more intense feelings than sticking a penis in a vagina. He taught me the difference between intercourse and making love.

He helped me understand that by taking his cock in my mouth, I was communicating acceptance and he was communicating trust. Sex with Dylan wasn't just a physical transaction. It was a deeply emotional experience.

I cupped his balls as my tongue teased his slit, tasting the saltiness of his pre-cum. It was something I never could have imagined I'd desire, let alone enjoy. But there was something so raw about sharing that much of our bodies with each other, and the more I sucked, the wetter I got.

Dylan's balls tightened under my fingers, and I knew I had one second to either pull him out or swallow him. I took him as far into my mouth as I could and felt his warm release hit the back of my throat. I loved easing him out in this state, when his cock was sensitive and still leaking, running my tongue around his head until he pulled me up to kiss him.

I was still dressed in my work clothes, but between us it took no time before I was on my back, naked on the bed, with his fingers between my folds.

"My turn," he growled.

I bent my knees and let my legs fall open for him, totally exposed. He was the only man who'd ever seen my sex. The only one to have put his mouth on it. I'd been shy and embarrassed the first few times, but he made it so abundantly clear that he loved every second he was there that I could now relax into the moment. And he could draw out that moment to half an hour of touching, teasing, tasting. Sometimes I had to beg for him to finish me when the painful pleasure at the edge of orgasm got to be too much.

Sadly, tonight would not be one of those nights. Tonight

was one of the very rare nights when Dylan did not bring me to completion.

*Beep, beep, beep, beep, beep.* The smoke detector screeched. Startled, I joined it with a shriek of my own.

"Shit, shit, shit," Dylan said, jumping from the bed and running naked to the kitchen.

That's when I realized that the faint smell of smoke I'd registered just a minute earlier was not from a neighbor's dinner disaster. It was from ours.

"Can I help?" I called to him.

"Nope. Nothing to save. Give me a minute," he said back.

I heard the kitchen fan come on and Dylan opening the living room windows. I was still on the edge and desperate to let this orgasm be free, so I pulled my bullet vibrator from my bedside table drawer. Dylan knew I had it, and I figured he knew I used it, but I'd never masturbated in front of him, so I pulled the duvet over me before I placed it against my engorged clitoris. I closed my eyes and imagined Dylan's tongue on me. It took seconds before I was pressing my hips down into the mattress, trying to pull away from the vibrator but also still holding it tight against me.

When I could breathe again, I opened my eyes. Dylan was still fussing in the kitchen. I called to him, "Should I order takeout?"

He came into the bedroom holding the remains of our burned-to-the-bottom dinner.

"Wok of shame," he said with a wry smile.

In my head I laughed, but before that translated to a smile, I burst out in tears.

*What the heck?*

Dylan looked at me like I was crazy and took the wok away. A minute later he crawled back into bed, handing me a piece of cheese. "You're hungry. And I left you halfway home. I'm sorry. Eat this and let me finish."

I rolled so my back was facing him. "Spoon me?" I said, wiping my runny nose on the back of my arm.

"It's just a bit of chicken. Nothing to cry about, baby."

"That's not it. I don't know why I'm crying. I'm not sad. I'm not upset. I'm not that hungry. I'm just ... I don't know. I feel so much, and I ... everything is so overwhelming right now."

Dylan wrapped himself around me and held on as I sobbed. Images and words popped into my head. After a minute or two they started to make sense. The tears were fear. I was falling so hard for this guy. I knew I'd never survive if it didn't work out. And I had every reason to believe that eventually things would go sideways.

Statistically speaking, this was a relationship that was doomed to fail. Because of my lack of experience. Because this was Dylan's first actual relationship. Because of the differences between the ways we were raised. Because he already had a successful career and I was still a struggling student who might never get her master's degree and a proper job. Because—

"Kama." Dylan interrupted my downward spiral. "I'd planned to surprise you with something next week, but I think you need it now."

# 31

## DYLAN

Two months ago, when Kama and I were reviewing all the films for the festival, there was one that she'd stopped to rewind so she could point out a piece of art. It looked like kid art to me, something drawn and colored by a precocious six-year-old with high-quality markers and an exceptional ability to stay inside the lines. It wasn't bad, it just didn't grab me. But when Kama described what she saw, I had to admit it was genius.

"Look," she said, pointing at the monitor. "It's a clever play on words. I'm shocked that you didn't catch it. It's exactly like the goofy puns you make."

"Umm ..." I stared at the picture.

"You don't get it? Tell me what you see."

"Okay, I see a man and a woman standing outside a house. There are musical notes floating above their heads and..." I paused and made my thinking face. "She has her mouth open, so I'm guessing she's the one singing."

"Yes! Do you get it now?" Kama bounced in her seat.

I shook my head.

"I can't believe it! It's so obvious. What else do you see?"

What else? "Okay, so the woman's purse has been

emptied on the ground, and the guy's pockets are hanging out, so I assume they're looking for something that they can't find."

"Exactly. You have to have it now. Come on! You're the pun master. I'm going to have to pun-ish you if you don't get this."

I'd seen Kama excited before, but not like this. She was bouncing like her side of the MPR couch had morphed into a trampoline.

I shook my head. "Nope. Just not seeing it."

She deflated but didn't lose her smile. "You want me to tell you?"

"Please. Let me in on this impossible joke."

She looked at the monitor. "What I see is"—she turned to face me and sang the answer in an unrecognizable tune —"She broke into song because he couldn't find the key!"

I groaned but had to admit that it was clever.

"When I can afford real art, that's the kind I want. Art that's full of energy and fun," she said as she hit play and got the film rolling again.

I'd been struck by how taken she was by that silly piece of art, so I went back to that film and found the scene with the picture. One shot was close enough to make out the name of the artist, who, it shocked me to learn, was an actual artist represented by a gallery.

Marker art. In a gallery. Granted, it was Australia, but still. Marker art in an art gallery.

I spent an hour looking at all of his pieces. His style was distinctive. Every piece was a play on words done with bright colors, sharp lines and—Kama was right—a joy that couldn't be mistaken.

The gallery was selling prints and canvases of all his work. I considered buying a print of the singing couple for Kama, in thanks for helping me watch all those hours of films, but something about it didn't feel right. I didn't order it and then forgot all about it.

But the day after Kama agreed to move in, I wanted to get her something to make her feel like the condo was as much her home as mine. That piece of art came to mind. I found the site again, and this time when I looked at the picture, I realized what had felt off about the two characters. The man looked as much like me as a cartoon-based, short-haired, white man could look. But the woman in the print looked nothing like Kama.

I contacted the artist and asked how much it would cost to replicate the picture but with one change: drawing in a tall, full-figured woman with long black hair instead of a petite woman with curly blond hair. The artist got back to me with a price. It was a lot more than I'd planned to spend —hell, it was an outrageous amount—but Kama would get original art, not a print. I did some gymnastic rationalization and decided that the art was an investment, no more or less risky than putting my money into the stock market.

The poster—if you can call something that costs over six hundred dollars *before shipping*, a poster—had arrived two days earlier. I'd planned to have it framed before giving it to her, but I felt like she needed to see it now.

I reached into the bedroom closet to find the mailing tube and felt strangely nervous. Spending the money had been uncomfortable, but giving the picture to her created an even more intense 'WTF are you doing?' feeling.

With my naked back to Kama, I breathed out slowly as I argued with myself.

*You can't buy love, you know,* one voice said.

Then the other: *She already loves me.*

*'Til you screw up.*

*Not going to ruin this.*

*Heard that before.*

"What are you looking for?" Kama interrupted the one-man tragedy playing out in my head.

Deep breath.

"I bought you something." I pulled the giant tube from behind my suits and held it in front of me.

Kama sat and pulled the duvet up to cover herself. Her eyes were red and her face blotchy from crying, but her smile was back. Not the dimple one, but at least the corners of her lips were turned up.

"Let me guess … is it a trip to the happiest place on Earth?" Before I could think of what to say she continued, "No, because I already live in the happiest place on Earth." The dimple threatened to make an appearance.

"Do you want to guess, or do you just want to see?"

"I want to guess. It's a poster. Obviously. I'm thinking… it's that charity picture of you and Nick without your shirts on, holding those tiny Dalmatian puppies for the SPCA! Am I right? A poster of my boyfriend to hang in my cubicle at work?"

I don't know what my face looked like to her, but disgust was the emotion her guess elicited. "Uh, that is *so* not going to happen, Kama. Just open it before this moment is entirely ruined. In fact, ugh, I think it might already be."

And there was the dimple. My heart felt better.

*Fuck you, voice of fear.*

She pulled off the end of the tube, and before she could pull out the print I said, "I hadn't planned to give this to you like this. I have an appointment on Saturday to have it framed. It's an original, so be careful not to bend it."

Her eyes opened wide. She unrolled the print. She stared at it for several seconds without speaking. No smile. No laugh. Her eyes got wet, and then she handed it back to me.

"Take this. I can't …" Her voice dropped off as she inhaled a small gasp, then cried even harder than before.

I took the print. Now I was wide-eyed and fighting every cell in my body not to cry. What was that reaction? Was it good or bad? It felt bad. It felt very bad. I rolled up the print, put it back in the tube, and placed it on the living-room table. I could always sell it.

"Dylan. Come back. Please."

I stood over her. "I'm sorry. I thought …" I had no idea what I thought. I felt a mixture of stupid and angry. How had I read her so wrong?

Kama stared at her hands. "Sorry? Why are you sorry? That's the most beautiful thing anyone has ever given me. Ever, ever." She met my eyes and sobbed again. "And you had the artist put me in the picture. With you."

I crawled back in bed and wrapped my arms around her. I'm not ashamed to admit that my cheeks were wet, too.

# 32

# KAMA

Another month passed. Dylan and I had been living together for seven weeks. On the surface, things were perfect. He was perfect. And it was freaking me out. I felt like I was living in someone else's psychology research project, waiting for the phone call to tell me I was being brought back to real life now after my participation in an experiment in alternate realities.

I'd met all of his brothers, and they were just as funny, smart, nice, and stupidly good-looking as he was. Even Chris, who shared no genetics with any of the other five, looked like he'd been beaten by the handsome stick.

Only Morgan and Nick had serious girlfriends. Tamara and Sophie were lovely and all too happy to share what dirt they knew about Dylan, which wasn't anything new to me. I guess when he told me he'd shared everything, he hadn't exaggerated.

It made me feel bad that I still hadn't taken him home to meet my family—well, my parents—but since I couldn't guarantee Rohan would be out, I wasn't willing to take the risk.

Dylan couldn't understand why I was so reluctant to have him meet my brother. "How much of a jerk can he be?"

It was hard to answer since Rohan seemed to direct all of his psychopathic tendencies at me. Everyone else saw a friendly guy who lived with his parents so he could help pay the mortgage and take care of the yard work. What a load of baloney.

Josh and Lizzy had seen each other a few times since the karaoke night. She said it wasn't anything serious, that they were just hanging out; that he wasn't interested in more. When Dylan and I asked them over for dinner, they were both quick to agree. This made us happy since I'd been missing my BFF and he'd been missing time with Josh. Double dating would allow us to get all the time we wanted with our favorite people.

I made a homemade beef lasagna and garlic bread. Lizzy brought a salad. And Josh said he'd bring dessert. I realized that his definition of dessert was a little different from mine when he handed me a bottle of Ardbeg single malt whisky. The way Dylan high-fived him, it seemed they shared the same understanding of 'after-dinner treat.' Who was I to argue?

Dinner conversation was fun and light. Once we cleared the dishes, we played Cards Against Humanity—the drinking game version.

"How do we play that? Loser drinks?" I asked.

"No!" Dylan and Josh answered together.

"It has to be the winner who drinks. Otherwise you ladies will intentionally lose," Josh said.

"And … he's projecting again," Dylan said. "We used to play 'loser drinks' until we figured out that lush over here was losing on purpose. So now best combination gets to drink. Losers stay dry."

"I plan to demolish this bottle," Josh said.

Several rounds in, it was Dylan doing the most damage

to the single malt. I'd never seen him drink that much. He was a fun drunk. Funny in a self-deprecating way. I'd started to intentionally lose because I wanted to be as sober as possible to watch Dylan get more drunk.

It was my turn to pull and read the black card. "Dear Modern Love, I'm having some trouble with *something*. What do you advise?"

"Read it again," Dylan slurred as he fanned his cards in front of his face.

"Okay. Ready this time? Dear Modern Love, I'm having some trouble with … something from one of your cards, Dylan. What do you advise?"

Lizzy and Josh looked at their cards, made faces. They looked at each other, made faces. They were cheating so hard it was ridiculous. All the nodding and winking and cards passed under the table to each other.

"Ready? Give me your cards," I said. I got a card from each of them and added a fourth from my pile. I didn't get to vote, but it made the game more fun to have four options.

"First answer: Dear Modern Love, I'm having trouble with my prostate."

Dylan was the only one to laugh. "I feel your pain, buddy."

"Right. Okay. Second answer: Dear Modern Love, I'm having trouble with Ryan Reynolds's dimples."

"My only problem with Ryan Reynolds's dimples is that they aren't pressed against my inner thigh," Lizzy said.

"Josh has dimples," Dylan said, pointing at his cheek and nodding at Lizzy. "He could be your surgogate Rynald Reynold," he slurred.

Josh looked horrified, then apologized to Lizzy. "It's not you. It's me," he said.

"Next: Dear Modern Love, I'm having trouble with my Instant Pot recipes." I shook my head. "Seriously, people, that's the best you could do?"

Dylan picked up the whisky bottle. "Hey, is this bottle less than half full or more than half empty?" He chuckled and looked right at me. "That should be a psychology test to help figure out how positive a person is, don't you think, Kama? You could do that research. You'd be really good at it."

I raised my eyebrows and held back a laugh. Lizzy gently kicked me under the table. Then Dylan turned to Lizzy and slurred, "She's super smart, you know. I feel terrible about her thesis."

Dylan leaned forward and gave me a sloppy kiss. "I love you so, so much."

"Love you, too, drunk guy."

Dylan sat back, then leaned the other way, over to Josh. "I have a secret." He sounded like he was trying to whisper, which he wasn't at all. He was just slurring more slowly. "I have to sue the dean of her department because my boss hates her. You can't tell Kama because it's her dating search... search?... *re*-search that's being used to humiliate her. I mean him. The lady at the university. Not Kama."

My body went numb. I felt like vomiting. I stood up so quickly I knocked the table, which toppled the bottle of whisky. Josh almost caught it before it hit the ground. At least he slowed it down, so the bottle didn't break, but enough poured out that both Dylan and Josh dove to save it. As they were arguing about whether to mop it up or lick it off the hardwood floor, I grabbed my coat and purse. I was out the door and into the elevator before I even took a breath.

Lizzy grabbed the elevator behind me. She met me outside before I could hail a cab. Good thing, too, since I had no idea where I was going. Just anywhere away from here. Neither of us said a word on the drive to her apartment. Once we were inside, I flopped onto her couch, and the gates of hell opened. I'd jumped right over the denial stage of grief and deep into rage.

"How could he not tell me about the case and think that was okay?"

Lizzy was her always-calm self, trying to understand Dylan's side of the story. On a normal day, in a normal situation, I loved Lizzy for her balance and open-mindedness. But today, I wanted to shake her.

"He bald-faced lied to me."

"I'm not sure that's technically true." She put her hands in front of her face.

"What? I'm not going to hit you."

"Yeah, but you spit when you yell."

I whacked her arm, and she yelped. "No, he lied. He promised me that he'd convinced both the client and the firm that suing me would be a waste of money and time."

"If I understood what Dylan slurred, they're not suing *you*, babe."

"They may as well be. Now everything makes sense. Why my advisor won't support my thesis anymore. And Dylan knew that, but he chose not to tell me. It may not be a technical lie, but he didn't tell me the truth." I buried my face into her throw cushions. "What do I do?"

"You're going to stay here tonight and settle down. You're going to talk it out with me, and I'm going to tell you to give him a chance to explain himself. And you're going to listen to me because you know in your heart that I'm right."

"Lizzy, I'm stuck with him. I have nowhere to go if this is a breakup. I don't have—"

"You're not breaking up, dummy. Did you not hear what I just told you would happen?"

"And did you not hear him admit that he's primary counsel on a case that put the kibosh on my thesis? If it weren't for him ..." I stopped to figure out where I was going with that.

If it weren't for him, I would have had to go toe-to-toe with Booker in court. He did put a stop to that. But that case I would have won, hands-down.

"What? What are you thinking?" Lizzy asked.

"I don't know. This makes no sense at all. He knows I've not done anything wrong—that's why Booker agreed to give up his bogus claim against me. So what now? I don't understand. And I don't understand why he's still involved and didn't tell me."

Lizzy leaned over and wrapped her arm around me, pulling me in tight. "It doesn't make sense because you left before he could explain. Maybe there's a perfectly logical explanation."

I scoffed. "He's way too drunk to explain anything right now. But fine, maybe there is a good explanation for why he took the case. Like, maybe being in charge gives him control to keep the case directed away from me."

"Exactly!" Lizzy said, pointing at me.

"But if that's the case, he's doing a terrible job. Nobody else's thesis got canned last semester, so it's still personal."

"Maybe it would have been worse if he'd not been involved." Lizzy shrugged.

"Yeah, well, maybe if he'd told me then we could have worked together to find a solution. He's always all about two heads being better than one—when it's *his* head that's being added on as bonus brains to my ideas. But does he ever bring a challenge to me and ask for my opinion?"

Lizzy made a face. "Rhetorical question, right?"

I glared at her.

"Look, I know you want me to side with you, but I think Dylan was put in an impossible situation by his work. And the way you met was basically a setup for you two *never* becoming a couple."

"Exactly. This should never have happened. So what—"

"Shut up. I'm not finished. And yet, here you are. And I

know you love him, and he is definitely head over ass into you."

"Funny way to show it." I could feel myself falling toward a full-blown rage. I could stop myself from going down that path, but did I want to?

"Yeah, hilarious. He asked you to move in, bought you furniture so you'd feel at home, had that custom-made art done for you, cooks your favorite meals, killed that bogus attempt to discredit you, and spends how many hours a week touching you? What a dick. I'd have tossed his ass to the curb months ago." Lizzy shook her head.

"He's not perfect, you know."

"Oh, and you are? Did you tell him yet that you were planning to go on five more research dates where you'd have to act like they're actual, real dates? Don't you think that's something your boyfriend might have some feelings about? Are you giving him a say about that?"

"Seriously, Lizzy? You want to go there?"

"Go where, Kama? To the fact that you have double standards? Yeah, I do want to go there. This guy is everything you could ever want in a man. He makes you happy—"

"He makes me crazy," I interrupted.

"This situation with his work? Yeah, it sucks. Seriously sucks. And maybe he could have told you it was happening, but maybe he really couldn't. Because of this little thing called confidentiality that you both take so seriously."

"And yet here I am, crashing at your place because he broke that confidentiality tonight."

"Oh my god, Kama. I love you, but you're making me crazy right now."

"I hate him."

"You love him."

"No, I hate him."

"That's why you're crying?"

"I'm crying because I have to find a place to live. I gave up my sweet dorm apartment, and now I'll have to move back home. I can't move back home, Lizzy. You know I can't. Can I live with you?"

Lizzy shook her head. "Live on my couch? No. I love you, but no. You're going back to your place—your place and Dylan's—in the morning when you're both sober, and you're going to talk about this. You'll figure it out. You know what I put my money on?"

I shook my head.

"I think he's involved so his control over the case will give him more power to protect you. Did you ever think of that?"

"I still think he should have told me. I don't think I can trust him now."

Lizzy rubbed my head and let me cry on her shoulder until I was ready to sleep.

# 33

## DYLAN

My head pounded like I'd been beaten by bags of rocks. I rolled over to say good morning to Kama, but she wasn't there. Probably already up. I didn't remember her drinking as much as I had. I went to the bathroom and realized I was still wearing my jeans from the night before. That was a first. With my face washed and teeth brushed, I looked at myself in the mirror. Why was the bathroom so damned bright? I looked like hell, even viewed out of focus and through squinting eyes.

I pulled off my clothes and put on shorts and a clean T-shirt.

"Hey, babe, do you feel any better than I do?" I asked as I walked out to the living room.

"I feel like shit. I need Tylenol," a gravelly voice replied from the couch.

*What the hell?*

"Josh? What are you doing here? Where's Kama?"

Josh rolled over, dropped his feet to the floor and grunted as he pulled himself into a slouching-slash-sitting position.

"You don't remember?"

"Mmm ... Gone for breakfast?"

"You seriously fucked up last night. She left. I'm guessing she's at Lizzy's place 'cause Lizzy left, too. Thanks for that. I was thinking maybe I might, you know, take the first step with Lizzy."

I shook my head, trying to make sense of what he was saying. "You and Lizzy? Really? That's ... unexpected. Why did Kama leave?"

"You have to talk to her. But I don't think you're sober enough yet, bro. Take a shower. See if you remember anything. And think of a damn good apology because you're going to need it."

"Seriously, Josh, don't be a dick. Tell me what happened."

"Short story? Actually, it is a short story. You told me, in a not-at-all-discreet way, that you're arguing a case against the dean of the psychology department, and that Kama's thesis was the genesis of this lawsuit, and that she'll never be able to find an advisor to complete her master's degree with that thesis. In pretty well exactly those words."

I'd fallen into the armchair halfway through Josh's spiel. Impossibly, my head pounded even harder.

"I'm a dead man," I moaned into my hands.

"Seriously, Dylan. Shower. Put your brain back in drive and figure this out. You cannot lose this woman. She is fucking perfect for you." Josh hit me with a throw pillow. "And her best friend is growing on me. If you fuck it up with Kama, then you've also fucked with my chance for anything more with Lizzy. Don't do that to me, bro."

I tossed the pillow back to him. "Maybe it's better for it to end now. One day she was going to realize I'm a fuck-up and take off, anyway."

"That's an excellent look on you, Mr. Pity Party. Get over yourself, Dylan. As much as you like to believe you ruin everything, you're no better or worse at it than any of us. Nick is more of a fuck-up than you, at least by Dad's gauge, which is the one I assume is feeding this idiotic thinking. And he seems to be doing pretty damned well with Sophie."

"Yeah, he lucked out with her. Odds that two of us would get that lucky? Zero. I'm taking a shower. Thanks for coming over." I looked around the living room and saw the Ardbeg, still with a quarter left in it. "And take that fucking bottle with you when you go."

I left Josh looking green. I don't know how long I stood in the shower. Ten, maybe even twenty minutes. I tried to think of a way to apologize to Kama, but what was there to say? It would be a lie to say I was sorry for arguing this case. This was the lawsuit my promotion was riding on, and I'd made a conscious decision to stick with it. Saying I was sorry would ring hollow.

I couldn't tell her I was sorry I hadn't told her about it since that would have been a breach of confidentiality. I couldn't apologize for not breaking the law.

It was a no-win situation, and the sooner I accepted that, the better.

I heard voices when I turned off the water, so I stood and listened before opening the bathroom door. It was impossible to hear what was being said, but it was clearly Kama and Josh. She wasn't yelling. Good sign? I couldn't tell if she was crying. I was inclined to get back under the shower and stand there until I drowned. Coward's way out. My head hurt too much to deal with this.

A knock on the door.

"You coming out soon? I want to brush my teeth." Kama sounded tired, deflated.

Standing in my towel, I opened the door to let her in. She didn't look at me. I grabbed my clothes off the toilet and stepped around her. I went to the kitchen and poured a glass of orange juice for myself.

"You want some OJ?"

No answer.

"Are you seriously giving me the silent treatment, Kama?" I walked toward the bathroom and realized too late that, number one, she couldn't answer since she had a toothbrush in her mouth. Number two, she would not be wanting orange juice after brushing her teeth. I felt like a tool. This was off to a shitty start. I had to pull it together and get out of defensive mode. "Right, that would be a no to the OJ."

She nodded and half smiled.

Back in the kitchen, I put the kettle on and dropped a tea bag into Kama's favorite mug. My head throbbed. I should have taken some ibuprofen before my shower. It was in the bathroom, so I waited for Kama to come out.

The kettle whistled. Still no Kama, so I made her chai latte and placed it on the bedside table before knocking on the bathroom door.

"You've been in there a long time. Can I come in?"

No answer. I knocked again.

"Kama, can we please talk?"

I waited and heard nothing from behind the door. I pushed it open and found her lying in the tub with her head under the water, so I turned the light off then on again to get her attention.

She sat up, looked at me, shook her head, then submerged it again.

I felt nauseated. My first fight with Kama. Hell, it was my first relationship fight ever, if you didn't count all the dumbass arguments I had with my brothers. I didn't count those since there was never a question that those fights would always end with us making up. This one I wasn't so sure about.

Should I force her to talk or listen, or let her come to me? I had no idea. All I knew was that I desperately needed ibuprofen and acetaminophen and lots of water, so I grabbed

the painkillers from the medicine cabinet and left her alone
to soak.

She woke me from a surprise nap by nudging my feet to
make room on the couch.

"Sorry," I said by force of habit.

"What are you sorry for?"

"My feet." By the look on her face, that wasn't what she
wanted to hear. "I mean, I'm sorry we're having this fight.
I'm sorry I got so drunk last night and said stupid shit.
I'm—"

"No. Stop. You didn't say *stupid shit*." She made air
quotes. "You told a truth that you'd been keeping from me.
Big, big difference."

"Well, it was stupid of me to say it." She met my smile
with a glare. "Well, it's true. It was unprofessional and
unhelpful."

"I just want to be clear about something. Can you answer
truthfully even if breaks client confidentiality?"

"I don't know, Kama."

She stood up. "Okay. I get it. *Your* work has boundaries.
But *mine*, apparently, is fair game. All right. I have to go."

"You don't have to go. Please don't go. I'll tell you
whatever you need to know. Just sit back down. Please?"

She sat cross-legged and pushed herself as far away from
me as she could. Her arms were crossed in front of her chest.
Her eyes were swollen. Her wet hair was pulled up in a
messy bun on top of her head. She was wearing a pair of my
sweatpants and a tank top. She looked so vulnerable. I
wanted to grab her and hold her against me.

"So talk," she said.

I told her all the actions I'd taken and not taken related to
the two cases she was connected to. I told her I'd had mixed
feelings about both of them, but that I thought I could be the
most helpful if I stayed on as counsel. I told her I thought

Bob Booker was an asshat and that my boss had a juvenile vengeance against her dean.

I told her everything—everything except that my promotion was now riding on this one case. I didn't think that was relevant or helpful to getting us through this.

# 34

## KAMA

Two weeks passed. Dylan and I survived our first fight. We were still living together, cooking for each other, making love, and laughing together most days.

But things weren't the same. And as far as I was concerned, resolving the conflict hadn't brought us closer together. It had put a wall between us. At least that's how I felt. I never mentioned it to Dylan, and I wasn't sure if he felt that way, too, but I was wary about us planning a future together beyond the summer.

One thing I'd done to ease my fear was put a deposit on an apartment in the same grad student dorm I'd been living in when Dylan and I met. That was the one upside of not completing my thesis by September first: I'd still be a student and could live in student housing. The deposit was nonrefundable, but it was only two hundred dollars. My mother would have been appalled, but I slept better knowing that if, by the end of August, Dylan and I weren't fully back to the way things had been, I'd have a safe place to live again.

I didn't tell Dylan about it. After all, he thought it was fine to keep an even more important secret from me. I could see what a slippery slope this was, but I had no motivation to move to solid ground until he admitted that some secrets were never okay to keep from a partner.

My job was going well, and I loved it. Since I was on probation until I had my actual master's degree, I had to shadow colleagues at meetings with the families we were supporting. But I was left on my own to do intake paperwork and write follow-up reports. A child protection worker with his or her degree always vetted and signed them, but I didn't mind. I was learning a ton. I loved the team and had connected with several of the kids in the system—kids whose families had let them down. I swore I would not be one more of those people.

And although I still hadn't found a new advisor, I hadn't given up hope. I worked on completing the first full draft of my thesis. And I'd planned to continue to do so. That is, until the dean's office sent me an email that told me I'd been kicked out of the psychology department's master's program.

I opened the message while I was cooking dinner. Dylan wasn't home yet. I stood, stunned, chopping knife in hand, celery washed but still intact. A minute later, maybe less, there was celery carnage on the chopping block, across the counter, and around my feet. I was done.

I turned off the oven and grabbed the key to our storage locker so I could get my suitcase. I'd pack as much as I could for now and come back for the rest later, while Dylan was at work.

When I got back to our suite, Dylan was sweeping up the mess I'd left on the floor.

"Hey!" he said. Cheerful. Exuberant, even. "Looks like the celery still had some fight in it. Actually, I'm glad, because I am taking you out for a celebratory dinner tonight. Anywhere you want. What restaurant have you always wanted to go to but haven't because it's too expensive?"

He stepped toward me for a hug and saw the suitcase. I guess he finally read my energy, too, since he took a step back and said, "What's going on?"

"You tell me," I said with no humor. "Why the celebration?"

He looked at me with caution in his eyes. "Umm, that promotion I mentioned a few times over the last months? I got it today. What's up with you? You don't look like you had such a great day. Something bad with one of the kids?"

"Something bad with one of the kids ... Yeah, in a sense, if I'm one of the kids. Which I am as long as I don't have a master's degree. Which I won't be getting now because I was kicked out the department today."

I was pleased with how well I'd kept my emotions out of the delivery of this information, something I'd learned to do at the ashram retreat.

"Oh, Kama, I'm so sorry." He rushed at me with his arms open.

I blocked him with my own arms—and fists—held up in fight position. "I don't want a hug. I need space."

"Why the suitcase?"

"I just told you. I need space. From you."

"But I'm here to support you, Kama. I want to—"

"Really? You're here to support me? Tell me with a straight face that the timing of your promotion and me getting kicked out of the department are not connected. Can you do that? Can you? Can you legitimately tell me that your career success is not directly related to my career failure?"

He stared at me.

"I'll be fired now. You realize that, right? I will be one more person in those kids' lives who's made a promise to be there and who is going to break that promise. But it's okay. I'll tell them that the Very Important Lawyer Dylan Rhodes got a promotion, so everything will work out just fine. Leave me alone, Dylan. I can't talk to you right now. There's nothing you can say that will make this better."

"But I—"

"Actually, if you want to help me, go. Call Josh or one of your other brothers. Take *him* out to dinner. I need to be alone to pack my things so I can be gone when you get back. I can't take it all right now so, if it's okay with you, I'll keep my key and come back for the rest while you're at work. Because, yeah, I'll soon have my weekdays free. Won't that be nice? I'll have time to work on my thesis. Except... Oh, right. I'm no longer a student."

I went into the bedroom and slammed the door. I listened for the front door to close before I let myself cry.

I hated that I'd been right about having a dorm apartment as a backup. And I hated that I'd have to wait before I could move in. At least, I assumed I'd still be allowed to move in. Figuring that out was something I'd tackle in a day or two as I navigated how to maintain my student status while I fought this decision. I hoped that not only was I still eligible to live there but that I could move in a month early, on August first. I could survive one week back at home with Rohan—but five weeks? I found my anxiety pills in the medicine cabinet behind the aspirin and dental floss. I rolled the pill bottle between my fingers, debating whether I needed one right now. I decided I didn't. I felt more dead inside than anxious.

# 35

## DYLAN

I woke up on my couch, confused and nauseated. I felt my face and temples to see if I'd been in a fight, because my head felt like it had taken a beating. Josh had met me at a bar, and I drank. A lot. That's all I could remember. I had no idea how I'd gotten home.

The bedroom door was closed but not latched. My first thought was that Kama had closed it because I'd been snoring and keeping her awake. That was followed by a niggling feeling that she wasn't there. I dragged myself up and pushed the door open. Empty room. Like, really empty.

Her dresser drawers were open and empty. Her side of the closet: empty. In the bathroom, the medicine cabinet had too much space in it. She'd left the acetaminophen but taken the ibuprofen. I swallowed two extra-strength tablets of the former with sink water and went back to crash on the couch.

I stared up at the artwork of Kama singing, trying to help me find my keys. Instead of making me feel better, it made me realize that this was the reason I didn't get serious. One fuck-up, just one mistake, could ruin everything. When I closed my eyes, I saw visions of Kama moving out. I couldn't stop them from coming, just like I couldn't stop her from leaving.

It was inevitable. Always had been. I'd been a fool to think otherwise. I was twenty-eight years old. I knew better. I'd let my guard down. I'd let her get too close and led her to believe that she'd be safe with me. Which she wasn't. She never had been, from the moment we met. Nobody was.

My phone pinged, and I picked it up, hoping it was Kama. It was Nick. I dropped it without reading his message. Nothing to talk to Mr. Happy in Love about. He wouldn't get it. I closed my eyes and willed myself to sleep, but my brain wouldn't shut off. That's when my condo door burst open and two giants came in, talking way too loud.

"See? Told you he'd still be asleep," Josh said.

"Looks like he's awake to me. Get dressed, little brother. We're taking you out for breakfast," said Nick.

"I thought we'd agreed we were taking him to the gym to beat the shit out of him."

"After breakfast. I'm starving."

"Not hungry. Not a good time," I mumbled.

"Yeah, well, too bad. I drove an hour to come cheer you up, so you'll drag your sorry ass off the couch, take a quick shower, and come for breakfast with us."

"And pack your gym gear because we're not letting Nick leave the city without getting in a few good punches for ditching us to live in the middle of nowhere."

"You're just jealous because Sophie is way cooler than both of you two put together," Nick said.

"Seriously, guys, I'm not in the mood."

"Seriously, Dylan, we don't give a shit what you're in the mood for. You had the perfect thing going with Kama, and you blew it. We're here to make sure you know it."

"I thought we were going to help him feel better," Nick said.

"Jesus, Nick, have you totally forgotten how to be the big

brother? We have to get you away from Sophie more often. She's a terrible influence on you. First we make him feel worse, so he doesn't do this again. *Then* we cheer him up," Josh said.

"You *love* Sophie and her influence on me," Nick said. He and Josh continued talking as if I weren't there. I buried my head under a throw cushion.

"It's true. I do. And I also love Kama and her influence on this idiot." Josh kicked my leg, "So, idiot, get up, get showered, and let's get going. This is your wake-up call. You don't get to opt out."

I knew there was no way these guys would leave without me, so I showered and got dressed in shorts and a T-shirt, like they were.

Nick and Josh helped themselves to the leftover ribs and coleslaw in my fridge. They also let me know I was out of juice, which I hadn't been before they'd arrived.

"I'm not hungry anymore. How about you, Nick?"

"Actually, quite full. Great ribs, bro. Did you make them, or did Kama?"

I shook my head at him and gave him my best 'don't go there' death stare.

"Wallet and keys secure in those pockets, Dylan? We decided you don't deserve breakfast. We're going jogging. Seawall. Just five miles."

"I hate you both," I said.

"Feeling's mutual," they said together.

The entrance to Stanley Park and the seawall was an easy jog from my place, and they weren't kidding. We ran the entire trail. There was no talking. At points I could barely breathe. They cut me no slack. This was not a hangover walk or even a jog. It was a run. When we got back to the entrance, instead of walking back to my place, Nick pointed to the parking lot.

"My car's here. Let's go, boys."

"Where are we going?" I managed to say between gasps.

"Shut up and get in," Josh said.

When Nick pulled into the parking lot of the gym where Josh and I sparred, I moaned. "I can't. I'm wasted. Josh, I don't even know how you're functioning today. You drank as much as I did last night."

Josh laughed. "I had three beers and switched to Coke. You had three beers and switched to, let's see, tequila, then vodka, then rum. And you should thank me. I saved you from spending a month's mortgage on the scotch you kept trying to order."

"Thanks but maybe you could have stopped me from ordering anything at all. I feel like puking."

"Get out of my car!" Nick yelled.

Josh laughed.

I dragged my ass into the gym, planning just to shower and watch them go a few rounds in the ring. But when I headed toward the change room, Nick grabbed my arm and pulled me back toward the lockers.

"Not happening," I growled.

"Not an option," he said, mimicking my tone.

Josh had three pairs of gloves in his hands. Nick waved to Dominic, the owner of the gym, to come and tie them on for us. He did Nick's first, and while he waited for Josh and I, Nick warmed up with a punching bag. Several minutes later, Nick, Josh, and I stood in the ring.

"So how's this work? You two just going to beat the shit out of me?" I asked, holding my arms in the air in surrender.

"Just like old times," Josh laughed.

I swung at him, but he moved too quickly. While I was regaining my balance, Nick threw a punch and connected with my left pec.

"Cheap shot, asshole."

"You want to talk cheap shots? What you did to Kama. That was a cheap shot," Nick said.

I drew my left arm back to hit him, but he was fast and I was moving in hangover slow motion. I decided not to bother fighting back, figuring they'd get bored and have fun pounding each other instead. It didn't go down that way.

"So, does it feel good being a partner in a fancy law firm, Mr. King of Shit? Everything you always wanted and more?" Josh spoke and swung, connecting with my side ribs.

"Fuck you," I exhaled as I fell toward the ropes, where Nick met me. I braced myself for a punch, but he planted his gloves moderately gently on either side of my head and said really slowly, "Stop living your life for Dad."

Then he punched me. Hard in the gut. I fell to my knees and had a flashback of us as teens during a high-school rugby game. It was right at the start of the second half. Nick was on the field, and I was on the sideline. A bunch of kids were half watching from the bleachers, and I heard this jackass, a grade ahead of me, announce to a buddy—across a distance of several people—that he'd nailed one of the nicest girls in my grade. A girl I knew would never have slept with him.

I turned and gave him a challenging look. "Like hell you did. She's too good for you," I said.

"I never said she did it willingly," he called back, laughing.

I lost my shit and ran into the bleachers. We both threw some good punches, and I broke the guy's nose. That earned me a one-week school suspension which, whatever. But it also earned me a month grounded, which included a week-long family vacation that I didn't get to go on.

Dad told me it didn't matter that I'd done the right thing. He even agreed that the kid needed a good ass-kicking. But he said that I shouldn't have been the one to give it to him because my actions reflected badly on him. I'd made him look like a father with an out-of-control son.

"You getting up?" Josh asked, reaching out an arm to help me up.

I accepted it. "Which one of you wants to stand in for Dad?" I said, anger overriding my hangover.

"There he is! That's the brother I know and love. I mean hate," Nick said, raising his arms to protect his core.

We only sparred for twenty minutes before I was done, wiped out. It was exactly what I needed, and those guys were exactly the people I needed to be with.

"Back to my place to change, and then lunch? My treat. Because Mr. King of Shit just got a raise, and since I don't have anyone else to spend my new riches on, you guys are it."

"I'm in," said Josh.

"Me too, but on one condition," said Nick. "You text Kama and tell her you're a shithead."

"Actually, tell her, 'Josh says I'm a shithead.' I want her to know I'm on Team Kama."

I grabbed my phone and texted Kama.

> All the brothers agree. Dylan Rhodes is a shithead. I'm sorry you ever had to meet me.

# 36

# KAMA

Dylan called several times a day and left long, apologetic messages that I let go to voice mail. In part because I still wasn't ready to talk to him, but also so I could listen to them over and over again.

How could I ever forgive him for not telling me that his promotion hinged on me being thrown under the bus? What kind of man does that?

He swore the dean's decision to kick me out of the department had blindsided him, too. He also promised that he was working to have me readmitted. He promised a lot of things in those messages, but I'd seen no evidence of anything but words. Words that sounded nice but meant nothing without actions.

I hadn't been fired and, according to my boss, I wouldn't be because I was doing a great job. But after my probation ended, if an internal candidate complained that I didn't have the required qualifications, union rules stated that I'd have to give up the position so it could go back out for a new competition.

I was an emotional basket case, and I couldn't bear seeing all those kids while I was grieving myself. And since there was zero chance I'd be defending anything before the end of my probation period, I resigned. More accurately, I quit without notice, which made me feel even worse about everything.

I'd been back in my old room at my parents' place for nine days, and things were going okay on the Rohan front. I ignored him, and he mostly left me alone, staying in his basement suite. He claimed to be working on some kind of online business that made no sense to me.

When the doorbell rang on Sunday afternoon and I looked out the living room window to see Dylan outside, my heart did a flip-flop. I jumped up and opened the door. I was greeted by a man holding a picnic basket and huge bouquet of wildflowers.

I wanted to grab him in a hug. I wanted to kiss him. I wanted to hit him. I was still angry, but I was willing to hear what he had to say while we ate and drank whatever was in the basket.

"Hi," I said.

"Hi," he replied.

We stood at the door, just staring at each other with tentative smiles. *Understanding begins with a shared breath*, I thought, so I moved my gaze to his chest to match the rhythm of his breath. And before either of us spoke, Rohan walked up beside me.

"This must be the brilliant lawyer who got you kicked out of your master's program. I'd like to shake your hand, sir. Kama didn't have the sense to see how ridiculous that research was. You were just the man she needed to meet."

Rohan extended his hand. I stood in stunned silence. Dylan didn't have a free hand to return the gesture, but he made no effort to either pass me the flowers or put the basket down. I could see his jaw tense.

"You must be Rohan," he said. "Kama barely talks about you."

Oh, dear. My stomach tightened. I did not want to witness an argument between these two, especially about me.

"Be right back," I said, and I bolted up the stairs to my bedroom to grab my phone. I was gone less than thirty seconds. Dylan was standing in the same spot, but Rohan had taken a step or two closer to him and was speaking too quietly for me to hear. I snatched my purse from the hook by the front door and dropped my phone into it.

"Tell mom I won't be home for dinner," I said as I tried to push past my brother.

Rohan grabbed my arm hard and held me in place. "While you're living under this roof, you follow our house rules. And that means you will be home for dinner." Then he faced Dylan and said, "Kama thinks that because she's so clever, doing a master's degree, she's above the law. Don't you, little sister?"

"Let go of me, Rohan." I spun, and he released his grip. Gaining confidence with Dylan there, I faced Rohan directly. "You are not the boss of me."

He grabbed my jaw and pinched my chin between his thumb and forefinger, squeezing hard. "Aren't I?" he drawled.

"What the fuck, man? Let go of her!" Dylan spat.

My head suddenly filled with helium instead of brain matter. My chest compressed, and the room closed in. I had two seconds to sit, or I'd fall. I leaned against the doorframe for balance as my knees bent. The last thing I saw was Dylan raise his arms as a beautiful bouquet landed beside me.

# 37

## DYLAN

I dropped the flowers and the basket, and put my hands against Rohan's chest as he bent over and grabbed Kama's T-shirt to pull her inside the house. He let go of her, but his fists were fast. His right hand found its mark beside my left eye. Surprised, I stumbled backward, and in the time I took to get my balance, Kama was inside and the door was closed. I banged with both fists.

"Open the door, you son of a bitch! Open the door or I'll call the cops."

Silence on the other side. Given Kama's and Rohan's relative sizes, I couldn't imagine he'd be able to move her somewhere more comfortable. I pictured her slumped over on the tile floor, rocking the way she had in the restaurant.

"Kama! Kama, are you there? Can you hear me?"

I pressed my ear to the door, hoping to hear her repetitive "yup, yup, yup," but there was nothing. Maybe she was speaking too softly.

"Kama, if you can hear me, kick or touch the door. Can you do that for me? Please, let me know you're okay."

I listened. I stood for a full minute, waiting. Nothing. I banged on the door again. The other side was still. Then I wondered if Rohan may have dragged her away. The thought enraged me.

I took my phone from my pocket to call 9-1-1 and stepped off the front stoop to see the street address. As I did, my foot kicked the flowers which had landed on top of Kama's purse. I stopped dialing.

How would Kama feel if I called the police to her house? Would she be humiliated? What would happen to her if I did? Would her brother do something? Or her father or mother? I had no idea. She rarely spoke about her family, always turning the conversation back to me and my brothers. I knew so little about this part of her life.

And now I'd shown up, unannounced, and created a shit show for her. *Dammit.* I picked up her purse and was about to hang it on the door handle, but I changed my mind. If I had it, she would have a legitimate reason to call me. I could tell she was not unhappy to see me. Maybe she wasn't delighted, but at least she didn't appear to be angry. How would she feel now? Would she be upset if I took her purse?

I was willing to take that risk.

I looked at the door and the window beside it. I didn't see a soul, so I put Kama's purse into the picnic basket, then picked up the bouquet of wildflowers and placed them on the railing, so they'd not be accidentally stepped on.

Walking down the front path backward, facing the house, I looked for any sign of her from a window. Nothing. Nobody. I dropped the picnic basket in the passenger seat, then got into my car and sat for several minutes, rolling around ideas.

It occurred to me that her brother might read her text messages. What could I say that wouldn't make her situation worse but would let her know I was here for her if she needed me?

I walked back to the house, phone in hand, took a photo

of the flowers on the railing, and added it to a new text message. I typed slowly, willing Kama to come to the door.

> I was out of line to come to your home unannounced. I'm sorry I overreacted and threatened to call the police. Your flowers are on the front porch. I hope you feel better soon.

I hit send and, as I walked back to my car, I touched my left cheek, which was feeling hot and sore. In the rearview mirror, I saw swelling and bruising around my cheekbone and below my eye.

Assault. I could charge that bastard with assault. I *should* charge him with assault.

But how would that blow back at Kama? There would be questions about why I'd shoved Rohan to begin with. There was no way to do this without Kama becoming the center of the story. I couldn't do that to her. Again.

With my plans for the day ruined, and angry energy coursing through me, my autopilot directed my car to the highway, Lily Valley, and Nick's place. I'd go for a hike. Or a beer. It didn't matter. I needed brother time.

Setting my cruise control at five miles over the speed limit, I launched Spotify and chose one of Kama's playlists at random. I'd downloaded them all so I could surprise her with music I knew she loved on our drive to the picnic spot.

Twenty minutes into the hour-long drive, I realized that these were the same songs, in the same order, that had been playing on our first date. As they played, flashes of conversations with Kama came back to me, including one from our second date when she told me that the panic attack she'd had with me was the first in two years. The first since she'd started grad school and moved into residence. She was disappointed because she'd allowed herself to believe that she'd outgrown them. And then I came along and showed her that all was not well in the state of Denmark. Or in her psyche.

The playlist reached the song that had been playing during the conversation that led to her panic attack. My tone, and her reaction, were indelibly imprinted on my brain since I'd listened to those twelve seconds fifty times over.

Me: "Women who would be flattered that I was imagining them naked while we ate our buffalo burgers?"

Kama: "You are not imagining me naked."

Me: "Aren't I?"

What had surprised and relieved her was that the panic attack hadn't triggered a general state of anxiety, like she had when she was living at home ... living at home ... with her brother. That's when it hit me: her panic attack today had nothing to do with me. Rohan triggered it.

When Kama told Rohan he wasn't the boss of her, he'd said the exact same thing, in the exact same tone, as I'd said on that first date: "Aren't I?"

That was it. I had no doubt. But what I didn't know was what he did *after* saying those words that would lead her to panic. Since the words themselves weren't threatening, it had to be the actions that followed that made her shut down.

*Dammit!*

I was already forty-five minutes from the city. The first place to turn around was Lily Valley, and that was still fifteen minutes away. Then it would take an hour to get back to her house. I swore at myself for driving away and leaving her so vulnerable with that bastard, but there was nothing to do now.

I tensed then released the muscles in my back and shoulders, encouraging them to relax. I needed a punching bag. Good thing Nick had one.

# 38

# KAMA

Ten, maybe fifteen minutes later, I pulled myself up off the floor, from the spot where Rohan had dragged me. It was far enough from the front door that I couldn't touch it or communicate with Dylan. Of course, Rohan wouldn't help me get to the couch or upstairs to my bed. At least he didn't try to carry me down to the basement. He'd done that enough times when I was small that I couldn't even look at the basement door without having a twinge of anxiety.

I hated being back here. And I hated Dylan for putting me in a situation that forced me home. What was I thinking, giving him a second chance? That was my problem: I was too forgiving. And even though Lizzy said Dylan deserved a second chance, she no longer had any interest in having a go with him, even though he was single again. I'd given her my blessing, but he was like a hot potato neither of us wanted to touch: "You go out with him." "No, you go out with him."

I listened to see if I was home alone. No sound from Rohan's suite. I relaxed a little.

Using all my energy, I made my way upstairs to my room and slumped on my bed. If I lay down, I could sleep. But then I'd wake up and have to deal with Rohan. Better to sleep on the couch at Lizzy's place for a night or two. I wouldn't need much, just a couple of pairs of underwear, a clean T-shirt, my computer. I stuffed the clothes into my laptop bag and pulled open my bathroom door to grab my toothbrush.

"Going somewhere?"

I jumped backward, and my ribs crashed into the highboy dresser.

"What are you doing in here? Get out!"

"Answer my question. Where do you think you're going?"

I bent forward to catch my breath and spoke into my legs. "Nowhere. I just need to brush my teeth."

"Liar! I saw you packing underwear into your computer bag." Rohan stood up from his seat on the toilet, opened the cover, and dropped my toothbrush into the bowl.

"Fine. I was going …" I didn't want him to know where I was going. "I was going back to Dylan's place. My place with Dylan."

"But you're not going now. You're staying here with me. Helping Mom make me a nice dinner. I think homemade pizza would be good, don't you?"

I sat on my bed. He was like a child who played a game by a set of rules he'd made up. But he never bent or broke the rules, and I could sometimes use them to my advantage. Like the rule that my bed was my safe place, a place he couldn't touch me.

Eventually, he'd get bored of watching me type and would leave me alone. Eventually, he'd get restless by himself in his suite and he would leave the house. Eventually, I'd be free to do what I wanted to do, and we both knew it. That was his game: control me until he got bored.

I flipped open my laptop. My messages app showed a new text from Dylan. I sighed and shook my head. What kind of lame apology was that? *I hope you feel better soon.* Seriously? You leave me on the floor, and that's what you have to say? That text didn't warrant a reply, so I deleted it.

"What's wrong, little sister?"

I ignored him. That was the way I took part in his game. I egged him on by pretending he wasn't there. It drove him crazy. But I was safe.

I texted Lizzy.

> Can I crash at your place tonight? Rohan is being Rohan. I had another attack. Meh.

She wrote back immediately.

LIZZY

> Shit. Come by Burgersio after 3 to get keys.
> I'm working 'til midnight. Love you.

I promised myself that no matter what, I'd have my own place by September first at the latest. And no matter what, I'd never spend another night back home as long as Rohan was still here. Frankly, I didn't expect he'd ever leave. Mom and Dad would never ask him to. They thought it was ridiculous to waste money on rent when they had enough space for us all. Rohan, being such a dutiful son, didn't argue with only having to pay a hundred dollars a month for his whole suite or with having his meals cooked for him.

The registrar at the university went above and beyond, returning my nonrefundable dorm deposit. I'd asked if that rule could be bent, since I was no longer eligible to live in the grad residence. News had traveled about how I'd been kicked out, and anyone with three brain cells knew exactly why—the case Dylan had argued against the psychology department's thesis standards got some publicity.

Dylan had lost the case, which didn't surprise anyone who knew me. What surprised us all was the dean's reaction of kicking me out of the grad program. Nobody saw that coming. And nobody thought it was right, but nobody had a say. Returning my dorm deposit was an act of administrative disobedience, the registrar told me, to communicate that she and her colleagues disagreed with my expulsion.

I had enough money for first and last month's rent in a small basement suite. Nothing as fancy as Dylan's high-rise, but possibly a little bigger. My challenge would be to convince a landlord I'd have a job by the time I needed it. And then getting said job. But I would.

As Rohan sat staring at me from his seat in my bathroom, I searched for bachelor apartments and suites on Craigslist. It didn't take long before he sighed and walked out, telling me I was too boring to hang out with and no wonder I didn't have a boyfriend. I didn't acknowledge him.

After he left, I closed my laptop and listened until I heard the deadbolt on the front door click closed. He'd gone out. Time to make my escape.

At the front door, I looked for my purse. It wasn't on its normal hook. Great. I couldn't leave without my wallet. My bus pass. My phone. I cursed my brother for having figured out a way to keep me trapped. This was a new low, even for him.

I screamed at the air. I would not let him win. I steadied myself and opened the door to the basement and his room.

"Hello?" I called. "Rohan, are you there?"

No sound. I took a deep breath and flicked on the light, then started down the stairs.

"Rohan, I'm coming down." I stopped in the middle of the flight and listened. He was sneaky. He could have slipped back in one of his windows without me knowing. He could be waiting to pounce. I'd have no protection from him on his turf. If I got all the way down and he caught me … Nope. I would not think about it. I turned and went back to the top of the stairs, heart pounding. I knew what I had to do, what I had to say, to see if it was safe.

I'd finally figured it out. All those years of panic attacks that had seemed totally random—aside from the Rohan connection—had a trigger. It was Dylan who'd inadvertently helped me figure it out, but I didn't see it until I saw the two of them together, and Rohan used his own Jedi mind trick on me.

Standing in the hall with the basement door open just enough to call down, I yelled, "I'm coming down … and …" I took a deep breath, "you aren't stopping me."

I held my breath, waiting for his answer. If he were there, he'd not be able to resist replying. And I'd not be able to resist panicking. But it was worth it. Either I'd be trapped by my fear or trapped by his sick desire to control me.

I let out my breath slowly. There was no sound. He wasn't there. I ran down the stairs as fast as I could, opened his bedside table drawer, and reached in the back. That's where he kept his cash. Ever since his first job, when he was fourteen and I was just eight, I'd heard him stash his money there a dozen times. It was hidden from Mom and Dad but not from me. He thought I couldn't see when I was having an attack. He was right about seeing with my eyes. But I'd learned to see with my ears. I could hear everything, and in that heightened state, with adrenaline pumping hard and all my nerve endings on high alert, every sound communicated all the information my eyes weren't seeing.

The sound of a drawer opening. A small drawer. A shuffle of items—a watch, a knife, condom packs, papers—and then paper flipping. His quiet voice, counting by fives and tens. An envelope being closed. His hand moving the shuffled items aside. The envelope dropped, and the drawer closed.

I reached into the drawer and found the money. I grabbed a twenty and stuffed it into my pocket. I was about to put the envelope back and realized that whether I took only twenty dollars or all of it would make no difference.

The outcome would be exactly the same: a psychological beating. My hand changed direction, and I stuffed the entire envelope down the back of my jeans, under my T-shirt. In case he saw me on the street. In case he took my laptop bag. Just in case.

I ran to the top of the stairs, turned off the light, and was out the front door within thirty seconds. Running to the bus stop. Running for my freedom. Running for my life. Not my literal life—he'd never kill me—but my metaphorical life, one I had full control over.

I walked into Burgersio and grabbed the table for one at the front. My waiting place. Lizzy had seen me from across the room and winked. She arrived a few minutes later with a pot of chai and cream.

"You look like hell," she said, forcing me to stand and giving me a hug.

"I'm never going back."

"Stay with me as long as you need."

"He stole my phone and wallet. This is a new low, even for him."

"Report him to the police."

"I can't." I imagined my parents' shame.

"Of course you can. And you know you should."

I shook my head.

"How do you plan to get your phone and wallet back from him?" she asked.

I shook my head again.

"At least report that you've lost them, so you can get all your ID replaced. And so he doesn't use your bank card and take your money."

That's when I remembered the money. "I stole the cash he had hidden in his bedside table."

Lizzy's face lit up. "You didn't! How much?"

"I have no idea." I pulled the envelope from my jeans and placed it on the table.

Lizzy picked it up and opened the flap. Without taking the money out, she flipped through the bills, counting out loud. "Twenty, forty, sixty, eighty, one, twenty, forty, sixty, eighty, two, fifty, three, fifty, four, five, six, seven, eight, nine, one thousand, one, two, three, four, five, six."

I stared at the envelope.

"Sixteen hundred dollars? I figured it was just tens and twenties." The blood rushed out of my head, and I felt faint.

"With this kind of cash, you can stay with me and pay rent!" Lizzy elbowed me gently.

"I have to get it back. That's ... he really *might* kill me."

"He's not going to kill you. But yeah, he'll be mighty upset. Keep it. Use it as leverage to get your phone and wallet."

"I need to think. And," I said, looking out the window, "I need to get going. If he comes looking for me, he'll start here."

"I'll get you my keys."

It was still way too early to go to bed, but panic attacks left me tired, and Lizzy wouldn't be home until midnight. Nobody would judge me for crashing under the blankets for the afternoon and evening.

Lizzy's pull-out bed was made. It had the same sheets I'd slept on a few months earlier after a particularly crazy karaoke night. Before Dylan.

Instead of curling into a ball and crying myself to sleep, I focused on canceling my debit and credit cards. They were easy enough. One call and done. Getting my driver's license and health card replaced would have to wait until Monday. A new phone would have to wait until I had picture ID again. That was the biggest pain. Except ... I did have a passport. But it was back at my parents' place. I'd wait until tomorrow for that, when mom would be sure to be home.

Seemed like a perfect afternoon to spend with Christian and Satine at the *Moulin Rouge.*

As I watched, I wondered what Dylan was doing, and if he'd gone on his picnic without me.

# 39

# DYLAN

Nick agreed to meet me at the fire hall in Lily Valley. His 'office.'

He was standing in the parking lot when I pulled up.

"Do we need to turn around and go back and get her?" Nick asked, looking ready to roll.

"I just don't know. If it weren't for me showing up, she'd be fine. I kind of think she's better off without me there. And her brother said her parents would be home for dinner so... I'm thinking there's nothing I can do that would make things better at this point."

"Have you called her?"

I shook my head.

"Call her, you dumbass," Nick said, hitting my ribs with his elbow.

"Can we go inside? I want a beer and to figure out what to say. How to not make things worse."

I tried calling Kama three times but she wasn't answering. Nick and I were onto our second beer and third rack of pool, and he was kicking my ass, which was unusual.

"You're worried about her." Nick said it as a matter of fact.

"Yes and no. I mean, I'm confident that she'll be okay, once she recovers from the panic attack. But I'm worried about us, her and me. I feel like a total tool. I never expected Kama would be so directly impacted by this pissing match that's been festering for ten years between my boss and her dean. It has nothing to do with her."

"Nothing to do with her? She was the fuel that relit the fire. What did you expect would happen to her? Did you really think she'd get out of this without being burned?"

"Seriously? Fire metaphors? You're better than that, bro. And yeah, actually, I did. Sure, she provided a vulnerability that my asshole boss could poke at, but I truly never expected it to touch her like this. In my perfect world, the only outcome would have been to shine a light on how juvenile these two old rivals were, even as grown-ass PhDs. It's pathetic."

"You're feeling guilty."

"Guilty? No. I'm mad. I'm furious with James, but I'm also mad at Kama."

"Kama? How the hell can you be mad at her? She's the victim here."

If we were still in our teens, before Nick started training to be a firefighter, I'd have jumped the pool table at that comment and gone a round with him. But I knew if I challenged him now, I'd end up needing his first-responder expertise to put me back together. God, how I wanted to punch something.

"Kama is just as much responsible for where we are now as I am. She didn't have to move back home. That choice was hers." I pointed at a pocket and missed the shot. I was done. I dropped my cue on the table and sat on the couch with my beer.

Nick shrugged, hung my cue on the rack, and lined up his shot, which he nailed.

"How many times have I offered you relationship advice?" he asked.

I thought for a nanosecond. "Never. Thank god."

"Pay attention, son, because I'm about to school you in Relationship 101."

"Not happening." I stood and looked toward the loft space, which was home to weights and gym equipment for the firefighters. "I'll be in the workout room."

From downstairs a man yelled, "Hello! Nick, are you here?"

Nick opened the rec room door and yelled down the stairwell, "Upstairs."

A few seconds later, an RCMP officer in uniform was standing with us.

"Hey, Larry," Nick said. "What brings you here? On break? Want to join us? My brother, Dylan here, is sucking wind." Then he turned to me. "Larry—Constable Aspen to you—is Lily Valley's resident police officer."

Constable Aspen looked at me, back at Nick, then took a step toward the balcony door that overlooked the parking lot. He pointed. "Is that your Audi?"

"It is." *Shit.* I wondered if I'd been citizen-reported for speeding. I ran through the drive up ... I was sure I'd set my cruise control to five miles over. Not enough over the speed for a personal visit.

"Can you come down to your vehicle with me, please? Bring your keys."

Nick dropped his pool cue, and the three of us headed downstairs.

In the lot, Constable Aspen asked me to unlock my car and stand back.

"What's going on, Larry?" Nick asked. I elbowed him, knowing it was best to remain silent and let the cop do the talking. I knew this not from personal experience, but from working with a handful of clients who'd had plenty of police interactions.

"A person and her cell phone have been reported missing, and the tracing app places the phone in this parking lot. Since there's only one vehicle here, I'm guessing the phone is inside."

Constable Aspen put on latex gloves and opened the driver's side door. He popped the trunk, looking directly at me as he pulled it up. He looked inside. I knew all he'd find was a first aid kit and an umbrella. He moved to the passenger side, looked in the glove compartment, and swept under the seat. Then he opened the picnic basket and looked up at me with questioning eyes.

"Do you have a date up here with you? Is she in the bathroom, maybe?" he asked, nodding at the fire hall.

"No. She … she, uh, was busy. Couldn't make it," I said.

Constable Aspen pulled Kama's purse from the basket.

"Shit." I'd forgotten I'd grabbed that.

He looked at me with eyebrows raised. He opened the purse and pulled out Kama's phone.

"Who gave you that bruise? Looks new. Was it Ms. Ray?"

My stomach sank. I shook my head. There was no easy way out of this. "It was her brother. Ms. Ray's brother, Rohan."

"Where is Ms. Ray?"

"I have no idea. The last time I saw her, she was at her house."

"And that was at what time?" Constable Aspen asked.

"Noon? Twelve-fifteen? Why are you asking where she is? Isn't she the one who called in the missing phone?"

"Sir, I need you to face the car and put your hands behind your back."

"I can explain," I said.

"Yes, you can. I'll take your statement at the detachment. Against the car."

"No, I mean there's a logical explanation. I picked up her purse so nobody else would steal it. It was lying on the front steps of her parents' house."

"Unusual place for a lady to leave her purse," Constable Aspen said.

"She dropped it."

"Just dropped it and left it there? Again, not making a lot of sense. I need you—"

"I texted her. Told her I had it. I didn't know the phone was in her purse. I assumed she had her phone on her." I stopped talking. Nothing I was saying was helping.

"Larry, seriously, there's got to be some mistake or reasonable explanation. Dylan's a lawyer. Kama is his girlfriend, sort of," Nick muttered. "He's not a purse snatcher."

"Nick, I'm sorry. I really am. But you know how this works."

Aspen gave me a look that was clear. I faced his car and put my hands behind my back. He cuffed me and opened the back seat of the unmarked Ford Explorer. I got in.

"Wait!" I said. "Nick, figure out how to get hold of Kama. She can explain."

Aspen spoke to Nick before he closed the door. "If you get hold of Ms. Ray, let me know ASAP. We care less about the stolen phone than we do about finding Ms. Ray. The fact that your brother has the phone and nobody knows where the young woman is …" I could see Aspen's face, and my gut twisted. He suspected I'd done something to her. "Just let me know if you get in touch with her."

Aspen wrote something on a business card and handed the card to Nick. We left the Lily Valley Volunteer Fire Department with lights and sirens. *Great.* I knew what came next. Photos, jail cell, investigation. And media coverage. *Shit, shit, shit.*

I needed a lawyer. No, I needed Kama to call and tell them this was a misunderstanding before they processed me. I hoped Nick understood the urgency. I could not let this get out. Even though I'd ultimately be found innocent, this was the kind of press that could ruin a career. A career I'd barely started. There would be no coming back from this.

This attention would thrill Dad. Not.

I had to call my firm to get a lawyer. I wondered who they'd send to represent me. That would be telling.

A baby lawyer would say, "You might as well quit since you're done here."

A junior partner, like me, would say, "You'd better have a damned excellent explanation for this."

A senior lawyer? I was under no illusion that they'd send a senior lawyer. I didn't like my options, not that I'd have a say in the matter.

At the detachment, Aspen took me to a holding cell. I was alone, at least for now, but I'd be here for hours before I'd have representation. I did some math. It was late Sunday afternoon. I'd give the lawyer an hour to wrap up whatever he or she was doing, another hour to get to Lily Valley from downtown Vancouver. And if the lawyer they chose lived in the suburbs, another hour just for travel time. Minimum two hours, but probably closer to four. I figured I'd be spending the night.

Unless Nick got hold of Kama. But someone had reported her missing. The only people who'd have called that in would be her parents or her brother. That gave me a bad feeling. If Rohan reported her missing, knowing I had her purse, there was no way I'd be getting out of here in time for work on Monday. He'd make sure she stayed hidden as long as he could. That was my bet.

Two minutes with the guy was enough to tell me he was

a grandiose narcissist. I'd met my fair share in the last two years. From the way he looked at Kama, it was obvious he derived pleasure from other people's pain. I bet he was hurting me to hurt her. Or not. Maybe he wanted to hurt me just for the sheer pleasure of it, because I'd challenged him.

And then I had a darker thought—that Rohan wasn't involved, and that Kama had set this up to get back at me. Ruin my life for ruining hers. For minutes my mind swirled down that path—that Kama was showing me what it felt like to be blindsided and have your career and life goals taken from you by someone you trusted.

An hour later, sitting in a cell while my name and mugshot were being prepped to hit the six o'clock news, I couldn't stop thinking Kama had picked herself up from under the bus, stepped into the driver's seat, and was running me down.

I needed to give my statement. Screw the lawyer. I wasn't guilty of any wrongdoing, and telling the truth wouldn't dig me any deeper in the shitter than I was now. If I could clear this up before news time, it might save my reputation. I'd get a slap on the wrist from the firm for not following protocol, but that would be much less damaging than a media story about Dylan Rhodes, jilted lover and primary suspect in a missing persons case. Even if the story *was* retracted a day later.

I looked up at the camera in the corner of the cell, waved my arms, and yelled, "Hello! I'd like to speak to an officer."

# 40

## KAMA

Christian and Satine were at the part in their love story where Satine had to convince Christian that she didn't love him anymore or else the man who'd bought her would have Christian killed. I'd watched the movie three dozen times, and I still didn't know what I'd do if I was ever in a situation like that. Could I give up my happiness and lie to the man I loved to save him? Or would I fight harder to save us both?

In theory, it seemed so obvious: I'd fight to save true love. In practice, though, things weren't as clear. I finally had a relationship that let me put myself right into Satine's head, and all I could wonder was if what Dylan and I had was love, or if it was just something that fed a part of me that had been starving.

If I were literally starving, would it make sense to fall in love with the first person who brought me a burger and fries? Of course not. But what if it was a free-range buffalo burger with all the fixings I love the most? And organic potato fries? That was a harder call, but it still didn't make sense to fall in love with the delivery man. What made sense was feeling such a deep gratitude for that person that it could be misconstrued as love.

I was grateful to Dylan for showing me what a loving relationship could look like. I'd thought I loved him. But maybe all I really loved was what he gave me. And all he loved was what I gave him. That was all that made sense now, since there was no way I could resolve what he'd done.

As I cried along with Satine, I felt a sense of relief that I hadn't gone on that picnic with him. The more distance I got from him, the easier it was to remember that I'd been happy enough before I met him. I had a goal and purpose. And since meeting him, I'd lost some of my drive to achieve that goal. I mean, I still wanted my master's degree in psychology. I still wanted to work in the field. But having gotten the chance to work with kids who'd been thrown into the foster care system, I had a desire to research something entirely new, something that would make me the best child behavior counselor any kid could ever have.

Satine had no doubt been one of those kids, scooped up by a man who loved her and took care of her basic needs but at a terrible cost—the loss of her innocence, her autonomy, and her self-sufficiency. What would her life have been like if, when she'd first been taken in by Zeigler, she'd felt empowered enough to say, 'No. My body is not for sale'? How different would her life have been? Entirely. Of course, she never would have met Christian and fallen in love with him. But she'd have met and fallen in love with someone else. And not had to die of consumption.

As I watched the movie and daydreamed about my own elusive, evasive happily-ever-after, a text message notification from an unknown number popped up on my laptop. I ignored it. It was probably informing me I was being investigated for tax fraud.

Twenty minutes later, my laptop rang: FaceTime. It was Lizzy.

"Did Nick get hold of you?"

"No. Why? And why are you calling me from the bathroom?"

"My phone was pinging like crazy, but I don't get a break until seven so I came in here to see what was going on. You need to call Dylan—I mean Nick. Or call the RCMP. Dylan's in jail, and they think he kidnapped you or something."

"You're kidding, right?" I wasn't laughing.

"No. Apparently Rohan reported you missing and they traced your phone to Dylan's car, with your wallet and everything. Everything except you. So now the cops are worried."

"That makes zero sense. How would Dylan have my purse and phone? Why would Rohan report me missing? I've not even been gone four hours. They're just having you on, Lizzy. Some kind of bogus manipulation to get me to call him."

"I think this is real."

"Well, if it's not Dylan behind this, then it's Rohan, and that's … that's new level disturbing. It's probably one of Rohan's friends. Nick doesn't even have your number, so it can't be him."

"He got it from Josh, who's on his way over to my place to tell you the same thing."

"What? Josh knows I'm here? Lizzy, why did you—"

"I have to get back to work. I'm texting you the number to call. It's some RCMP guy. Just call? Please?"

"I don't have a phone, remember?" I rolled my eyes. This sounded ridiculous.

"FaceTime him, then. Or wait for Josh and use his phone. He should be there soon. Gotta go. I love you!"

She closed the app. My laptop pinged and notified me of a new text message.

UNKNOWN

Kama, this is Nick. You need to call RCMP
ASAP. Dylan's in jail. They think he hurt you.
URGENT. 250-555-0196

Before I could write a reply, FaceTime chimed again:
Unknown Caller.

I hesitated but covered the camera and answered. It was
Nick.

"Okay, what's the—"

"Thank god you're okay. I've been worried," he said, and
he actually looked relieved to see me. "Did you call the
number I gave you?"

"No, I—"

"Kama, you have to call it right now. Like, right now.
Dylan is in jail in Squamish. And until you show the RCMP
you're okay, he'll be staying there. Just please. Call that
number I texted to you."

"I can't. I don't have my phone." This was all too
confusing to process.

"Text them. FaceTime. I'll call Constable Aspen and tell
him I just talked to you. But you need to tell him yourself
that you're okay. Please, Kama?"

"I don't understand. Why would the RCMP think Dylan
kidnapped me? That's ridiculous."

"Of course it's ridiculous. That's why you need to call, or
text, or something right now before your name is top of the
six o'clock news as a missing person—"

"I'm not missing."

"Kama," Nick said with force, he looked scared, "please
call or Dylan will be named as a suspect. It would ruin him.
His career."

I thought back to the argument Dylan and I had about
that film we watched for the festival selection. Trite quotes
popped into my head. *An eye for an eye leaves the whole world*

*blind.* Dylan had said that. *Without justice, there is no peace.* I'd said that. I sighed.

"Fine. I'll contact him."

From my laptop, I texted the number Nick had given me, said I was fine and that Dylan had nothing to do with my supposed disappearance. I got an immediate reply.

> UNKNOWN
>
> I need your address so I can send an officer over to talk to you.

Josh and the police arrived at the same time, but I didn't get to talk to Josh since the police asked him to leave, and I didn't see any reason to argue for him to stay.

Ten minutes later, after first assuring the police I was fine, that I'd left my parents' house willingly, and that Dylan had nothing to do with any of this, I was being escorted from Lizzy's apartment. Josh was sitting on the front steps, presumably to talk to me after the cops left.

"Kama, what's going on?"

"Looks like I'm being arrested." It was all I could say before they placed me in the back seat of a police cruiser. I was being taken to a pretrial holding center, accused of theft under $5,000. That, I learned the hard way, was a criminal offense. When I was found guilty—which I would be, since I was—I'd be facing six months in jail and a criminal record. I was too stunned to react.

I found out that Rohan was the one who'd reported me as a missing person. But not really. He'd called to report that I'd stolen several thousand dollars from him and disappeared. I tried to correct the officer. I gave her the envelope with the money in it, minus bus fare and an Uber lift.

Rohan had also spun a good story about me being in no emotional state to be on my own. He told them he'd left me in bed after I'd had a panic attack brought on by Dylan.

Rohan suggested that I'd stolen his money to get away from a dangerous ex-boyfriend who was stalking me, and that Dylan must have caught me.

At least, that's what I could put together based on the questions the police had asked. When I tried to explain that I'd only meant to take enough money to get a cab, then had a moment where I thought I could use my brother's money to help me get my wallet back because I thought he'd taken it, the officer told me to wait to tell my story to my lawyer.

I laughed.

"I used to have a lawyer boyfriend, but I just got him out of jail for supposedly kidnapping me, which seems to have put me in this position of needing a lawyer." Then I got serious. "I don't have money for a lawyer. So what now?"

"We'll get one to come and see you on Monday."

"Does this mean that my brother is pressing charges against me?"

The officer driving looked in the rearview mirror and made eye contact with me. She nodded.

They dropped me off at what they called a holding center. To me, it just looked like a jail. A guard processed me, took my clothes, and gave me a pair of light-blue, elastic-waist pants and a matching short-sleeved shirt. Then she took me to my cell. I was happy to be alone.

I felt numb. No emotion. One question ran on repeat in my brain, and I needed to stop it: What did you do to create the situation you're now in?

I sat cross-legged on my mattress and closed my eyes, trying to imagine I was back at the ashram in the meditation class. I tried to focus on the mantras they had us say in our heads.

*I change my thoughts, I change my world.*

I repeated it in my mind for ten breaths.

*I am brave, I am whole.*

I repeated it in my mind for ten breaths.

*Breathe in compassion, breathe out hurt.*

As soon as I started the breathe-in-breathe-out mantra, all I could see was Dylan's face in my mind's eye. As I breathed in, I smelled his skin. As I breathed out, I felt his lips on mine. And then, when I was supposed to be letting thoughts pass without judgment, our song played in my head.

My mantra changed to *breathe in Dylan, breathe out a piece of myself.*

Opening my eyes to break the spell, the shock of seeing myself in this prison cell finally hit me.

How could I possibly love a man who'd chosen his career over me? I told myself I hated him, but the feeling in my body didn't match the words in my head. Closing my eyes again, I decided I'd focus only on the first mantra.

*I change my thoughts, I change my world.*

And after several minutes, I realized that whether I loved him or hated him didn't matter. I was Satine, walking away from Christian. If I didn't walk away from Dylan, we would destroy each other.

# 41

## DYLAN

Monday morning couldn't come fast enough. As soon as Josh told me Kama had been taken away by the police, I emailed Barb, my boss's assistant, telling her I needed to see Mr. James as soon as he arrived in the office.

I'd found out from Lizzy, who'd found out from Kama's parents, why she'd been arrested. I couldn't sit by and let her deal with that on her own.

I was at my desk before seven, my new normal since my promotion. Some days I wasn't even the first one here. Junior Partner was a nice title with some sweet perks—this executive office, a parking spot close to the elevator, a company credit card, a monthly dry-cleaning budget, stock options in the company—but the downside was that for the next couple of years, I'd be living in this office. And holidays? Not likely, at least for the foreseeable future.

Even though I'd only been in the new position for a week, I already understood why James had been so interested in my relationship status. Good luck finding a girlfriend who'd put up with only being able to see me when I was sleeping.

Kama. She haunted my thoughts as I tried to focus on the

details of a case I'd be arguing in three days. Normally, I turn off my email program after checking first thing in the morning, but today I kept it open, so I'd see when Barb replied.

It was 8:07 a.m. when my laptop pinged. She wrote, 'Right now.'

I bolted down the hall toward Mr. James's office, still uncertain how I would address two topics in one impromptu meeting. I'd start with the non-news news and move on to the topic about which I felt I needed guidance from senior counsel.

"He has his first meeting at eight thirty. Head on in," Barb said.

"Thank you." I knocked on Mr. James's door and entered when he said, "Come."

"You getting settled in okay?" he asked.

"Yes, thank you. Look, I know you don't have a lot of time, and frankly neither do I, but I thought you'd want to hear it from me. I was arrested on the weekend—"

"You were what?" James inhaled so hard, his face looked like someone had punched him in the balls.

"It was a misunderstanding. It got cleared up. Nothing to worry about."

"Nothing to worry about? A partner in this firm is arrested, and you're naive enough to think there's nothing to worry about?"

This wasn't going the way I'd expected it to. I didn't want the focus on me. I'd wanted to focus on helping Kama, and I didn't want to say she was the source of the misunderstanding.

"I wasn't charged. Like I said, a misunderstanding. But that's not—"

"Were you photographed and printed?"

"Yes, but—"

"For fuck's sake, Rhodes. Why didn't you call the firm? Tell me exactly what happened."

As much as I didn't want to share the details, there was no way to avoid them. As I told James the story, he scribbled notes. Then he held up his hand in a clear 'stop talking' movement. I stopped mid-sentence.

"She set you up. This was a clear tit-for-tat revenge move. You ruined her life, and she acted to ruin yours," he said with a knowing look.

"Sir, that's not at all what happened. She was an innocent victim in this."

"Victim?" he spat. "You're the one who got printed. You're the victim here, Rhodes."

"Sir, she's in jail because of this. And—"

"Good. That's where she belongs. Glad to see our justice system is working."

My entire being vibrated. I could feel the fight, flight, or freeze hormones coursing through me, from the top of head to my fingertips and toes. I was not in a state to argue, so I did what I had to do to find my balance. I stood and stepped behind the chair I'd been sitting in. I knew it would look like an aggressive move, but I didn't care. Standing with my legs apart, I pulled my shoulders back, made fists, and flexed my biceps a few times, like Bruce Banner before he transforms into the Incredible Hulk. It was the Superman pose on steroids.

"Rhodes?" Mr. James sat back in his chair, looking at me through squinting eyes.

"Kama Ray needs a lawyer, and I want to be that person."

James's expression didn't change for several seconds. My words hung between us. And then he laughed. It wasn't a jovial sound, like he'd just realized he'd been punked. It was maniacal, like he'd just found a piece of evidence in a murder case that would make his argument a slam-dunk win.

"You're not joking, are you Rhodes?"

"I'm deadly serious. I'm the reason she's in this situation. And I understand she is guilty of the charge against her—"

"No," he said.

"No? No what?"

"No. Our firm will not represent this woman."

I grabbed the back of the chair, having found my grounding.

"Sir, with all due respect, as a Junior Partner, I understood I no longer needed yours or anyone's permission to accept or refuse cases. I'm here as a courtesy to—"

"You're skating on thin ice, son."

Oh, that did it. How many times had my dad said those same words to me? Dozens. Probably hundreds. They were fighting words. The teenager in me wanted to stomp and yell, 'You're not the boss of me,' but the man with the law degree understood that this grandiose narcissist *was* the boss of me.

I had an image of Kama doing the Jedi-mind-trick hand motion. I felt some of my anger dissolve, replaced by a feeling of amusement at the thought of what she'd say if she were in this situation.

I raised my right arm and faced my palm toward Mr. James. Then I slowly moved it outward, away from my body. "You want to rethink your position on this."

Part of my brain was horrified at what I'd just done, and the other half was killing itself laughing, imagining how Kama would laugh, too, when I told her.

I couldn't see how this conversation could be salvaged, so I turned and left Mr. James's office without saying another word. Adrenaline coursed through me again as I walked back to my shiny new partner office. I couldn't think clearly.

Had I just invited my boss to fire me? A sick feeling told me I had.

I sat down at my desk and stared at my laptop. I had a case to prepare. This was not the time to worry about Kama. But if not now, in her time of greatest need, when *would* I make time to worry about her?

I tapped my mouse pad and entered my password. The email app popped up with the message from Barb: 'Right now.'

*Right now.* Thank you, Universe. I'd make time for Kama right now. I had no choice. Her situation was urgent. The case I was preparing was important, but any other lawyer in the firm could do the work. There was nothing special about my skills on this one.

I hit reply to Barb's message and started typing. My hands seemed to know what I would say before my brain did.

*Must withdraw from the Apex Heating v Johnson case. Files on my desk. First court date on Thursday. Leaving the office to see a client at the GVRD Correctional Facility. Will not be back today.*

I read and reread the message several times but didn't hit send. I organized my case files and placed the folder on the edge of my desk. I saved and closed all the open digital files, so they'd be available for another lawyer to work on. Spinning my chair to face my wall of windows, I looked at the view of downtown Vancouver. This was the dream. I'd achieved it in record time. My dad was so proud he'd started organizing an event—not just a party, but something worthy of his reputation. I had finally earned the Rhodes last name.

And in that moment, none of it was what I wanted. I didn't give a rat's ass about the promotion or even Dad's slap on the back. All I could think about was the fact that my success had destroyed the only woman I'd ever loved. And that she had loved me—until I betrayed her. I'd betrayed Kama so I could get this office.

What the fuck was wrong with me?

I was under no illusion that I could get her back, but I had to do anything and everything to get her name cleared. I couldn't leave that to a province-appointed lawyer. It had to be me. The realization that I would probably lose my promotion, possibly even my job, didn't faze me. Not one bit. In fact, I felt relief that I could start fresh in any career I wanted once this was over.

But right now, I had to be the best goddamned lawyer I could be.

# 42

## KAMA

*onfused* didn't begin to describe how I felt when I entered the room to meet my free legal counsel and saw Dylan looking out the window of the small meeting room. He turned when the guard opened the door to let me in.

I wanted simultaneously to run into his arms for a long, hard hug—and tear the leg off a chair and stab him in the heart with it. He looked as unsure about how to approach me, though I didn't see a weapon behind his back. We settled on a handshake that turned into holding hands after we both sat down.

"Why?" It was the only thing I could think to say.

Dylan pulled his hand out of mine and sat back in his chair. "Sorry."

"For what?" I asked slowly. In my mind, I thought of a dozen things he could be sorry for. I was curious to know which one he thought he should lead with.

"Sorry for holding your hand. That was inappropriate."

I'm certain my face betrayed how I felt. *That's what you're sorry for?* I shook my head and wondered how much worse my sentencing would be if they added assault to it.

"And," he continued, looking at his hands, "I'm sorry that you're here. I'm not sure if it's my fault, but I know that if I hadn't showed up at your place, I wouldn't have taken your purse and your phone and… I'm just sorry." He finally looked up at me. "I'm sorry I ever thought I was smart enough to protect you from a system hell-bent on finding scapegoats. I'm sorry I didn't tell you what was happening and ask if you had any ideas. I'm just so fucking sorry, Kama, for it all."

I'd never seen this repentant side of Dylan. As the woman who loved him, who had loved him, I liked it. There was a softness, a vulnerability about him. But as a woman sitting in jail, guilty of a crime that could ruin my life, I wanted to see the cocky, self-confident lawyer version of Dylan.

"Why are you here? You know I can't pay your firm's fees. And wouldn't it be a conflict of interest? Or are you not actually here as my legal representation? Did you just say that to get in to see me? I'm confused, Dylan. And angry—at Rohan and at you. And I'm really freaking scared because I'm guilty. I took Rohan's money."

I hadn't cried since being brought in. Here it was, Monday midmorning, and it was only now, with Dylan sitting across a metal table in his suit, that the gulf between where I was and where I should be, became crystal clear. The emotion hit me hard and fast.

Dylan didn't speak while I cried. He reached out and took my hand again. I let him. When I caught my breath and could focus my eyes, I saw Dylan wipe a tear from his cheek. He hadn't been sobbing like me, but he wasn't unmoved.

"Will you allow me to represent you, Kama?"

"Why, Dylan? Why now?" My heart wanted to believe it was because he loved me and wanted the best for me, but my brain was quick to interrupt that thought. "What's in it for you?"

He squeezed my hand and held eye contact. I looked for the answer in his eyes and saw as many emotions in them as I was feeling.

Dylan didn't speak for a full minute and when he finally did, he said just one word.

"Justice."

I rolled that word around and connected it to every hurt and betrayal I'd experienced from Rohan and my thesis advisor and the university and even Dylan. I wanted justice. That was exactly what I wanted. It was all I wanted.

"How is this going to work?"

"You'll accept me as your legal counsel?"

"Am I still eligible for your friends and family discount?" I tried to smile, but I'm not sure how well it came across since I was fighting back tears.

Dylan pulled a legal pad and pen from his briefcase and placed his phone on the table. He hit record. "Do I have your permission to record this conversation?"

I nodded.

"Can you say yes to indicate you agree, and then state your name and birthdate, please?"

Dylan-the-ex-boyfriend vanished, and a man I'd seen hints of but never actually met in person took over: Dylan Rhodes, kick-ass lawyer.

In his effort to paint a clear picture of why I might have been pushed into taking that money from my brother, Dylan asked questions about my family that forced me to tell him things I'd never shared with him. I had an image of the two of us as characters in a movie. In one scene, we were sitting in a cozy restaurant on a date, and I was pulling all the details about his life from him. As we talked, the background morphed into a soulless meeting room. His casual clothes became a suit and mine became prison wear, and now I was the one answering all the questions. It was a small epiphany. Until this moment, I'd never let Dylan see behind the curtain. My curtain.

We talked—I talked—for over an hour before Dylan stopped recording and put away his pad and pen.

"Why didn't you tell me any of this before? I'm troubled that you kept so much of your story from me. I told you everything about me."

I didn't have an answer for him, at least nothing that didn't sound and feel either selfish or hurtful. Or both.

"Kama, did I not make enough space for you to be this honest with me when we were dating? I feel like I tried to get to know you as well as you got to know me."

"You did," I whispered, staring at the table.

"You're the one who's so hell-bent on the whole 'secrets are lies' idea, and you kept so much from me. I'm not sure how I feel. Actually, that's not true. I'm hurt."

I nodded.

"So why? Why did you keep all this from me?"

The reason repeated in my head, over and over: *I didn't trust you.*

And then another voice: *And he proved himself untrustworthy, so you were right, weren't you?*

*But maybe I wouldn't be in this situation if I'd been as honest with him as he'd been with me.*

*He threw you under the bus.*

"I didn't trust you." I said it out loud.

Dylan pushed his chair away from the table and ran his hands over his face. He looked wrung out. "Do you trust me now?"

"Do I have a choice?"

He stood up so quickly his chair fell over, making a loud crash of metal on concrete. The guard overseeing the room walked toward us.

"Sorry. Clumsy." Dylan waved to the guard, righted his

chair, and sat again, this time two feet from the table. "Yes, Kama, you have a choice. Just like you've always had. You had the choice to trust me during all those months we were together and, apparently, you chose not to. Nothing's changed. You still have that choice." His voice was curt and sharp. "Do you trust me now?"

"The truth?"

"Yes," he sighed, heavy and loud, "the truth."

I met his eyes and told the truth. "I don't know."

What I saw now in his eyes and on his face was not what I'd seen when he first sat down. His jaw tensed, and his forehead highlighted his stress lines. He looked defeated.

"I'll take that under advisement and get back to you with a plan of action. Thank you for your time, Ms. Ray."

I felt like throwing up. "That's not what I meant. I mean—"

He stood again, placed his hands on the metal table, and leaned toward me. "I can't represent— Actually, that's not the truth. I *could* represent you, but I *choose* not to if you don't trust me. So please tell me what you mean, Kama. I'm dying to understand." His anger was palpable.

To his credit, he gave me at least a full minute to answer. The truth was still that I didn't fully trust him, and there was no other way to say it. What if I told him I didn't fully trust anybody? The voices in my head fought, and then I realized why I felt so desperate to tell him I trusted him now.

I looked up and said, "The truth? I trust that you're the best legal counsel available to me."

He held my gaze for several seconds. I wanted to mirror his breathing, but it looked like he was holding his breath.

"That's not good enough," he said, as he reached out to shake my hand.

I stood, never breaking eye contact, but my arm wouldn't move to take his hand.

He dropped his arm and nodded to the guard, who opened the door, then turned to face me. "I'll inform the appropriate people that you'd like to talk to a legal aid lawyer."

# 43
---
# DYLAN

I was furious when I left the pretrial holding center. I'd pictured that meeting going quite differently. I didn't expect to learn she'd held so many secrets from me. I knew she'd lost trust in me after the university mess, but I was shocked to learn that she'd never trusted me in the first place. I wondered how I could have been so blind.

I was in uncharted territory, but I knew just the person to talk to about this: Josh.

Of all my brothers, Josh was the guy for this situation. I was less than one year older than him, so we had that twin thing going on. We just got each other. Also, Josh knew what it felt like to be in love and then get blindsided and lose it all. I figured he'd be able to relate.

I parked in the guest spot at his live-work loft and let myself into the building using his access code. It was afternoon, so the odds were fifty-fifty that he'd be awake. And easy money that he'd be alone, so I didn't bother knocking on his door. Again, I used the keypad code he'd given me one drunken night after I promised never to abuse the knowledge. And I'd kept that promise. Mostly.

I swung open the door to his loft, a huge, industrial-looking, concrete room where he worked, slept, ate and, on very rare occasions, entertained. He wasn't in the room, so I peeked into the bathroom. He was showering. I made myself a cup of coffee, logged onto his Wi-Fi and searched for 'how can I make women admire me,' 'what is kink,' and 'sex no-strings.'

I got an inordinate amount of joy from messing with Josh's search-engine algorithms and imagining the ads he'd now see based on my suggestions. Last time I was over, I'd searched for 'healthy cat food' and 'best cat litter.' He had to reboot his modem since funny pet videos suddenly overtook his YouTube feed. Just being here made me feel better.

And when a buck-naked Josh walked out of his bathroom into his giant everything space and saw me sitting in his gaming chair, he jumped and yelled like a cartoon cat surprised by a mouse. It made me spit my coffee. I could always count on this brother to be the salve for any of my woes. He was the best listener. His advice was sometimes hard to decipher since he wasn't one to go into great, long explanations about his unusual logic patterns. But when I took the time to let his ideas settle, they were good.

"Jesus, Dylan. You're lucky I'm naked, or I'd kick your ass."

I stood and assumed a fighting position, legs wide, fists up. "You've got the perfect advantage since I'm all constricted in this suit and button-down. Let's go!"

Josh shook his head and turned his ass toward me. "Not on your life. I don't trust you won't go for my balls." He pulled on jeans and a T-shirt.

There was the trigger word. *Trust.* And just like that, I didn't feel better anymore. I knew he'd said it as a joke, but he also had a point—I *would* have taken a cheap shot at his nuts if he'd left them exposed.

But he'd have done the same. Was it really that he didn't

trust me, or was it that he *did* trust that I'd be an asshole if given the chance?

"Seriously, bro, why are you here? Am I being served?"

"I need some advice," I said, sitting on Josh's couch. He'd taken a seat in his chair.

"Why aren't you at work?"

"I'm not sure I have a job anymore. I kind of challenged my boss and then walked out."

His eyes went wide. "Dad is going to go apeshit. What do you need to know? Where to hide? Venezuela. That's my vote."

I laughed. "You'd have me go to the most dangerous country in South America? You're such a jerk. But no, this isn't about Dad. Although I suppose I should put some thought into how to deal with him. This is about Kama. I royally fucked up."

"Ya think?"

"I don't mean the case with the university."

"Neither do I. I was talking about the fact that in saving your ass from jail, she landed there."

"Yeah. Well, I went to fix that this morning but made things worse."

Josh buried his face in his hands. "What did you do?"

I told Josh everything, breaking every law of confidentiality in the process.

"So? Your best advice?" I asked.

"Save yourself the airfare to South America, get to your office early tomorrow, tell your boss you were high on painkillers when you stormed out, and forget about this chick. There is no way to come back from this, bro. Time to move on."

He looked genuinely sad for me. But I didn't feel sad. If looks could kill, Josh would have been a corpse, lying in the middle of a smoking pile of hard drives.

"That's your best advice? Move on?"

"You said it yourself: she'll never forgive you. I was just agreeing."

I stood and paced.

"What?" he said. "You want me to argue with the great Dylan Rhodes, who never loses an argument?"

"I want you to tell me what *you'd* do, asshole."

"I would have quit the case after the first date, when you knew she was innocent. Then—"

"I stayed on the file to protect her," I interrupted.

"You keep telling yourself that. But we all know that's bullshit. You stayed on the case because your promotion hinged on it. And, you kept going out with her because you liked her. You didn't do any of that for her—you did it for yourself."

I sat back down, knowing he was at least part right.

"If I'd been you, I'd have told my boss to go fuck himself when he told me to argue that case against the university. If you cared about Kama as much as—"

"I do care about her! And maybe it's too little, too late, but I did, for all intents and purposes, tell my boss to fuck himself this morning." I realized that I hadn't been thinking about my job when I was taking Kama's statement and that she didn't know I'd quit so I could help her.

Josh lay back in his gaming chair so he was virtually supine and crossed his arms over his chest. He closed his eyes, and for several seconds, I wondered if he'd decided to take a nap. He spoke without opening his eyes.

"How smart is Kama?"

"Very."

"Is she smarter than me?" Josh asked.

"This feels like a setup."

He shrugged. "No. Would you say that she's better at connecting dots than I am?"

That was an easy answer. "One hundred percent."

"So here are the dots I see. You might not have known

what the outcome of that case between the asshole and the university would be, but your job as a lawyer is to anticipate as many outcomes as possible. Right?"

"One of my jobs."

"And to have contingency plans for all of those outcomes, even if they're long shots. Right?"

"So?"

"So why the fuck would you have not thought that one possibility would see Kama taking the fall for this grudge your boss has against her dean? Shit, Dylan, it took me twelve seconds to see that. Do you think that maybe Kama had the same thought when she found out she was being scapegoated? That maybe you could have helped her, but you just stood on the sidelines and pleaded the fifth?"

"We don't have the fifth—"

"Shut up, asshole. You let her burn to protect yourself. To get that promotion. And you wonder why she's pissed?"

"Yeah, well, she's no angel." Adrenaline coursed through me, and I fisted my hands. "She used me, too, you know. And that doesn't seem to compute with her."

"Of course it doesn't. She was honest with you from that first date. You knew you were only a test subject, that you were under a microscope or something. If she was using you, you'd agreed to it. You even signed some piece of paper, didn't you?"

"Yeah well, she didn't tell me that her experiment was to cast some voodoo love tricks on me and make me care about her. She wasn't honest about *that*, was she? You know, fuck it. She may not have broken any rules in her research, but she sure as shit broke dating rules."

"Oh, yeah? How so?" Josh asked, looking at me with skepticism.

"She manipulated everything about the dates to get me to like her more than I should have. She played certain music. She asked specific questions. She ... I don't know what the fuck else she did, but you know me, I don't get attached. And she tricked me into getting attached. Ergo, she manipulated me. And that's not cool."

Josh slid from his chair and pressed up close to me on the couch. "She got under your skin." He pinched my arm. I punched his hand. He laughed and jumped away. "I say good for her. And I say with love, big brother, that whatever trickery she used has been a long time coming. Before Kama, did you ever let anyone in to get to know the real you?"

"Fuck off," I said. But I knew he was right. "So what? She got me to talk about things I don't talk about. And then she did exactly what I should have known she'd do with that information. She threw it back in my face and walked out. She as much as said I wasn't good enough for her. Well, news flash, Kama fucking Ray, nobody will be good enough for you."

Josh walked to the fridge. "I disagree. I think you're perfectly good enough for her. Beer?"

I grunted, and he threw me a can.

"The problem is," Josh continued, "you don't believe you're good enough for her."

"Since when did you become a psychology major?" I spat.

Josh sat back in his chair, and we drank our beer in silence until he spun his chair away from me and clicked on a bank of video monitors.

"If this conversation is over, I've got work to do. You may be out of a job, but some of us still have deadlines. You're welcome to hang out."

I leaned back on the couch and watched as six computer monitors came to life, running a variety of programs and apps. Nothing about the way Josh's brain worked made any sense to me. He thrived on information overload and puzzling out multiple problems at the same time. He was designing a new video game, one he'd been handed a ridiculous investment to create, and he seemed to work best when he was streaming two sitcoms, engaged in a group chat on WhatsApp, and playing a first-person shooter game that had nothing to do with the game he was creating.

I'd watched him work before, and although it appeared he was ignoring his actual task-at-hand with all the distractions, now and then he'd stop everything, stare at the ceiling, talk out loud to himself, and then type like a maniac on his work keyboard. It might only happen once or twice a day, but apparently that was enough progress for him to keep his investor happy.

As I considered how differently Josh and I interacted with the world, how differently we saw things and processed information, I had an epiphany.

When Kama was telling me her story, I wasn't angry. I'd felt sympathy for her and understood why she struggled to trust people. I'd only lost my shit when she said she wasn't sure she could trust *me*. It made me realize I was focusing my anger on the wrong people.

I was angry at Kama for not giving me a second chance to prove myself. I was furious with James for having used Kama as a pawn in his personal vendetta. It enraged me that Rohan had subjected Kama to two decades of emotional abuse. But when I really dug down, all of that anger was sitting on top of deep disappointment in myself. Because Kama hadn't been wrong not to trust me. She'd actually been right. I was just one more person who'd let her down.

I'd been singularly focused on winning just one game—my career—and I'd let all my other games—specifically, my relationship with Kama—fall out of focus.

And now I had to figure out how to prove to us both that I was good enough for her.

# 44

## KAMA

I'd been in the pretrial center for three days, and no other lawyer had come to see me. It worried me since Dylan had been clear he would not represent me. But my dad had visited every morning and assured me that things were being taken care of.

"Last night we had a pleasant talk with the young man you used to live with."

"Dylan went to see you? Are you sure it was him?"

"He said the lavender plants are healthy. He's a caring man," Dad said.

"Papa, why were you talking to Dylan?"

"Beta, he loves you. You know that?"

I huffed. "Well, did he mention that he's the reason I won't be getting my degree? He might love me, but he loves his career more."

"And what do you love more, Beta—your career or this man?"

"I don't have a career. And it's because of this man. So I love neither. Can we talk about something else, please?" I was irritated with the conversation.

"Okay, fine. Your mother wants to know what you'd like

for dinner tonight. Do you prefer tikka masala or vindaloo?"

"Since we're dreaming, tell her I'd like steak and lobster with gulab jamun for dessert," I scoffed.

Dad smiled and bobbled his head from side to side. "She will not like that, but I'll tell her."

I shrugged my shoulders. "You still haven't told me why you were talking to Dylan."

"And you didn't answer which you love more, your career or your boyfriend."

"He is not my boyfriend!"

"Of course he is."

"Papa, I moved out. That means we broke up."

"You were upset."

"Yeah, I was upset. He betrayed me."

"He had poor judgment, but I don't believe he ever betrayed you. You didn't let him tell his side of the story before you decided he was guilty."

"You're taking his side? I can't believe this is happening again. You *never* believe me. You always believe the man."

"Beta—"

"Stop calling me that! I'm not a child. You give Rohan the respect of using his name, but you never call me anything other than 'child.' I hate it."

Dad looked hurt by my outburst, and even though I was sorry, it was something I'd needed to say for years.

"I had no idea the pet name upset you so much. I wish you'd told me. And you know what else I wish you'd told me, Kama?" He gave me his serious stare.

I rolled my eyes and shook my head. Somehow I knew this was headed into territory where I'd done something wrong by not doing something.

"I wish you'd told me how Rohan treated you when we left him to babysit."

I was stunned. Why was he mentioning this now? Dylan must have told him. Another betrayal of trust. I'd told him my secrets in confidence, which he then shared with my family. I wanted to hit him.

I inhaled deeply. How to answer that question twenty years after the fact?

"I *did* tell you, Papa. But you and Ma didn't believe me."

"This abuse, locking you in the bathroom or a closet, happened every time we left you with him?"

I shrugged. "Not every time. Not if I had a friend over. That's why I always wanted Lizzy to come when you and Ma went out."

"But Be— Kama, how many times did you try to tell us? I don't remember more than once. And my darling daughter, I remember that conversation so clearly since it was the first time my heart broke for my little girl. I remember like it was yesterday, telling you to tell me if Rohan ever did that to you again. And you nodded and said you would. But you never did. For so many months after that time, I'd ask, 'Beta, did your brother treat you well?' and you always said, 'Yes, Papa. He was good.' Do you not remember that?"

I had a flash of knowing that Dad was right. He had asked every time for a long time. Which meant he had believed me. It also meant that for whatever reason, I'd lied to him. I'd lied and then painted my father as the person I couldn't trust.

I felt faint.

"Did Dylan tell you everything I told him?"

"He told me nothing. Your brother told us. Dylan came over to explain what could happen to you if Rohan didn't withdraw his accusation."

"Wait. Dylan is still working on my case?"

Dad looked confused. "Of course. Did he not tell you? He left the firm so he could represent you. He gave up his recent promotion." Dad raised his eyebrows and looked over his glasses at me. "The boy would do anything for you, Kama."

"I'm so confused. Dylan quit? Rohan told you everything?"

"I don't know if it was everything, but it was enough to make your mother leave the room crying. It was enough to make me put my foot down and tell him it's time he finds his own place."

That made me smile a little. "You finally kicked him out?"

Dad answered with a head bobble. "And it was enough that Dylan threatened to charge Rohan with I don't know what"—Dad waved his hand in the air—"if he didn't withdraw his accusation of theft against you. He's a talented lawyer. Rohan signed a paper right then and there."

My chest constricted. "Does that mean I'm getting out of here? No court? No record?"

"Why do you think I asked what you wanted for dinner tonight?"

"I thought…"

"You thought, you thought. You know what I think? I think you think too much. Turn off your brain for a little while and use your intuition, Kama. Listen to your heart. As smart as your head is, your heart knows better."

"I'm so sorry I forgot that you believed me, Papa. I don't know why I lied after that. And for all these years I thought you trusted Rohan's word more than mine."

"I'm sorry too, Beta, that I didn't try harder to see the truth. You know, your mother and I worried constantly about your anxiety and moodiness, but everyone told us it was a thing you'd outgrow. We should have looked harder to find the truth."

It was impossible to name the emotions I was feeling. It was a mix of relief that I'd be going home and not have to face a judge with grief that I'd made my parents worry about me when I'd had the power to make everything all right. I'd always been in control, and I'd chosen to sabotage my own life. I wished my psychology degree had helped me see that.

"What do I do now, Papa?" For the first time in years, I wanted my dad's advice.

"We wait until the paperwork is taken care of, and then I take you home. And," he said with a smile, "I think I'll let you tell your mother you want steak and lobster for dinner."

"Tell her tikka masala." I gave dad my dimple smile, which he never said no to. "And can you ask if she'll do her mint and cucumber salad, too?"

He nodded and shook his head at once, making it clear he knew my tricks.

"Thank you, Papa. But that's not what I meant. What do I do now about Dylan? Do you and Ma like him?"

Dad put his hand on my arm and looked at me with a long, serious stare. "Kama—"

"You can keep calling me Beta if you want."

His stare relaxed. "Beta, you can't make your decision based on how your mother and I feel."

"I know, but I'm confused. I don't know if I should give him a second chance, or if the way he treated me is the way he'll treat me in the future. Maybe it would be better to leave things as they are now."

"And how is that? How are things now?"

"Broken up."

"I don't understand. If you feel broken up, then fix it."

"No, I don't mean I *feel* broken up, I mean we *are* broken up. We broke up." As I said the words, though, I realized Dad was right. I was broken up about not being with Dylan. I didn't want to end what we'd had, but I wasn't sure it would be possible to fix all the things we'd broken, including each other's careers.

How do you come back from that?

And at this point, would Dylan even want to? I felt like every time he looked at me, all he'd be able to see was the person who'd ruined everything he'd been working to achieve. He'd look at me the way I look at Rohan: with caution, always ready to step behind my wall.

"Should we invite him for dinner tonight?" Dad asked.

I was surprised at my gut reaction. "No."

"But you're coming home because of his work. His help. His sacrifice."

"I just need a few days to think, Papa. I'm not ready to talk to him. I need to know what I'm going to say first."

"Oh, Kama, get out of your head for once in your life and let your heart lead your actions."

"I'm trying, Papa. I am."

# 45

## DYLAN

Listening to my dad pontificate about how I'd ruined my life and my future by effectively quitting my job one week after being promoted to junior partner was probably the most freeing hour of my life. I was no longer the golden boy. In Dad's eyes, 'choosing a piece of ass' over my career was hands-down the most idiotic thing I'd ever done. And, he reminded me, I'd made some terrible decisions in my twenty-eight years.

With the celebration—an event that had never been about me—canceled, I felt a relief that I imagined could only be surpassed if Kama accepted my apology for ever having allowed her to be used as a pawn in James's retribution.

I didn't hold much hope that she'd accept me as her boyfriend again, but at very least, I hoped she'd accept me as a friend. And maybe, if I was really lucky, a friend with benefits.

I still hadn't spoken to her since the day I took her story at the holding center. I filed the paperwork that allowed her to be released, and her dad was there to take her home. Her mom had invited me to dinner that night, but as much as I wanted to be there, I knew I had to give Kama the time and space to process everything she'd been through without me influencing her thoughts or feelings.

I took solace, knowing that her parents were rooting for us to get back together and that they'd be dropping hints to that effect.

She'd been out for almost two weeks and hadn't texted or called. I was starting to think that the only way I'd ever see her again was to hang out at the restaurant where Lizzy worked and hope that Kama might drop in to visit her BFF.

So when I saw her standing outside the movie theater on the night that the films we'd co-curated were being screened, I almost cried.

When she saw me looking her way, she smiled and waved me over.

"I'm glad you came," we both said as a greeting. Then we laughed.

"I really didn't expect to see you. I hoped to, but ..." I shrugged, knowing I didn't need to say more.

"Wouldn't miss it for the world. That was a lot of hard work, and I want to bask in the audience's awe of how great a job we did." She smiled and showed her dimple.

I wanted to grab her in my arms and tell her I was never letting go. But I didn't. She had to be the one to make the first move.

"Are you meeting someone?" she asked.

I shook my head. "I'm trying to stay kind of invisible since I don't know who's coming from the firm. I don't want to make anyone uncomfortable."

"So it's true? You really lost your job, not just your promotion?"

"Sort of. Not sure I lost it as much as I tore it up, peed on it, and threw it back at the boss."

Kama looked away and shook her head. "I'm sorry," she whispered.

"Don't be. You have nothing to be sorry for. I'm sorry that I ever got the damn job."

We stood in awkward silence for several seconds.

"Are you waiting for anyone?" I asked.

"Nope. I was just sucking in the festival energy and"—she shrugged and gave me her dimple smile again—"hoping to meet someone who looks like a safe bet to share a bag of popcorn with."

"Someone who agrees that the butter has to go in the middle as well as on top?"

"That's a good start. Also, someone with clean hands and fingernails."

I held my hands up and turned them to show her both sides.

"You'll do. You want to find seats or …?"

I resisted taking her hand. I resisted putting my hand on her lower back. It almost killed me, but I even resisted leaning in to smell her hair as we waited in line to get popcorn.

With drinks and snacks, we headed into the theater. We were early enough to have a good selection of seats, but as we stood and scoped the rows, an usher tapped my shoulder.

"You have a VIP pass, sir." She pointed to the best seats in the house. "You get to sit in the middle row here."

I looked at Kama. "You want to be a VIP tonight?"

She looked at the seats and saw two people sitting in the row of twelve. "Won't that be awkward for you?"

*No more awkward than sitting beside you for two hours and suppressing every cell in my body that wants to touch and kiss you.* "I'll be fine."

Kama looked at the usher and said, "Can you please give our VIP seats to two people who look like they don't usually get VIP treatment?"

"I can do that," she said, and she walked away.

Kama pointed to the very back row. "I mean, since we've already seen the films, I feel like the back row is good enough. And I like the idea that nobody will be behind us if, you know, I might want to steal a kiss ..."

I grabbed her hand and virtually dragged her to the back of the theater.

# 46

## KAMA

I had never experienced so many butterflies in my belly as I did in the fifteen minutes before the lights went down. I was checking my phone virtually every minute, waiting for the trailers to start. The fact that Dylan wanted to sit with me and grabbed my hand when I mentioned maybe kissing him helped me relax a little. But not entirely. The risk I'd taken was next level. Way scarier than Saturday-night karaoke.

This was my Super Bowl risk. The equivalent of my million dollars for thirty seconds of an audience's attention. But it was just one person who I needed to see what I'd made.

The theater was packed when the lights went down. Not an empty seat in the house. I closed my eyes and held my breath. I had no idea where in the trailer sequence my piece would run. Or if it even would.

I'd contacted the festival coordinator a few days after getting home from jail and explained what I wanted to do. Tanya, who I figured out was Dylan's Saturday-night friend, told me that to screen a thirty-second ad would cost thousands of dollars. I'd figured as much but had hoped they might cut me a break since I'd helped Dylan with the selections. She was lovely and apologized for not being able to bend the rules.

Later that same day, though, she called back and said that if my piece had a strong social justice message, it could run as a public service announcement, which would be free. Still, there would be no guarantee it would screen if they filled all the slots with paying films.

Taking Dad's advice, I took a chance and listened to my heart, not my head. Since getting home from my forced time-out to sit and think about life, the universe, and everything, the idea of making a film for Dylan would not leave me alone. If it wasn't screened at the festival, I'd just have to upload it to YouTube and send him the link. Since I hadn't even known if he'd be at the screening, that was my Plan B anyway.

I spent virtually every waking hour for ten days working on this project. I'd never made a film, but I'd done at least ten thousand hours of research with all the happy-ending movies I'd watched in my life. And after having seen what got submitted to festivals, I knew I could produce something good enough for theater projection with just my phone and a proper mic.

The first trailer thanked all the festival sponsors, and the firm Dylan used to work with in particular, for sponsoring this showcase of films about justice. It was shockingly boring, just a voice-over on top of logos. The audience ignored and talked over it. That calmed me since that meant ninety percent of the people here probably wouldn't even register my thirty seconds of fame. But it also made me more nervous. What if Dylan was part of the ninety percent?

The next trailer was a preview of the feature film that was considered the gem of the festival, and it was beautiful. It was art. The entire audience went quiet but for whispers. The blood left my face. The anticipation of whether my 'public service announcement' would be next made it hard to breathe. I put my hand on Dylan's leg to ground myself. He turned to look at me but kept his own hand on the bag of popcorn.

I held my breath as the most beautiful preview in the history of film ended and several people clapped.

*Please don't let the next one be mine.*

*Please don't let the next one be mine.*

I squeezed Dylan's thigh.

"You okay?" he whispered, pushing the popcorn between himself and the arm of his chair so he could put his hand on top of mine.

I exhaled and closed my eyes. *If I can't see it, it won't be there. Or better yet, I won't be here.*

But it was, and I was. I heard the strum of an all-too-familiar guitar string. My stomach tensed, and before film-Kama sang, tears filled my eyes. What if he didn't accept my very public apology?

I regretted having chosen these seats, right in the middle of the row. What if I needed to get out quickly? I felt like vomiting as I heard my voice fill the theater, followed immediately by Dylan's shocked, "What the …?"

I couldn't bring myself to open my eyes. I didn't need to. I could see what the theater was seeing in my mind's eye since I'd spent at least eighty hours recording and editing this thirty seconds. I knew exactly what Dylan was seeing. Every frame. But I had no sense of what he was feeling. I'd taken my hand off his leg so I could hug myself. If we'd been in the comfy VIP lounge chairs, there was no doubt I'd have been rocking.

After the opening close-up on my hands with the superimposed words *Grounded By You*, the rest of the shots were of things that elicit a feeling of calm: trees swaying in a lush evergreen forest, cumulus clouds changing shape, ocean waves lapping the shore. I edited the video footage, so it flowed like a breath: long inhales and slow exhales, that matched the rhythm of my song.

*Grounded by your touch*
*You branded love and justice*
*On my heart*

*Trust was broken by words unspoken*

*I'm here now to say the words I could have*
*To listen to the words I should have*

*You are the calm in my chaos*
*The trust in my suspicion*
*The forgiveness in my revenge*

*Understanding begins with a shared breath*

*It hurts to breathe without you*
*Our story can't be over*
*We deserve our happy ending*
*Be my partner in life's duet*

My piece ended, and I honestly couldn't tell if anyone had been listening or if the crowd had talked over it.

The next trailer started, and I finally had the courage to open my eyes and face Dylan. He was staring at me wide-eyed, slack-jawed. I couldn't read his expression. He blinked once. I blinked once.

"We need to talk," he said, standing.

"Now?"

"Right now."

I picked up my purse and soda. He carried the popcorn and his drink. We excused ourselves past a dozen people with Dylan leading the way, saying, "Excuse me," with such conviction I felt like I was about to have a strip torn off of me. He threw the popcorn and his soda into the first trash can we saw, so I did the same.

We didn't speak as we walked through the now-quiet lobby. We didn't speak when we got out to the sidewalk. Dylan looked up and down Granville Street and waved at a cab, which we got into without a word until Dylan gave the cabbie his address.

## 47

# DYLAN

I was speechless. I had no idea how to respond to what Kama had done. And I was never without words. No matter how tense a situation, I was the guy who always had a comeback, even if it wasn't always the best thing to say.

We sat in the cab without touching, each securely belted on our sides of the car. It was a quick ride, a distance we could have walked in under ten minutes, but I needed to be at home, needed to have the freedom to express my feelings without restraint.

I looked at Kama. She was staring out the side window. Was she still crying? Her cheeks had been wet after her 'public service announcement' ended. I watched the rise and fall of her chest and abdomen. She was barely breathing. I inhaled hard through my nose and exhaled loudly out my mouth. A second later she did the same. Good. She'd need oxygen in her for what was about to happen.

The cab pulled up to my building. I gave the driver a twenty for the seven-dollar ride and got out. Kama stayed in her seat, looking from me to the driver and back. I opened the door again. "Are you coming or what?"

"But you just paid him to take me home." Tears streamed down her face. "Didn't you?"

"Oh my god, woman, get out of the cab." I would have laughed at her ridiculous assumption, but she looked so sad my heart broke. I reached into the car and motioned for her to come out my side. She scooted across the seat and as soon as she was in touching distance, I reached in to help her out. My hand slid down her forearm until it was holding hers. She gave it a squeeze and I led her with purpose to the elevator.

She didn't speak, and I still hadn't found my words. Nothing that felt like it was the right thing to say. And I needed to say the right thing, now more than ever. More than any case I'd ever argued for a client.

I could not lose Rhodes v. Ray.

We rode to the twentieth floor in silence. My heart pounded. Adrenaline coursed through every cell in my body. Everything was at stake and would be decided in the next few minutes. Fight, flight, or freeze... None of those were viable options for dealing with this fear. There had to be a fourth way.

I fumbled with my keys, inserting the wrong one. Kama stood behind and hummed the song 'Everlong' by the Foo Fighters. It made me stop, turn, and look at her. I breathed out. She breathed in.

Her eyes were glassy, and her voice was barely more than a whisper. "I'm trying to help you find the right key."

That was it. I dropped the key chain on the floor and grabbed her in my arms, hugging her so hard she squeaked.

"I never want to go more than twelve hours without breathing the same air as you." My lips found hers, and she kissed me back with so much intensity I had to brace myself against the wall. It was hard to pull away, but I needed to be inside the condo to finish that kiss.

I picked up the keys, got the door open, and pulled Kama

inside.

"You're not upset?" she asked.

"I'm only angry with myself for not having called you two weeks ago. For not having accepted your mother's invitation to have dinner with your family the day you were released. For having put you in—"

She pressed her fingers against my mouth.

"Shut up and kiss me."

Kissing Kama was always a full-body, multisensory experience, but this kiss was next level, like we were a single organism, contracting and expanding together, moving and breathing as one.

With my eyes closed, I saw the universe swirling as greens and blues and violets. The world outside of this kiss, this touch, did not exist. And I never wanted to leave this place, to go back to the real world.

It was Kama who broke away. I fought to keep the connection, but she was insistent. Without words, she undressed, and I followed her lead. Silently, she took my hand and led me to the bedroom. I couldn't let her pull back the covers and climb under them.

"Wait. I have to put on fresh sheets. They're kind of… gross."

Her head tilted, a question in her eyes.

"I haven't changed them since you left. At first it was because I didn't want to wash your scent from the pillowcase and the duvet. There's no logical reason for having left them this long, but the illogical one was that I'd decided I didn't deserve a comfortable bed if I was sleeping in it by myself. And since there is no woman other than you I want to sleep with …"

"You haven't changed your sheets in twenty-six days?" Her expression was one of disgusted amusement.

"Well, I don't know if it was twenty-six days *exactly*."

"I do. It's been twenty-six days since I stupidly stormed

out. And there hasn't been a single night I didn't wish I was here."

I'd moved to the closet to pull out the fresh bedding while Kama stripped the dirty sheets. We worked seamlessly, as a team, making the bed.

"Do we need to talk before what I hope is happening happens?" I asked as we crawled under the duvet.

"I already said all I could think to say in that song. And since I'm here, I assume you forgive me. Maybe we still need to talk, but what I really want to tell you is better said with my hands and the not-voice part of my mouth." She smiled and gave me her dimple.

"I don't deserve you."

"Deserve? There is no one else in the world who deserves me more than you do. You earned me, earned my trust, and that was not an easy battle. And now that you have me, you're stuck with me. I have a strict no-returns policy."

"Kama Ray, I promise I will never put my ego ahead of your trust ever again."

"I know. And I promise I will never put my fear ahead of your love ever again. But can we talk later, please? Every one of the thousands of minutes it took me to make that thirty-second love letter in a film, I was wishing my mouth was on your body, breathing you in."

She leaned on her elbow and kissed the right side of my neck. Then my collarbone. Then my shoulder. She kissed, nibbled, licked, and sucked her way down my right side to my belly button, then up the left side. I ran my hand through her hair and rubbed her back to have as much connection as possible.

*I deserve Kama. She said I deserve her. She said she trusts me.*

The thoughts played over and over and over.

*I deserve her. She trusts me.*

If there was a Top Thirty Under Thirty for happiness, I'd be the hands-down winner.

· · ·

*Thanks for reading Second Breath: Dazzled by my Blind Date.*

*If you're not quite ready to say goodbye to Dylan and Kama, I have a treat for you—a bonus chapter that's only available to people like you, who've read to the end of this story!*

Geni.us/2nd-breath-bonus

**Josh's second chance romance picks up in THIRD PARTY: Merry with the Millionaire.**

Paige was the love of my life for eight years. When her short-term, overseas work contract was extended, I stupidly told her to come back *now*—or not at all.

It's been two years. She's home for the holidays and I'll do anything to have a second chance with my first, my one, my only love.

*Have you read all the brother's journeys to their happily ever afters?*

- Nick & Sophie, his and hers firefighters, in FIRST IN: Cheeky with the Fire Chief.
- Dylan & Kama, enemies with chemistry, in SECOND BREATH: Dazzled by my Blind Date.
- Josh & Paige, the love that never waned, in THIRD PARTY: Merry with the Millionaire.
- Adam & Lizzy, fake marriage, true love, in RHODES TO LOVE: Daring with the Single Dad.
- Morgan & Tamara, forced proximity, friends to lovers, in FRISKY WITH MY BESTIE.

# GET A BONUS CHAPTER!

**Thanks so much for reading Second Breath: Dazzled by my Blind Date.**

If you're not quite ready to say goodbye to Dylan and Kama, I have a treat for you—a bonus chapter that's only available to people like you, who've read to the end of this story!

Geni.us/2nd-breath-bonus

love&stuff,
*Danika*
DanikaBloom.com

# ABOUT THE AUTHOR

Danika Bloom is a *USA Today* bestselling author who always wanted to be the mom in The Partridge Family or The Brady Bunch.

Since she only had one child, she lives out her mom-of-many fantasies in her rom-com series about bands of brothers ...

Actually, that's kind of creepy when you think about it ... Shirley Partridge (aka Shirley Jones) writing spicy stories about her hunky son Keith (aka David Cassidy, her real-life stepson) and his brothers ... ?

Hmm, she might want to rethink this bio.

Danika Bloom lives in a small village in BC, Canada. In an alternate reality, like Kama, she completed a masters degree focused on dating expectations in modern times. She falls in love with all the heroes she writes and has a very patient husband.

Find all her books at DanikaBloom.com

www.ingramcontent.com/pod-product-compliance
Lightning Source LLC
Chambersburg PA
CBHW072108020726
47501CB00003B/764